PENGUIN

LAST RI

Clare Boylan has worked for rad~~io~~
and magazines. She won the Benson & Hedges Award for outstanding work in journalism. She is now well established as a
short-story writer, her stories having appeared in magazines in
England, America, Denmark, Australia, Sweden, South Africa
and Norway, and in anthologies such as *Winter's Tales*. Her
first novel, *Holy Pictures* (1983, Penguin 1984), which received
immediate critical and popular acclaim and has been translated
into several languages, was followed by her collection of short
stories *A Nail on the Head* (1983, Penguin 1985).

Clare Boylan lives in Wicklow with her journalist husband and
two cats.

LAST RESORTS

Clare Boylan

Penguin Books

Penguin Books Ltd, Harmondsworth, Middlesex, England
Viking Penguin Inc., 40 West 23rd Street, New York, New York 10010, U.S.A.
Penguin Books Australia Ltd, Ringwood, Victoria, Australia
Penguin Books Canada Limited, 2801 John Street, Markham, Ontario, Canada L3R 1B4
Penguin Books (N.Z.) Ltd, 182–190 Wairau Road, Auckland 10, New Zealand

First published by Hamish Hamilton 1984
This revised edition first published by Penguin Books 1986

Made and printed in Great Britain by
Richard Clay (The Chaucer Press) Ltd,
Bungay, Suffolk
Filmset in Monophoto Times by
Northumberland Press Ltd, Gateshead,
Tyne and Wear

For my sisters

ONE

In darker moods Harriet felt she had been placed by fate under a leak in the world. How else would the slow drip of adversity have found her soft skull so unerringly and marked it with the slopes and furrows of its path?

She always pulled herself together very quickly and told herself her earlier struggles were a strengthening process which built up endurance and cultivated in her a taste for (when it came) freedom. She had read somewhere that freedom was a woman's right.

For a long time after she arrived at the cottage on Keptos she stood leaning against the porch letting the sun burn her eyelids. A little branch of crumbling roses, grizzling with bees, pushed its dowager's scent up her nose and now and then Kitty's moans, like the lament of an imprisoned veal calf, drifted at her through the blue shutters.

After a while her head felt thick, as if it was being slowly cooked, so she picked up some cases and went into the cottage. It was clean but it smelled faintly. She lugged the baggage to appropriate rooms, leaving Kitty's outside her door, and then went into the room she had allotted herself.

She loved this room. She had been coming here for ten years and was always refreshed by its convent sparseness, the thick geometric slab of sun that came in on the bald pink rug. This year she had to consider its features in a new light. Would the narrow bed, that had treated only her tiredness in previous years, be big enough for two? Would the room look mean if allowed to grow untidy?

She had kept it scrupulously neat, adding only a glass of wild flowers to the dressing table for ornament. Such things had been important. Everything, in the past, except herself, had been important. She went to the dressing table and stood with her hands flat on its surface, frowning into the freckled glass. She had pale red hair, grown long to cover her face, and big eyes. She narrowed her eyes to examine herself in soft focus, to take away a superficially fair impression. It was no use. Even if the lines on her face and the

7

set of her mouth were not those of one who had vanquished continents, crawled through deserts, eaten maggots, there lived behind her, like images in a hall of mirrors, a long line of narrower selves; cartoon figures – burdened and battered; femininity whittled down to its strongest and stringiest. Her face was warped by vicissitude, her body wrought by combat. She did not care. She had come through. She had brought through her salvage.

Her children were great big rosy brutes; her face and body, a small sacrifice. In any case, Joe Fisher fancied her.

She went back to the kitchen and emptied on to the table the contents of the remaining bag; an odd-looking lot of things, spaghetti and tinned tuna fish, tomatoes, coffee, condensed milk – a bottle of white wine. The children were always disagreeable on the day of arrival and it was easier to pack enough food for the evening than to goad them with forced cheer to the shops.

She poured herself some wine and put the bottle in the bucket of water under the sink, which was there to keep milk cool. For a few minutes she contemplated the tins and packets she had laid on the table, the empty fire grate that needed setting. She lectured herself on freedom while she flung sticks at the gaping mouth of the hearth. Then she went outside again and sat down on the step. After a moment or two she opened the top buttons of her dress and kicked her shoes off into the dirt. She dabbed at the top of her chest with wine to keep it cool and thought about Joe Fisher.

The thing she loved about him was his ordinariness. He directed a company. He had a selection of suits in his wardrobe and money in the bank. He owned a hat. He even had a wife. He belonged in the financial world and spoke in terms that women love to hear; bonds and securities.

All through the harrowing, mothering years she had been forced to take her sex wherever she could find it. Normal, decent men fled in the sight of her poverty, her victimized state. She did not blame them or call them cowards. She thought they were right. They would be affected by her plight. The one or two normal men with whom she had been involved – her husband, an accountant whom she had once begged to straighten out her affairs – had been contaminated. Her husband, who was not energetic, had run off with another woman. Her accountant joined a charismatic movement and urged her to sing and pray with him. She had been compelled to lie down with eccentrics, men with dirty fingernails and peculiar habits, men who made love to her with their feet in her face or else shouted dirty words in her ears. Because she was polite, none of them would ever guess how disagreeable this was to her. At heart she herself was deeply ordinary. She liked a head beside her on the pillow, a ring on her wedding finger, and meals with the right knives and forks at the proper hours. The only thing she lacked was the veil of implacability with which respectable women hide their faces as do the Muslim wives of Arabia. It had been ripped from her in her battle for survival and her naked face was disconcerting.

If she had not been a respectable woman Harriet supposed she would have had quite a happy life with the children. There were communes nowadays where abandoned women could go with their children and have such good times that drunken husbands and negligent lovers came banging on the doors at dead of night, begging for entry. Even a generation ago poor women on their own managed. They lived on cream sherry and chips and went to the pictures, donating their children to the streets or the state prisons at the earliest possible age. The more conscientious mothers had comforted themselves by bringing lovers home to bed now and then. She could not do this. She could not present herself as a loose woman in front of the children when they were small. Her own sexual affairs had been hidden and hurried, squeezed into lunch-times, allotted the most uncomfortable locations.

It was different now. The children were big. They were beginning to have lives of their own.

She remembered, with regret and relief, when those lives had been entirely hers. She was so proud of them, but the responsibility was immense. It seemed vital that no cold wind should touch them, no unpleasant truth crack their shell of privilege. When Martin went away she was a plucked hen sitting on an egg. Once, a few years after he had left her, she ran into some people who had met him with his new family on holiday in Greece. From that moment it became her duty to give her children holidays in Greece. She had a job in the day and at night, when the children were in bed, she took up the watercolouring she had done for pleasure in more

9

leisured days. She sold some of her work and made a little money. She found out that although the fare to Greece was costly there were islands, once you got there, where you could live for next to nothing. By letting her own house for a month in the tourist season she was able to take her children to a cottage on the island of Keptos.

She had not much enjoyed those early holidays. She was still bitter and lonely and she lay awake in her solitary bed thinking how much the trip had cost, how many the bills that would await her return and how unfair. Her mind was pestered by the thought that Martin might by now have moved his preferred wife and children on to some more exotic spot so that they languished in hot baths and the pink towels of a grand hotel while she had to bathe in the sea. The children grew lovely and brown, though, and she was convinced that their golden skin, their immunity to rashes and drips and their talk of holidays abroad gave them an edge with the other children, which having no father might have cost them.

As they got bigger they grew very close. The island was their home. London and school and work and even Harriet's growing success as an artist were looked on as exile. From year to year they counted off the months on the calendar until they got to Keptos. For a few years, when Kitty was six or seven and the others not quite teenage, Harriet had been happy.

For a while she forgot about men. She piled the bed up with children and they talked of how they would buy the island, the farm they would have with goats and cats and honey-coloured cows. She lived in a children's world, associating only briefly with the opposite sex when her body made unpopular demands.

Tim and Lulu became teenagers. Overnight they grew big and bloodyminded and costly. The shame of having a mother altered Lulu's voice to a maddening whine. 'Oh, *Mum*!' '*Why, Mum*?' she would grate constantly at the unfairness of Harriet's each single action; while Tim's voice, broken suddenly to a derisive trumpet, pronounced everything – and especially Keptos – a fucking bore.

Harriet was terrified. She never expected the children to turn against her. She could no longer be sure that this anarchy and vulgarity would not progress until one night she would be torn to pieces by two werewolves. Afraid of making a wrong move she grew addict to routine. Everything that had represented security – especially Keptos – became essential drill.

It was not easy. Lulu and Tim threatened violence and suicide. When she finally hauled them on to the island, Lulu walked around with a pair of shorts and a bare chest, making the old women who lived there curse and bless themselves and the old men's mouths crumple dangerously. Tim would not come out at all. He lay on the bed in his boiling and barred room masturbating all day. At this stage Harriet did not like them. They were only a duty. She would have told them so but she was afraid of them. She was hurt and lonely and she was frightened. She clung to an assortment of men and fell in love with them if they were weak enough to cling back. One of them gave her a child which was born dead and reproachfully monstrous.

On top of that there was the cost of everything. The children now required extra tuition for exams and money for tennis racquets and clothes and a social life. For a time she was dreadfully poor. She had to buy her clothes from the racks and boxes of Oxfam, which reinforced her reputation as a Bohemian.

In the past year things had begun to improve. The children went to university and their animosity (and interest in her) dropped off. Kitty was now a teenager but Harriet had come to accept this as merely a difficult phase and she worried less.

She was recently making a small name for herself in the art world (although she still kept her office job) and for the first time since Martin left, money was not critical. She was able to buy some new clothes. She was having her attic converted to a studio; and in keeping with the limited repertoire of the roles of fate – Scrooge or Santa – she almost had Joe Fisher.

She met Joe Fisher in a hotel where she was having a drink with another man. The man, whose name she couldn't remember, although she recalled his tie, wanted to go home with her and she protested that he couldn't because of the kiddies. 'Are you ashamed to confront your children with your sexuality?' he said and she, astonished, had said, 'Yes.' He left her then to go to the lavatory and from there he vanished, via the lavatory window, into the night. She learnt this from another man who, returning from the gents to the bar, recounted the story to the barman. 'Was he wearing a yellow tie?' she demanded and when this was verified (and for no reason directly connected with the athlete) she burst into tears.

The informant was Joe Fisher. He looked kindly at her with his ordinary grey eyes and asked her if she was all right, if she would like a drink, if she wanted to talk, and at last she felt it was safe to say yes.

They scrupulously told each other about their families, speaking loyally of their children. He said his wife was a wonderful woman and she accepted gleefully that he was bored and burdened by this paragon. One day she could no longer deny herself his touch so she leaned close with a cigarette in her mouth and took his hand which held a lighter. He withdrew the hand. 'If you come any closer I'm afraid I shall have to kiss you,' he warned. Harriet was so enchanted she almost fell off her stool, but she had grown cunning in adversity and she took her bold, hungry eyes off him. 'I am respectable,' she said, remembering a line in an old film; 'but I am not untouchable.'

He told her she had Botticelli toes, her skin was milky as the waves of the ocean, her eyes were the colour of cornflowers painted on china. He held and stroked her, sometimes humming as he did so, until each muscle released its punishing grip and her body began to feel like a curved and soft and pleasant thing, not the aching and angular workhorse she had turned it into. In other ways he was not a remarkable lover but this, like his wonderful wife, she appreciated as tokens of ordinariness. He loved being with her, he said, and sighed because their opportunities were so few.

At first she did not mind. She was so unused to happiness that she felt she must take it in tiny doses or it would make her ill. Then she grew panic-stricken and wanted to run away with him, leaving the children to starve to death if necessary. She could not afford to wait until they were fully grown before thinking of herself. Tim and Lulu had already forgotten her. If she waited for Kitty to grow up she would be too old, her toes would be gnarled beyond the regard of Botticelli.

She made up her mind that she was going to marry him. It was not that she was indifferent to his wife. She thought she must be quite a nice woman to have imparted so little resentment to her husband. Harriet believed she had earned a respite. She could not be expected to endure more. Mrs Fisher, having already enjoyed

12

twenty years of peaceful marriage, her children sleek with parental care, would be better equipped for a few years' hardship; and it was a well-known fact that one got it in the teeth one way or another. If it wasn't the loss of Joe Fisher now, it might be cancer or arthritis in a decade or so.

She needed time to woo Joe, to make him forget about his family. She needed to draw him so deep into her love that he would imagine he could no longer live without her.

Once he said so, it was only a matter of organization: a little dallying in a place where time stood still, where the air was dense with pollen and fecklessness. She invited him to Keptos.

'Lulu!' she called out. 'Timmy!' They were on the beach. On the first day of the holiday they always went for a swim straight away although for the rest of the time they tended to complain about the poor quality of the beach and wish for a swimming pool. She went into the cottage again and opened bags and tins, dumping tomatoes and garlic and tuna fish into one pot on the stove and a sheaf of spaghetti into hot water in another. She added a slosh of wine to the sauce pot and filled her glass again. She had started to light the fire when a great furious howl from Kitty's room summoned her.

She left her task and hurried to the child's side, approaching the limp figure on the bed with trepidation. 'What is it, kitten? What's the matter, little lamb?' She put out a cautious hand and stroked a big bare back.

'You sod off!' Kitty turned to her, and the pink face, still full of the dimples of childhood, was livid with pique.

She pulled back her hand as if it had been engulfed in flames and put the fingers of both hands defensively between her knees. 'Come on now, Kitty,' she said cheerily. 'You're too big a girl to carry on like this. Tell me what's the matter.'

'You go away. It's all your fault.'

Harriet's heart began to thump. The child was pregnant. 'What's my fault?' Her voice was a chalky scrape.

'You ruined my bosom.'

'I ... what?' She could feel the little pink spots of confusion and offence coming out on her face. Pop, pop, pop.

'You ruined my bosom.'

'I never touched . . .'

'You made me wear a bra when I was twelve. *Twelve!*'

'You were a big girl.'

'You made me wear a bra instead of making me take exercise and now I'm all misshapen and deformed.'

'You're lovely, Kitty, you have a lovely shape.'

'Fat fucking lot you know about lovely shape,' Kitty said bitterly. 'There!' She jumped on to the floor with a crash and stood facing Harriet, hands on hips. Harriet had to put a hand over her mouth to stem a heartless laugh. Kitty wore a bikini made of two bandages of cotton. Her big bust and bottom fell out drunkenly over these wispy slings.

'You can't go out in that,' Harriet said. 'It's too small. Your bosom is falling out all over the place.'

'Of course I can't go out,' Kitty said. 'I'm a freak. And my bust is not falling out. It's caving in.'

Harriet sat on the hard wooden chair and eyed her daughter wearily. 'I am not alone,' she told herself. 'Centuries, civilizations of women have put up with this.' But then she thought angrily; 'Look at them! Look at women's faces – they're all wrecked, preyed upon until there is nothing left but the polite ruin of a powdered sponge. I've had enough. I'll kill her with my bare hands. I'll strangle her with her own bikini.'

Kitty fell back on to the bed and began to sob once more. Her cries were now tiny tired mews. 'Oh, Mummy,' she begged. 'What will I do? I'm so ugly. I'll never be as pretty as Lulu.'

Harriet flew to put her arms around her. 'Of course you will, you're a beautiful little bird. You just try on a swimsuit that fits you and see how pretty you look.'

'I haven't got one,' Kitty hiccoughed intently.

'Never mind. You can have mine.'

As the spaghetti simmered, Harriet seethed. The swimsuit was one she had bought especially, in a very expensive shop, for the benefit of Joe Fisher. It was a lovely swimsuit which had cost the earth, and was the colour of blue flowers painted on china.

Selfish, scheming (fat) little bitch must have put her eye on it the day it was bought and connived at possession. Harriet now had no

14

swimsuit. She set the table, lit a candle, emptied a tin of raspberries into a bowl. The treachery of children was worse, even, than that of men for at least one had not sat up all night with the men when they had measles, nor spent years of one's life training them to use the lavatory and eat with a knife and fork.

Kitty came out of her room in a white dress and sat at the table prettily. Her pink-rimmed eyes glittered. When Lulu came in with Tim and presented Harriet with a loaf of bread which she had bought in the village because she thought it might be needed, Harriet almost wept with gratitude. 'Thank you, darling. What a lovely, thoughtful girl you're growing into.' Lulu backed away, looking worried. 'You never remember bread,' she argued. 'There's never any bread in the house.' But Harriet went back to the stove smiling. She held the loaf against her breast like a long-stemmed rose.

TWO

The island was shaped like a small animal that had been run over by a motor car. The body part was unnaturally broad and flat and four poor little squashed paws dangled out to sea. In the pit of one of these limbs all life was centred. Here the boats came in, bringing fishes or tourists. On the gritty beach was evidence of pessimistic efforts to disarm the tourists. A monastic bar supported the baggy behinds of old men and a taverna, set up in a shack of wood and tin, was open only in the day as though accepting that no one on holiday would dream of staying overnight. In any case there wasn't an hotel. A few of the locals offered bed and breakfast but seen from the harbour Keptos was not where one would choose to wake. Food and accommodation were very cheap and those with the persistence to climb out of the armpit and on to the back of the beast were rewarded with enchantment.

The village was hidden behind two wharfs where fish were sorted and boats repaired. An alley between these buildings was used as a market. One had to pick a path through boxes of fish and jaundiced chickens and thin, opportunistic cats to reach a bright square dominated by a white church with blue ikons set like eyes on either side of its peeling door. Heaped about this was a charming disorder of little wedge-shaped houses as satisfying as slices of birthday cake.

Dark holes in house fronts signified shops. Open tins of olives and pickles fumed amid sacks of nuts and spices. Rags of octopus were slung over make-shift clothes-lines to dry. A slatted wooden box heaved from within as its contents of snails circumnavigated a shit-covered shovel. A crush of grey-shelled pistachios were heaped like dead beetles inside the window of the liquor store.

In the drapery shop a statuesque plaster of Paris woman kept perpetual vigil in an outsized wedding gown of bristling white nylon. The baker too, sustained faith in romance with a display of old, exotic chocolates exhibited on a shelf above the unhealthy white bread and rolls.

Although the women had put their hands over their mouths and squealed with derision the time Harriet brought a Tampax box to the general shop seeking replacement, there was a feeling that anything short of cosmetic surgery could be supplied on the island.

Civilization came grudgingly to Keptos. There wasn't a telephone and the recently connected electricity was a delicate and humoursome element. Progress was a poky coffee bar where the young men listened to old pop music and whirled their strings of beads. When they were not drinking coffee they made noise, grinding fire crackers beneath their feet and herding their few growling motorbikes through the narrow streets.

There was a souvenir shop offering from season to season the same anaemic postcards and ugly rugs and pots.

Houses grew out of the village in narrow mouse tunnels around the main street. Little girls sat in doorways stitching circles of embroidery. Dilated black shapes in dark windows were the ever-watchful black-clad women and clothes-lines supported the mournful festoons of their thick black tights.

Although the insides of the houses were dark and the women dressed for bereavement, the exterior view was childish and clownish. House fronts were painted in white or pink or brilliant blue. Doors and shutters bore naive patterns of flowers and curving lines. Flowers grew profusely out of plastic buckets and empty olive tins. Lambs with brightly-coloured knitted pom-poms tied around their necks were tethered in front gardens and patted by children, and on flat roofs were perilous, card-house dovecotes and sometimes a rabbit hutch too, so that one looked up to the improbable overhead view of rabbits bouncing amid palpitating doves.

Only those who had to – a few farmers and shepherds – travelled further afield than the village. The rest of the island was covered with rocky bumps, not significant enough for hills, which grew lemons and olives and goats and wild, wise-looking children, and tiny, unusual flowers flourished out of the stones.

Harriet's house, which over the years had given up its architectural identity to roses and creepers and virile weeds, occupied, from a tourist point of view, one of the best sites on the island. A stony path led from her front garden straight down to the village where a shadowy route through two narrow streets brought her to the beach. In all, the distance was so short that one could start walking with a cup of coffee in hand and arrive on the beach with the coffee still warm and Harriet often did this when she awoke early and wanted to have her breakfast without the children arguing for a share.

The back garden rose on a slight elevation and joined, at its boundary, a rocky, hilly field with a tree and a few matted lambs and goats. From here you could reach one of the highest points of the island, just two fields above, and the view was wonderful. Below, the little hills, dusted with a filigree of wildflowers; further down, the roofs of houses, the squashed-paw profile of the island and, all around, the simmering, light-veined sea. In the far distance one could see the island of Psiros rising like some noble vegetable out of a buttery sauce.

Around its shores the sand was fine and pale and on its brow, accentuating its natural claim to nobility, was what looked, from their distance, like a little damaged coronet. It was the remains of a Doric temple. Seven steps of white marble survived and in spite of some collapse the lovely stone arrangement of the central colonnade could still be admired. The children best liked the fragments of fruit and lions' faces that had fallen at its base and Harriet loved its crowing proclamation of the island's beauty. It was Psiros they all depended upon. Psiros kept their dreams intact.

Because of the hardship of their earlier days, it had been impossible for Harriet to properly guard Keptos for the world beyond. There were years when they had not enough money for wine or meat and they ate endless vegetable stews which the children reviled. There were times when they hated each other and squabbled and snarled and the little dark, damp-smelling inside of the cottage became an evil chamber of depression. The island was still a magical place but they knew it as a limb of the world. It was not impervious to misery. In times of disillusion they had to pin their hopes on Psiros. When the children were small Harriet used it as a location for the stories she told them at bed-time. The people on Psiros were all princes and princesses. They ate off golden plates, afterwards flinging them into the sea to save washing up. Once, like Keptos, the islet had had its share of rats scuttling out of the rocks, but now they were gone away. The inhabitants, too well-bred and sensitive to set a trap, had trained their cats to menace the rats and the cats pulled faces at them and taunted them with loud and dreadful songs. The rats lined up on the edge of the shore and, as the golden plates were sent spinning on to the waves by idle diners, the rats would leap on board, two by two, and sail away to Rhodes or Crete.

Later, when they visited Psiros by boat, Harriet found it difficult to disbelieve what she had invented. There were scarcely any farms or cottages – and of course there wasn't an hotel – but villas with their own swimming pools. The brown, sleek people who peered at them from their terraces looked as if they might well throw golden plates at them if they did not leave. They went quickly before they could find out that the islet was attached to the world in a different and more dangerous way. They did not go back to Psiros but continued to use it for their own purposes, remembering the feathery texture of the sand, its goosedown colour, and the pearlized shells that ornamented it, but they watched it through Tim's telescope and kept to their cottage where the only real threat came from a bad goat in the field behind.

The cottage had been built by a farmer for his son, but the boy's wife died along with the baby she was bearing and he went away. The farmer would not confirm the unlikelihood of his son's return by selling the cottage. Now the farmer was ancient and his son had been gone for twenty years. A female relative looked after the old man and rented out the cottage in the season to help pay for his upkeep.

It was Harriet's plan to buy the cottage when the old man died. Up to now it had been an indigestible dream. Sooner or later the children would go away. The island would become a place for her to be lonely. Astonishing how, in the length of time it took to catch a man's attention, the dreaded loneliness became the longed-for freedom. Already, guiltily (but *thoughtfully*) she was placing the children in their future lives. Her arms were outstretched to briefly bless shadowy grandchildren.

On the first morning of their holiday she rose early, left the cottage by the back door and climbed over the hedge and into the field. Striding through a grumbling clump of sheep she walked to a north-westerly point and there flung herself on her back and gazed at the sky. When this occupation had exhausted its function she stood up, shaking out her hair, and moved towards the field's single olive tree. She shaded her eyes with her hand and gazed down to the sea. She looked like a mad woman or perhaps a merchant shaping his own miniature empire, plotting out the site of the house he would build to demonstrate most impressively his gains. In fact her pursuit was equally powerful. She was preparing the settings for her affair.

In spite of the fair count of men who had engaged her in the pursuit of lovers she had never had a proper affair. She had not mended a lover's shirt nor brought him coffee in bed nor sat wordless but content by a flickering fire. She believed in these activities and many others which she would devise and direct, using every feature of the island's beauty to compensate for the erosion of her own. Here she would prepare a picnic for him, pink tablecloth (specially bought) smoothed over the lumps, roses in a bowl, strawberries in another, fresh bread and cheese, wine in a bucket. Later they would carry the cloth to a farther and more private field, which she had marked out for making love. She would spread it as a sheet beneath a tree with healing needles of sun poking through the leaves. The remains of the wine would be propped at arm's reach in the shade and between kisses she would fetch it to cool his tongue, to cool his back. The site she had elected for this phase was one where, opening his eyes afterwards, he would feel as if he had conquered the world. There was a tree on a sort of earthy ledge and, looking down, one saw only cowering shrubs and the infinite, empty sea. She was happy to lie under Joe Fisher, to be dominated by him. She had no desire to wrestle for equality. She could not work up a passion for what was merely her equal. She wanted the luxury of looking up to a man.

She rolled around, wildly murmuring, 'Joe, Joe,' to rehearse this transport. Without the tablecloth the grass was harsh and it smelled of sheep droppings. She scratched her arm where an indignant insect had defended its home and allowed herself to imagine the touch of his sunwarmed skin as she massaged it with oil while he confided the troubles of his married life. They would sleep together in the sun and get burnt. They would swim and play in the moonlight. In bed they would bring each other comfort and love, kindness and comfort.

20

'Mummy! Mummeee!' A warrior cry sliced into her lush imagi-nings and she sat up to see Kitty standing on top of the high field looking statuesque and forbidding with her crown of morning tangles and a long, swirling white nightie.

She pulled down her skirt prudishly. She felt exposed by this discovery. How long had the child been there watching her odd behaviour?

'Come quick! Come and see this, it's blooming mental.' Kitty roared down to her mother.

'Please, darling, not now – not today,' Harriet begged, but she did not voice this plea for she knew her entreaties provoked the girl.

'It's ruined!'

Harriet pulled weeds from her hair and wondered if Kitty's bosom was still the object of contumely and whether, perhaps, having yielded her swimsuit she might now be expected to offer her breasts, like Saint Agatha's, on a plate. She noted with interest that Kitty had erected Tim's telescope, a costly and advanced piece of star-gazing equipment which Martin had bought the boy as a bribe at the time of his desertion. In fact, Tim's astronomical period had been at an end around then and he had brought the telescope to Keptos on the first year of their visit and then just left it there. They had enjoyed using it on the island for games of 'I spy' – particularly in regard to Psiros.

In recent years the telescope had been forgotten. What was Kitty up to now? Who had she been spying on and what frightful magnified slice of life had been offered to her?

'It's awful,' Kitty moaned and jiggled with impatience.

'Tell Mummy.' The day was growing hot. Harriet wanted coffee.

'Come and *see*!'

'Coming.'

She told herself it must be a carnal alliance between a man and a goat (for there was gossip about such things) and to tell the truth she was quite interested. When she got to the top she was panting with effort and scathed with branches and the hill was bereft of goats. She began to feel unkind.

'There's nothing here,' she gasped.

'No, Mummy!'

'You conniving little . . .'

'There, Mummy!' Kitty swung the snout of the telescope in the direction of the ocean's succulent pet.

'Psiros!' Harriet reached for Kitty's hand. 'Poor baby ' Kitty let her hand be held but she remained aloof in her distress and Harriet was filled with love and guilt. She and the older children were caught up in their own lives. Only Kitty remained dependent. Harriet sometimes forgot that she was still child enough to spy on the island for comfort when the rest of the world was not up to scratch.

Kitty urged, 'Look!'

At first she enjoyed herself in the way she had taught the children to do, eking out the view, admiring first the smug contours and blonde fringe of sand before jealously attending to its features.

She counted the fairytale houses with swimming pools, marzipan cottages, the patchwork of pretty gardens and the – 'Oh, golly!' she cried out (she was incapable of swearwords. Her mouth would not cooperate with her mind in the utterance of the satisfying words the children used, though she thought them in her head) and she pushed the lens of the telescope from her face in fright. The temple had vanished. Climbing into the sky in the prettiest part of Psiros was a grey phallic tower. It was a crippled structure held together with splints of scaffolding but already, like predatory insects on an injured animal, it swarmed with life. Even now, the plump white bodies had been chivvied out of the boat and were settling into the finished part of the building while on its other face giant machines slopped out fistfuls of concrete and spread sand over rocky ground, patting it down with patient metal paws. Already a giant blue square like a supermarket car park showed bobbing pinhead faces and tiny cleaving feet.

'What is it?' Her throat was dry, the beat of her heart hysterical.

'It's an hotel.'

'On Psiros? It can't be.' She squinted once more at the telescope. Even as she spied, she expected to see a cascade of golden plates slice the air and fell the intruders. But all she saw, stitched on to a metal frame in shivering blue sequins, was the name of the monster – The Paradise Hotel.

'A giant-size, *package holiday* hotel.' Kitty's voice was bleak, and accusing, 'There's a bus. They have coach rides around the island.

They'll come here on day trips and ruin the beach with coke cans and rubbers.'

'Kitty! Don't talk like that.'

'Don't start on me, Mum. This is very heavy for me.'

Heavy. Harriet sighed. Did Kitty know already that experience was not light but weight? Certainly it was heavy for Harriet. She could no longer offer Joe Fisher perfection. He would have to make do with her.

'I don't understand it.' She struggled to collapse the telescope and marched angrily back down the field, dragging Kitty. 'They're so rich on Psiros. They wouldn't let a stray dog on the island, never mind that concrete vulgarity.'

Kitty's large hand hit her back. 'Poor dear,' she said. 'There's a recession. We didn't like to say. The lords of the island have fled. The villas have been sold or left to the cats and the rats. You never even looked at Psiros last year, did you? It was dying. Now it's back from the dead. It's hard times, old mother.'

Harriet thought of all the plotting and conspiring to pay school fees and fill the children with vitamins. She thought of the dreadful men she had slept with in return for dinner so the children could have the eggs. She thought of nights spent weeping with worry over rent and rainwear. 'Don't condescend to me.' She was furious. 'I know about money. I do.'

But she didn't. She had no broad view of the world. It never occurred to her that the rich could be threatened. She balanced her pile of coins, guarding it with her elbows, and when it was knocked down she built it up once more.

She put an arm around Kitty and they paused in the place where she had earlier imagined herself with her lover. They stared desolately out to sea as women in a younger century might have watched the slurping approach of longboats full of bearded Turks coming to rob their honour and dismember their menfolk.

In the hotel people would be coming out to breakfast, bagging white chairs and tables jammed together on a patch of concrete under an awning. An ant-size waitress would battle between them with trays of things.

She pictured them rubbing fat paws together and asking the waitress where the action was. She felt vengeful toward them. Even

23

though the view through the telescope was hazy she could guess that they were what her mother used to call the lower orders, that the men would bet on dogs and the children snort glue.

'Common,' she thought bitterly. 'Coarse and common. Coarse and common and . . . carefree.'

THREE

As a child Harriet had been taken each year by her parents to the sea. They did not look forward to it, so far as she could tell, nor enjoy it, but there was satisfaction in its accomplishment. It was central to their lives as was her own pilgrimage to Keptos.

She remembered grey skies and glass-topped tables in damp cafés; sand the indigestible texture of failed brown bread. She ran about with a girl called Hawna Maroyle whom she had invented. She could never understand why a companion of her own imagination should be so unpleasant and provoke so much disturbance. Hawna Maroyle was tall with prominent teeth and a different party dress for every day. She was good at thinking up adventures which always appeared exciting at the outset but ended up causing trouble and by then she would have vanished from the scene. Her parents took very little notice. Suspicious in regard to the outdoors they engaged in a united front against the elements. They wore newspaper cones on their noses and donkeys' hats. Sun or rain were kept at bay with umbrellas. They were successful. No trace of weather stuck, no sodden grain of sand adhered.

Harriet herself was less fortunate. At the end of a fortnight she had been permeated by the grey of her surroundings. 'Chicken legs, chicken legs!' Hawna Maroyle would taunt when she was sent out to play in shorts and her thin legs showed bluish and goose-pimply.

She remembered a boarding house where she was sick on her pillow in the middle of the night and another (or perhaps the same) where her father cut up liver on her plate and she used it to make chimneys on a house of mashed potato. Green peas, acacia trees; grey knees masked with lisle, poking out in a row from the white-painted garden bench – old lady guests who prodded her with their walking sticks, lost their spectacles, found, instead, bags of matted boiled sweets one of which, if she could get at it, she got.

There never seemed to be children in the places where they stayed (she suspected her parents did not like children) and nobody at all who looked remotely like a person. The men were bullies or buffoons. The women were plump caricatures of politeness with crooked fingers and a great appetite for cakes. None of them kissed or wept or went to the lavatory. There must have been sex. Seaside resorts are famous for it. One could no more connect it with those remembered clockwork comics than with the Swiss Family Robinson.

She had a sudden extraordinary recollection – an adult evocation in her limbs and not in her head – of a comical old fellow who used to pull her on his knee while he played the piano and he jiggled her about, stretching the elastic of her panty with an unseen paw while the other executed a thumping reel and the room full of grown-ups showed their artificial teeth in appreciation and beat their heels on the floor.

She could not recall how she felt about this, only that afterwards she would often sing for the company and she remembered that the man's name was something to do with lighting; Lantern, she imagined; Reggie Lantern.

It was a very long time since Harriet had thought about those distant sunless summers. She could not see them as being useful to anything. Now she drew vigorously on memory. Every shred of unpleasantness was vital evidence towards the case for Keptos. Not that she needed much in this regard. She only required, as all of us do, to know that she had done better than her parents.

When she got back from the hill with Kitty, she feverishly set about making coffee, gathering roses, warming yesterday's bread, so that the air of her cottage would be both inviting and exclusive. With the great boldness born of desperation she then risked an invasion of her sleeping children's bedrooms.

Luckily they were both deeply unconscious. She was able to love them and feel they were worthwhile. She sat on the edge of a chair in Lulu's room listening to her own wary breathing whistling through her nose. She had lost all sense of property. She was a thief now.

She tried to think of the time when motherhood had been a right. All she could recall were nights of frozen feet when she had sat up through sick and tears. Babies, the love and the boredom; who could remember? Foolish details lodged in the head but the heart's memory was buried deep as nuclear waste – deep as the memories of a grown-up love affair.

Whenever she tried to think of Lulu as a little girl she could find only one picture in her head – a girl of eight or nine in a blue velvet coat with braided frogging. She was a child who took a serious delight in life. Once, someone brought her a present and she unpicked the twine and peeled the paper to find a toy baking set. She was speechless with satisfaction. (The gift-giver took her silence for disappointment.) There were miniature tins with fluted edges and a tiny rolling pin. She had spent the day baking – child's pastry, grey and unbreakable and then with solemn glee she had placed the scorched miniature tarts and biscuits in front of her dolls.

She wasn't a child any more. With her voluptuous hair and puffed-up cheeks and breasts she looked like a creature made for sex. But she was beautiful, she really was. She had come out of Harriet and had been cared for by her, a milk-fed lamb, and she was flawless.

Unlike Lulu, Tim still carried a direct line back to childhood. He slept with his fist in his mouth and he looked innocent when his mind was absent. Tim had been Timmy, a fat baby, staggering and chortling, ravenously hungry and usually stinking of shit. Martin used to call him a jolly little beast, and so he was. In spite of the smell, he had been very good company.

It was the smell that now pushed Harriet back out of her reverie. Not the happy farmyard milk-and-knickers smell of babies but a close, territorial odour that stifled and disgusted her. She had her hand poised to push back a wave of hair that rested on her son's forehead, considering whether she dared to touch him, but now she took her fingers back, coldly unforgiving. It had been the same, she had to admit in Lulu's room, she could barely restrain herself from flinging open their windows and abusing them. But for what? Their rooms smelled of sweaty sweatshirts, of the workings of adolescent glands. They couldn't really be blamed for the fact that they no longer smelled like children.

She withdrew herself stiffly from Tim's room and went to the kitchen where she sat, snorting with irritation at the way Kitty mutilated the bread and dipped it in her coffee.

'Do you have to do that?' she said.

'No.' Kitty's blue eyes were luminous over the blue of Harriet's swimsuit. Her hair was tied back with a blue ribbon which perfectly matched the swimwear and must have been bought earlier by her for that purpose. 'I don't have to do anything.'

'No.' She wanted them to be free and untrammelled, not strait-jacketed by manners as she herself was, although she sometimes wondered if it was not possible to be free and polite as well.

'What's wrong?' Kitty watched the small nerves jumping in distress under her mother's skin.

'It's nothing,' Harriet said; 'it's stuffy in here.'

Kitty shrugged. 'Why don't you go and sit in the sun?' Harriet shook her head. She wanted Joe. The sun was for Joe. She had arranged it for him. She did not want to start without him.

Unfairly she rounded on the child. 'Life's not like that, you know. There's such a thing as facing facts.'

'We could clean the place,' Kitty said.

'It's perfectly clean,' Harriet snapped.

'I've thought about it.' Kitty waved her wet bread. 'It needs more light. We could cut back the leaves and whitewash the inside.'

'Oh no! You'd spoil the character.'

'We'll give it our character then; buy some of those funny lace curtains from the village. We could put them on the windows and the beds. A few bowls of lemons and some pots of leaves and Zorba's your uncle.'

'Oh, well.' Harriet was impressed. Her dark adolescents still had secret doors that opened accidentally, pouring sunlight out. 'Who'd do it? Do you suppose we could ask some local man?'

'We'll do it.'

'Us? Lulu and Tim?'

'Ask them.'

It was a huge surprise, almost a shock, to find the bigger children enthusiastic about the idea. 'Good old Mum, a plan of campaign,' said Lulu, leaping splendidly on to the floor. Even Tim, after he had opened a hostile eye to inquire what the fuck, relented. She was so pleased that she left them to their breakfast and hurried to the village to drag back, single-handed, the substantial burden of their decorative supplies.

When she had finished shopping she went to see Melina, their landlady. Melina was the niece of the old man who held title to their cottage and who had built it as a wedding gift for his son, Stefan. She was a ruin of a woman, a widow with resentment. Four generations lived in the farmhouse – the old man, his niece Melina, Melina's daughter Persephone and a baby grandson, Horace. No wonder Melina was resentful. All the men in the family were dead except the one who had lived too long and the other, only recently born. It was a mystery why so many of the island's men wore out at an early age considering the slow pace of their life and work. It was also a mystery why the women kept up such penitentially high standards of housekeeping when there were so few men around to criticize or praise. Melina and Persephone moved about their gloomy house like nuns at an altar, polishing floors and tables, putting flowers into shadowy recesses and ironing endless useless white squares to smooth over tables or the backs of chairs.

Melina opened the door and clutched her heart, ready to receive news of a tragedy. 'Something is wrong?' she said eagerly.

'No,' Harriet panted. 'Everything's lovely.' She realized then that she herself was clasping her breast and breathing in an unnatural manner, having just released her grip on the enormous parcels of lace and whitewash and a bag of lemons, as well as the day's groceries. 'I am sorry,' she said. 'No breath.' She beat her chest in demonstration.

Melina brought her into the parlour. It was liquorice dark and Harriet blinked after the brightness of the day. The only light came from a big vase of greenish lilies in whose blossoms was wedged a bleaching photograph, from long ago, of a young man: Stefan. It was a shrine for Stefan who had snatched himself from them when his own family had been robbed by death.

'The cottage . . .' Harriet identified a chair by its waxed lustre and she sat.

Melina glanced automatically at Stefan's picture.

'I want to make some changes.'

The woman watched her sadly. Embarrassed, Harriet moved her gaze to the window. She could see Persephone slowly pegging napkins on a drooping rope line, strung from the main building to a wooden shed which housed the lavatory. The baby crawled in and

29

out of the washing basket and occasionally clutched at the leg of a dozing donkey for balance. Harriet was brought back from this pleasant picture by a series of awful wailing noises. Melina was crying. 'Change!' she lamented. 'Always change.'

'Improvements,' Harriet tried gently.

'Stefan's cottage,' Melina said. 'Forget Stefan, you are saying. Stefan never come home.'

'No,' Harriet said. She opened her bag to take out a cigarette and managed, quite inoffensively, to transfer a pile of paper money to the table. Melina took the money and counted it. She put it away. 'Stefan come home,' she said defiantly.

'Of course.' Harriet was impatient to get away. 'We keep the cottage nice for him. Just as you keep it nice for us. We are very grateful.'

When she got back to the cottage the children were already at work. Open windows were being recklessly sluiced from full buckets by the girls while Tim, half soaked from the window-washing operation, was at work on the roses and the creeper with shears. In the dizzy, sleepy heat of the day, they worked to the contenting slap-slap of the whitewash brush. Kitty sat frog-legged on the floor, wafting long arms back and forth, hemming the lace in horse stitches.

She could hear the children's soft, satisfied expletives when whitewash got in their hair or on the floor. Great tides of sweat flooded their armpits – not the furtive bedsweat which alarmed and excluded Harriet but healthy peasant seepage. Harriet's narrow arms ached and she had a pain in her head – she was working harder than anybody – but there were tears of foolish happiness in her eyes. It was years and years since they had done anything as a family. She told herself it was all because of Joe. If Joe hadn't been coming she would not have cared what the house looked like and she would never have dared ask the children to effect its improvement.

By early evening they were finished. The cottage was lovely. The wooden floor and table were fresh as trees. The windows gleamed through the dewy privacy of lace and the walls had the crumbly whiteness of wedding icing. A huge pottery bowl which Lulu had unearthed supported a display of lemons.

'It's lovely, darlings. Thank you.' Harriet splashed out remunerative helpings of yellow wine. As she handed round the glasses she saw to her dismay that the darlings had assumed their collaborative sibling scowl.

'It doesn't look right,' Lulu said.

'Frigging twee,' Tim boomed and he scratched at his crotch reflectively.

'It's not *us*,' Kitty said.

'Us.' Harriet spoke lovingly, forgetting about the dirty habits, the slovenliness and swearwords that were the children's everyday household contribution. 'Why don't each of you go and buy something for the cottage and then it really will be you?' She dug another pile of money from her bag. She knew she was paying for peace but she was pleased to see them go, to have a little time for herself. She wanted to savour the purity of her surroundings alone before the bickering broke out again.

When they had departed – dirty and paint-stained and noisy – she washed slowly at the stone sink and put on a yellow dress. She left a skinny chicken in the oven and made a Greek salad. She cut up some peaches in a bowl and sprinkled them with wine and sugar. Then she returned to the table and sat by the lemons to catch their colour and she drank a glass of wine.

'No fucking bread,' Lulu grumbled, head in the cupboard as the others were seated at the dinner table, mistily bathed in candle and lamplight. She turned a sour face. She had been for a swim and her wet hair hung like threadworms.

Harriet brought the chicken to the table.

'Yeuch!' Kitty made a throwing-up noise. She had recently turned vegetarian and was graphic on the subject of flesh. 'Bird murderer! Cannibal! Poor little battered, burnt-alive birdie.' She stood up and leaned over the table to inspect the abject fowl. 'My God!' Her eyes grew huge with horror. 'It's a canary!'

'Sorry, darlings,' Harriet said dreamily. She drank her wine and chewed on a miserable little yellow leg, like a canary's leg. She did not mind. She was at peace. She forgot about the Paradise Hotel. She could not remember a single day in which she had been more content. Contentment was more nourishing than joy. Being in love was not very peaceful. At times like this – or in this particular

31

moment – she thought she might be prepared to live her life at a low emotional level, down amid life's ganglions if they could be relied upon not to go awry.

FOUR

The following morning something happened which made her change her mind. She woke early, slipped into her yellow dress and went outside to smell the sea. Kitty came after her and stood beside her silently and held her hand. 'Will we run away?' Harriet said.

'Yes,' Kitty said so quickly that Harriet felt sorry for her and made amends by promising the child the special treat of breakfast on the beach.

When they were passing the farmhouse a figure emerged, fluttering like an injured bird. It was Melina. As she advanced, she appeared to unfurl. Her arms stretched out and her whole being seemed extended with happiness and relief. 'He is coming,' she cried. 'Yes! He is coming.'

They watched in amazement for a while and then Harriet thought, 'She knows about Joe!' After the momentary shock she was infected by the woman's spontaneous celebration and she turned to hug her daughter but Kitty glowered. 'Who's coming?'

Melina's expression had changed too. It appeared that she had been talking to herself and had not noticed her tenants. When she saw them her dance fell away and her pleasure turned to trepidation. 'He is *coming*,' she asserted on an altogether more wary note.

'Well, yes,' Harriet confessed. She ignored Kitty's heavy breathing.

'He is *married*,' Melina protested.

Harriet was aghast. To have come in planes and boats halfway around the world to avoid scandal and now find it had preceded one and awaited one was a blow. She was further distressed by Kitty's menacing whine: 'Mum? What's she on about?'

'How do you know he is coming?' she demanded of Melina. 'Did someone tell you?'

The woman shrugged. 'The boatman. He has heard. He hears all things.'

'The boatman . . .?' For an instant she was more confused than ever and then it was gloriously clear. Joe was already halfway. He

33

had spent the night on one of the larger islands and had booked his passage on the boat which would bring him to Keptos this morning. She could no longer attend to the demanding looks of her two companions. Her knees grew weak. She felt dithery as a girl. 'Oh, Lord!' She gripped her arms to make sure of their substance. 'Oh, Joe!'

'Mu-um?' Kitty's voice rose to a battle cry.

'It's all right,' Harriet spoke with forced authority. 'All will be well.' She managed a cool, ladylike smile for Melina. 'Good morning. Thank you.'

It appeared to be effective. The woman bared her teeth in sheepish placation and backed away. Harriet grabbed her daughter and proceeded down the little flinty path. She felt foolish about the huge grin that was plastered to her face but there was nothing she could do.

'*Mum!*' Kitty shook her off with such vehemence that she almost rolled to the bottom of the slope but she clung on and kept her balance.

'I've got a visitor coming, darling,' she said nervously.

'You what?'

'His name is Joe Fisher. He's my friend and he's nice.'

'A man? Mum?' Kitty adopted her hands-on-hips pose. 'Wait a *min*ute . . .'

She had not told the children Joe Fisher was coming. She had been afraid; afraid that they would stay behind if she told them she had a friend – afraid they would come and he would not and she would look a fool. She was afraid they would make fun of her.

'Where's he going to sleep?' Kitty demanded.

'He can share with me,' she said carelessly.

'He's your fancy man, isn't he? You're moving in your fancy man. You couldn't bloody wait for me to grow up. Why did you bother to have me at all, that's what I'd like to know? Why not flush me down the toilet and save yourself the trouble?'

She broke away and thudded back up the hill to the cottage.

'Where are you going, precious?'

'I'm going to kill myself.'

She forced herself to follow as slowly as possible. Freedom, she admonished herself severely. She must no longer allow herself to be bullied by the children. It was unlikely that Kitty would kill herself before breakfast.

Already a part of her mind had forgotten about Kitty and was planning for Joe's arrival. She needed to shop; fish and water melon and peaches, a piece of lamb. She would have to get the big children out of bed and make them wash and dress. She would have liked to look a vision with a white dress and a tan and paint on her toes but she sensibly told herself that could come later.

When she got to the cottage she was surprised to find that Lulu and Tim were up and setting breakfast on an old sewing table they had brought into the garden. As always, she was caught in admiration of the two dark heads, the tall bodies and insolent faces. They were also very clean. Lulu wore a pink peasant dress and Tim had pale blue jeans and a white vest. She still had her silly smile on as she climbed up to greet them and she simpered quite idiotically when Tim pulled out a rickety chair for her to sit on.

'Coffee, old dear,' Lulu smiled.

She sat. 'Where's Kitty?'

'Locked in the toilet.'

'She went to kill herself.'

'Oh dear.' Even at the thought of the little girl hanging from the rafters in the gloomy closet, her tongue blackened and eyeballs bulging, Harriet was unable to erase her smile.

'Oh *dear*,' Lulu teased.

'It's all right. She brought an apple with her,' Tim said.

'The lamb.' She sipped her coffee. It was nice coffee. Now that they had ceased to reproach her, she sometimes felt that Tim and Lulu were her mother and father, that she no longer had to earn their sympathy, but only to win it. 'There's an hotel on Psiros,' she said. 'They're building a new hotel. It's upsetting little Kitty.'

The teenagers exchanged glances. 'Nice, is it?'

'No, it's simply horrid. It's a great ugly grey tower. It ruins our view from the top field. You can't see the temple any more. It's got coach tours and all sorts of cheap and nasty types and ...

Lulu patted her hand. 'Don't take it so hard, dear.'

'Well, naturally I'm upset,' Harriet said. 'On Psiros!'

'Is that why you're grinning like a fiend, venerable Ma?' Tim said. 'Last stages of despair, is it?'

'No,' Harriet smiled.

'Something else, then? Got a secret? Out with it!' Lulu descended on her and began to tickle. Tim joined her. She felt her ribs bounced against their pillaging fingers. 'No! No!' she shrieked with uncomfortable mirth. 'Come on, Mum,' Lulu cajoled. 'Tell us about your fella. Tell us about your bit on the side.'

Harriet stopped laughing, feeling embarrassed and annoyed. So they knew too. Had news of her affair been broadcast on the radio?

'All right, children,' she said with vague authority. 'That's enough.'

They retreated good-naturedly but their looks were full of bait.

'I've got a visitor coming,' she confessed. 'A gentleman. His name is Joe Fisher.' She looked into their teasing eyes. Her smile was gone and her own eyes filled with tears. 'I want you to be nice to him. Please. It's important to me.' She suddenly felt like death. To her relief, Lulu did not snort with amusement. 'We know,' she admitted. 'Kitty told us. Poor old Mum. You've fallen in love.'

'You don't mind, darling? You'll be good?'

'Course not, Mum.' Lulu winked at Tim. 'Love makes the world go round. It's what holidays are for, taking care of the old night starvation.'

'That's right, dear,' Harriet said shakily.

Lulu refilled her coffee cup and Tim serviced it with milk. When she murmured a query about her white dress, Lulu offered to iron it. 'I'll buy something nice for lunch,' she promised.

'I'll cook it,' Lulu volunteered.

Harriet could not believe her luck. Normally the teenagers competed in sloppiness. Today they were conspiratorial in the deftness of their housekeeping. She wondered what example they had pursued in suddenly achieving such maturity since she herself mostly felt a child.

She felt foolish now about her earlier doubts. She was too close to despair. It snapped at her heels like a starving dog. Up to the moment when Melina had announced his coming, she had not really believed that Joe would turn up. He was an indispensable person to the many accredited members of his life. It was difficult for him to get away. He had to set his business in order and tell lies to his wife. He had been vague about the date of his arrival. She would have understood if it failed to materialize. She looked on lies as politeness more than treachery. She did not expect people's feelings towards her to last any longer than the time it took to express them and she was skilled at budgeting small rations of happiness, smearing them thinly over greater periods of time.

Walking down to the harbour where she would meet Joe when the boat came in, she experienced a strange magnification of sense. The sun pricked like drizzle on her arms. The sky twanged off the sea in layers of brilliance, bouncing on the white of the houses.

All around were offerings to her senses. The little houses, cool as lemons, offered up their smells of washing and boiling meat and garlic. On the dusty track, two small brown girls bartered earnestly with stones and flowering branches. Pink and purple shifts hung on them like bells. When she was happy like this she could reach out and touch life and help herself to its elements. Grief was a prison. It sealed you off in a black bag so that you could not even feel sun or rain.

She had plenty of time. The boat did not come in until twelve. She dreamed and dawdled, imagining the fattest pieces of fruit and fish which she would buy with care; a great expensive slab of meat. Even before they made love she would have to fill him up with the choicest food to show her gratitude. Other women flattered their lovers in bed with coarse language. She kept her mouth shut. She could not trust herself to say anything in case it was 'thank you'.

When she got to the village she descended into the dark pit of a produce shop and headed for a basket of huge peaches, fat and furry, nesting in straw. The fruit and vegetables on the island all had a sluttish, overblown look but the big, battered porous oranges, the bulging red and green tomatoes, the muscled cucumbers and blotched, tartily rouged peaches were marvellous to eat. She picked six of these – one for each of them, two for Joe.

She had moved on and was promiscuously eyeing some figs when she got a feeling she was being watched. She gave the fruit a worried squeeze and put it in her basket. Ridiculous. The whispers came at her in a rush like wings. There was Melina, holding up her bag of potatoes for weighing, involved in some private mirth with another put-upon member of her sex. 'I'm imagining things,' she thought, moving on to the tomatoes with purpose, but when she glanced again Melina pointed theatrically in her direction and shook her head and rolled her eyes. Harriet smiled and nodded stiffly but the women stared at her in the tragic manner they had perfected, as if she was one of their dead. She flung the rest of the fruit in the basket, not bothering to test it, and paid without bargaining and ran from the shop. The incident honed her already-humming sensitivity until she felt transparent. Afterwards she stood outside the butcher's shop, with her hands on her chest, gulping down the hot air in an effort to recover, but its ragged offerings had an appearance of violent mishap which heightened her dismay. She decided to go straight to the harbour and wait for Joe. She would finish the shopping when she had him on her arm for protection.

When she got to the shore she could see the boat glued like a little paper one to the horizon.

It moved so slowly it appeared to be going backwards but she had to accept that it was faithful after its fashion to its schedule. In the dazed half-hour before his arrival her agitation was so great that she could not separate need from desire. She could no longer think of him as a person and when she tried to do so the outline appeared too large and plain and she forgot whether she liked it or not. All she understood was the immensity of her discomfort and the fact that his coming would relieve it.

She compelled herself to return to the village and buy some sweet confectionery from the baker. She walked rigidly back to the beach and ordered coffee at the bar. At this hour the bar was attended by fishermen, shy tribal men who muttered a dignified greeting and then ignored her. She felt quite comfortable with them. She began to breathe again. She remembered she was hungry. There had been no bread in the house for breakfast. While she waited for her coffee she took a little almond cake from the baker's bag and chewed on it from its paper square.

Scents of just-dead fishes, which smelled to her like female sex, rose from the hands and vests of the fishermen. As she sipped coffee, she studied them covertly. She noticed, for the first time, how beautiful they were. Apart from the older women, the people on Keptos seemed particularly attractive.

The men had strong bodies and the upper part rose like a flowering instead of the hunched congealing of the bodies with which she was familiar. The fishermen had innocent faces and the names of gods. One man had a mouth so perfect that when he pouted it towards his glass of wine one could not help thinking of its contact in a kiss (although she had never thought this way before) and, containing a little shudder, she leaned back her head to tip the honeyed crumbs of her cake off their paper square, feeling restored and much more relaxed.

As she did so this man, whose name was Apollo, moved forward and tensely touched her hair. 'You have lovely arse,' he said. She straightened herself so quickly that the crumbs of cake fastened to her nose. 'I beg your pardon,' she appealed. 'Your arse.' Earnestly he stroked a gleaming clump of her hair. 'Very beautiful.'

'Oh, my hair,' she apologized, retrieving her hair like a child removing its pigtail from a tease. The man gave her a harsh look and brushed her arm and the side of her breast with his fingers. She was speechless with shock. Immediately it seemed that all those simple men converged, grinning, leering, lusting – the toothless and the virile.

She smelled sweat and garlic and coffee, the fleshness of fish and the aniseed waft of ouzo. She knew that they knew. Apart from whatever underground information network the island carried, it was broadcast on her face, on her scent. She was waiting for a man.

She picked up her bag and hurried from the bar, apologizing. She was afraid. What if one of these good men should follow her and attack her. What would she do? She had been brought up to believe that men's sexual urges were a woman's business and that only a negligent trollop would allow a man to fall into the grip of his passions without so much as lowering a hem to help him.

She did not return to the harbour but went instead to sit on a wooden crate behind one of the wharfs, away from the painful blue of the ocean. She felt she was being watched as a madwoman or followed as a bad one and she did not know which was worse. She opened her handbag and concentrated on the disorder within. Some day soon she must clean it out. She picked over bills and letters, the cream comb with bent teeth, a broken powder compact, several lipsticks, a tourist's fathomless pile of notes and coins, all of it lightly greased and dusted in 'Honey Beige' from an earlier disaster with the powder compact.

She took out the compact to examine herself. Even the lines on her skin, the fact that she had not washed her hair, could not diminish the enamelled brilliance of her eyes and the triumphant lift to her lips. The sun yesterday had smeared her cheeks and nose with pink. She was admiring this effect when she saw in the dusty saucer of the mirror that she was not her only admirer. Apollo, the fisherman, and his brother Aristotle lounged at the corner of the wharf. She snapped the compact shut and dropped it into her bag. Busily she pulled out a letter and mouthed its contents with a screwed-up expression. It was an old letter and she knew it by heart but women alone everywhere defend themselves against pity by circling past appointments in their diary or reading old letters. The letter, like most of those in her bag, was from Joe – hardly a letter really, he was too busy for that; he wrote notes, but he put his heart in them.

My darling silly, she read. *Of course my feelings haven't changed. Of course I miss you. I thought you understood. Georgie had arranged some candlelit event. I'm keeping my fingers crossed for Tuesday. Be ready as I only have an hour. With xxxxxx and xxxxxx – Joe.*

She smiled tenderly as she put it away but then a tiny frown began to settle in. It was nothing, really. She wished he would call his wife Georgina and not Georgie. Georgie sounded too good a sport. What on earth was a candlelit event?

Cautiously she unfolded another. *Our stolen hours were heaven, darling. I can still taste your kisses. They are sealed in my mouth as bright sunlight stays locked behind the eyelids.* The letter was from a musician who had once given her a marvellous weekend and a nasty lingering infection.

She probed another envelope. *Dearest H.,* the page invoked mutely. Dearest H? Harriet had often left initialled notes to trusted and disliked business colleagues but it was surely an unusual form of address for a lover. All the letters looked the same to her. At the time of receipt they had seemed warm and reassuring. She had never really read the lines, let alone reading between them. She extracted what was necessary for herself – dates and times, a kind of continuity. Now she could see only impetuous summons,

40

impervious rejection. She was a squash ball, caught and thrown. 'No!' she chided herself. Joe's love was true, if measured. A woman had told her once that only shits (the friend's word) wrote good love letters. Nice men felt the burden of responsibility in their words and kept them to themselves.

Had he ever actually told her he loved her? Yes. There were the confessions-under-duress of their squeezed minutes of ecstasy. He had never interrupted anything mundane – helping her on with her overcoat, say – to assure her, 'I do love you, you know.'

Of course she knew. But what did she know?

Her knees were littered with scraps of paper, smoothed dreadfully by her caressing fingers as she searched the hearty memos for some tiny intrusion of irresistible emotion, when she heard the din. There were cries of greeting and discovery, the whine of Keptos' lone souvenir seller, sounds of daytime revelry at the little bar. She stood up abruptly, clapping a hand over her mouth, waste paper cascading from her clothes. The boat had come in. She fell to her knees, scooping up her letters and cramming them back into her bag, and stumbled forward to find him.

The harbour was choked by the jostling crowd of animals, traders, visitors and homecomers. Some of the people were dressed in the colours of a circus troupe and were loud and disorderly. She could tell immediately that these came, like her, from some civilized part of the world. The boat growled in the harbour, showing toothlike rows of seats on deck.

'Excuse me. Excuse me.' She pushed her way through a block of people united only by their lack of purpose. She was terrified she would miss him, that he, with his busy schedule, would turn and go back if he failed to identify her. In her anxiety she grasped beseechingly at the shoulders of nut-brown youths or pulled husbands round to face her, commanding the dangerous alarm of their wives. She had the foolish thought that she had only seen him in business suits and might not recognize him in leisure wear. She even investigated a beige, slackbellied old man pouched into dreadful shorts. Joe was not there. She ran between the wharfs and looked about the village streets where an impatient and energetic few had already advanced. She went back to the beach and tugged at tourists and smirking fishermen at the bar. He had not come. She clung on to the wooden counter, faint with shame.

'Are you all right?' said a middle-aged American. His eye, trapped in a face of damning goodwill, was frightened and hopeful. She shook her head. 'No.'

'Can I get you something?'

She nodded. 'Brandy.'

'It's the heat,' he reassured himself. 'Betsy, my wife suffers with the heat. At your age ...'

She nodded. 'Yes.' She seized the brandy and absorbed it in a burning, distracting balloon. 'Thank you.' She trailed away with bag and basket. As usual, in life's frightful moments, she resolved to reduce herself to convenience, to insinuate herself beneath the children's lives. 'Pull yourself together. Brave face,' she instructed herself, trying out a ghastly smile. 'Nourishing lunch. Keep up appearances.' It was not their fault that her fancy man had let her down. They were her first responsibility. It was ridiculous at her age to go gadding about with married men. When she got to the foot of the hill, she paused, wrestling with herself, not wanting virtue nor its wretched rewards. The pause gave the American, who had been pursuing her, a chance to catch up.

'Ma'am?'

She swivelled bad-temperedly to arrest his wistful gasp. Things had not yet declined so far that she was available for the offering of a glass of brandy. 'What do you want?'

He looked around as though seeking rescue or some object of his requirement. 'Nothing.' He blinked at her. 'I just thought maybe ...'

'Thought what?'

'You might be Miss Bell.'

'Mrs Bell.' Her impatience turned to curiosity. 'Who wants me?'

'A man.'

'What man?' Harriet had to clench her teeth to keep her jaw from trembling and she knew that her face was wild. The American stepped back fearfully.

'Young English fella.'

She took his arm. 'Please,' she said. 'Find him for me.'

'Sure thing,' he said doubtfully.

'You've been very kind.' She kissed his cheek and he flinched. 'I don't know how to thank you.'

'Delbert J. Mallard,' he sighed; 'at your service. Always happy to serve a lady.'

He looked around to get his bearings and proceeded up the hill in the direction of the cottage. Harriet hung on to him trustfully. 'Tell me, are you happy?' she asked.

'Beg your pardon?'

'Are you happy?'

'Happy?' His eye bulged gloomily.

'Yes. You can tell me. I'm a stranger. Are you really happy? Do you like living with Betsy?'

The children were always trying to stop Harriet from asking questions like this. They said it was rude and it upset people. Harriet couldn't see the point to any other type of conversation. She was nonplussed when people discussed the weather or the view, which was perfectly obvious and shed no new light on anything. She was always hungry for information about other other people's feelings. It helped her to get her bearings.

Delbert shook his head. 'Sure I'm happy. I'm on vacation. I'm happy.'

She nodded. 'That's good.'

'Are you happy?' he said with trepidation.

'I'm the happiest person in the world,' Harriet glowed. 'And all because of you.'

'Yeah?'

'And this English fella.'

'There he is!' Delbert looked up suddenly and pointed up the hill with relief. Harriet shielded her eyes to gaze. At first all she could see was Lulu running down the path. The sun kept striking her at angles as she ran between trees, catching in her hair, on her bare feet, outlining her body under the cotton frock. She was leaping more than running and she was smiling.

'That's my daughter,' Harriet said, distracted by pride from her purpose.

'There's your friend,' Delbert said, pointing to the shadowy figure of the man into whose arms Lulu swooped.

43

'Oh!' Harriet cried. 'Oh, golly!' She began to run. Her rigid hand would not release its hold on Delbert and she sprinted up the hill, the American lolloping and gasping at her side. 'Lulu!' Harriet cried out in distress. 'Joooe!'

But it was not Joe. Lulu paused briefly in her kissing. 'Mum! Hi!' It was a tall boy, very thin, with a pointed face, who absorbed her.

'Oh,' she said, 'I don't understand.'

'This is Roger, old dear,' Lulu shouted at Harriet. 'He's my friend.'

'Oh,' Harriet said.

'Roger, this is my mad mother,' Lulu told the boy. 'And this –' she put a friendly arm around the dangerously wheezing Delbert – 'is my mother's friend, Mr Fisher.'

Delbert could only raise an eyebrow but he did so with desperate appeal. Harriet began to cry. 'He's not my friend,' she whinged. 'I've never seen him in my life before.' She turned furiously on Delbert. 'You told me it was someone for me. You said.'

'*He* said.' Delbert found his voice and used it to accuse Roger. 'He said he was looking for Miss Bell.'

'What are you on about?' Lulu grinned. 'I'm Miss Bell. He was looking for me.'

'He never came.' Harriet sat on the grass verge and put her head on her knees. 'He never came.'

'Lulu Bell?' Delbert said and shook his head in wonder.

'He's not yours, Mum?' Lulu made sure.

'No.' Harriet was emphatic. 'He's Betsy's.'

'I guess I'd better go, then.' Delbert lingered, almost regretful. He held out his hands to say goodbye but Harriet had wrapped her arms around her knees. He ambled back down the hill, his hands still extended, like Rupert Bear in quest of butterflies.

'Mum?' Lulu said.

'Go away.' Harriet withdrew an arm and waved it to repulse her daughter.

'Mum!'

'How could you do this to me?' Harriet unravelled and sat up, full of fury.

'Do what?'

'Invite your young man to stay without so much as a word.'

44

'Invite? Young man?' Lulu spluttered derisively. 'Don't be so weedy, Mum. No one invites anyone any more. They just turn up. I told Rog where I was off to and he said "see you". That's how it is now, Mum. Laid back!'

'I see,' Harriet said beadily. 'Then how did you know he was coming in this morning? You came here to meet him.'

'Well, that's funny all right. It was that old bat Melina who told me he was coming.'

'She meant Joe,' Harriet said. 'She told me Joe was coming.'

'Yeah, that's what I thought she meant so I asked her. She didn't understand me very well, but she was very definite that it wasn't a Joe. That's when I thought it might be Rog. That's why I came down here.'

'I don't understand.'

'Never mind. It's a bit tricky all right. Melina doesn't seem too pleased. She says we'll have to go. But I thought, with your bloke coming, one more wouldn't make any difference.'

'What do you mean?' Harriet's voice sounded shrill and strange. 'Where's your young man going to sleep?'

'*Please*, Ma. Take no notice, Rog,' Lulu said sharply.

'You can't go living like a prostitute,' Harriet rebuked; 'not with little Kitty in the house.'

'Don't be disgusting, Mother,' Lulu snapped. 'Just because your bloke let you down.'

'Lulu!'

Roger watched them. With his pointed nose, his black tee shirt and drooping neck, he reminded Harriet of a young vulture. In her day a young man out of turn would have whistled through his teeth, admired the view and tapped his toe. He had neither embarrassment nor impatience. He waited for the outcome.

Laid back? she explored. No, he was a watcher, an old hunter. He made Harriet uneasy. She felt he was a stranger who had come to take away her property, who would wait until there was an unguarded hour. Well, she was old too – older than anyone. 'Wouldn't you prefer to stay in a nice hotel, Roger?' she said.

'What hotel?' Lulu said.

'There's a new hotel on Psiros. All the rooms have bathrooms.

Why don't you stay on Psiros, Roger dear? You can visit us on the boat three times a week.'

At length Roger was forced to look away from her glare. 'Well, perhaps, you know ... look, Lulu!'

'No, Roger,' Lulu snapped. 'Mum said the hotel was rotten – didn't you? I'm afraid you'll have to crash down with us.'

'Lulu ...!' Harriet cried. She had merely been going to say that they must not fight, they must make the best of things, but Lulu could only see trouble coming and she seized the white wrist of the languid young man. 'Come on, Rog. Let's show you the homestead.' She turned her sweet-snotty face on Harriet. 'Coming, Mum?'

'No thank you.'

'All right then.' She marched off with Rog leaving Harriet alone, alone. Once she appeared to relent. She paused, near the top of the track, to look back and, although Harriet's expression was solid ice, her maternal heart cried out for them to come and retrieve her.

'Bring us back some grub, Mum,' Lulu shouted.

Time passed. Harriet ate a piece of fruit from her basket and scratched her leg. She had lived long enough to know that life goes on even if you do nothing more than wait. If she sat until Tuesday the rubbish cart, drawn by a grinning, dowdy little donkey would pass by and someone might haul her on board. But it was more than a dilemma of the moment. She needed a prescription to get through hours and days and years. Other people did washing on Tuesday and baking on Thursday and put meals on the table every several hours. Their families kept them going in between with small demands ('Be an angel, Mum, and wash out my tennis shorts'). Other women had husbands whose eyes lit up when certain favoured dishes were prepared, who kissed the cheek, grazing the skin with a warm pipe-bowl. She had tried to give her life a structure but the architecture was wrong. She hadn't the patience to lay foundations.

She could not believe that other women were shaken by emotion as she was. She knew that their lives were not easy but she did not think they ached to be held, to be accepted, to be forgiven; that they howled (inwardly) from the pressure of the moon.

They were better than her. She accepted that; but they were better used than her. Not that she was abused, not that. She was like a judge about definitions. Everything was black and white. Unless someone actually assaulted her she could not claim to have been badly treated. When her husband left her for someone else she told herself that we are all victims of love in one way or another. The children's hostility was understandable too. She tried to be a good mother but she was a poor model for family life. Her mind wandered. She was still looking for a life of her own. And Joe? Oh, Joe. Of necessity her mind had blacked him out so that she would not feel grieved by his absence but merely chide him for his absent-mindedness. It was not Joe's failure to arrive on that particular boat that erased him from her hopes. She understood now that Melina's warning had been in regard to the children's friend. It was his letters re-read, his evasiveness remembered, her children's mocking, knowing laughter – Mum's bit on the side. He had probably sighed with relief the moment she had gone; the burden of his passion – or pity. Heavy.

Harriet was not one to feel sorry for herself. She expected little from life and was not offended when that was what she got. She was upset, though, by the possibility that life had run out, that she had outlived her usefulness; all the children so big and engrossed, her lover hung about with wife and securities. She understood suddenly the awful truth about Whistler's Mother. Once the artist had been hers, her subject, tottering with pencilled scrawl for her approval, and she, stifling boredom, had praised it, for he was her clay and her words, his sculptor. Now she was his subject. It was her only function. Young models scratched their buttocks, changed shape, scrambled off to sit on the lavatory, make love, cook supper, but she was constant unto death. Even landscapes changed, trees grew and leaves fell, but Whistler knew that, while life was glorious, his mother was resigned.

'I am not resigned,' Harriet said loudly. Persephone, the terribly beautiful widowed daughter of Melina, passed by with heavy grace with her baby and her bag of shopping in her arms. She stopped politely on hearing the growl of the foreigner.

Harriet held out a peach and the young woman, already schooled in selflessness, stooped and held out her baby to let him take it. The baby's strong fingers punctured the fruit and his single tooth seared it. In a second his coffee-coloured face was a pulp of yellow mush and pink juice sluiced his little smock. Having achieved this, the child pursed his mouth and offered a heavenly smile. 'Oh, how stupid I am. How long since I had babies,' Harriet reflected guiltily, thinking of the young mother's work in scrubbing the infant and his clothes, but the girl only looked pleased at the child's achievement.

It was odd to remember that she had once been like Persephone, young, pretty, bursting with pride at having produced two large and remarkable children. There was a husband then to cheer — although he quickly grew bored with the business – and the rewards of brand new smiles and little patting hands. She remembered her dismay the first time they wandered off in some game and forgot about her when they were three or four. Her husband did the same and almost at the same time too, just after she had had Kitty to console herself for the twins' defection.

It would happen with Persephone too. It was the scheme of things.

Within fifteen years she would be twisted and ravenous, wandering alone in the desert of the heart.

It was then that Kitty came, running crookedly, that trick of her age that made her look a young woman in one moment and a little girl the next. She sat beside Harriet on the bank and dumped her head on her chest. 'I'm not going back there,' she said, her voice thin as a wire. 'Not on your life.'

'Why not?' Harriet stroked her back.

'They're at it. Fatty and the beanstalk.'

'You mean they've gone to bed?' Harriet was appalled.

Kitty said nothing. 'I can't go home either,' Harriet said. 'Not yet. My fella stood me up.'

'Maybe he'll come later.'

'No.' It was the reasonable view but Harriet did not entertain this hope. She could see now that the plan had only been a holding one, to keep up her spirits while the remains of her family were crumbling away from her, leaving her only Kitty to clutch on to, like a dangerous toy.

Strong as she was she could only manoeuvre Joe Fisher from one direction. She could force him to accept her invitation to Keptos but in the same way his wife could prevent him from turning up.

'Nobody wants us,' Kitty mourned.

'You're not to say that,' Harriet warned. 'You ought not to be cruel to yourself. It sets a standard. In any case I love you. I really do.'

'I love you too,' Kitty complained in a tiny voice. 'But you don't seem to care any more. You're always off after something – men or booze or art or something.' She emphasized the three pursuits with equal contempt.

'I have to protect myself,' Harriet said. 'Soon you'll be gone.'

'I have to protect myself too.'

'I know. I know.'

She remembered guiltily that she had promised Kitty breakfast on the beach before Melina had disturbed them with her unreliable news. She could not go back to the house immediately because she feared that her shock would show and her jealousy.

It stung her to think that the years of self-sacrifice, of denying herself a night's comfort in her own bed with a friend, had failed to give the children any kind of standards. All they thought of her was that she was dull old Mum who couldn't get a man. Except for Kitty, of course. Kitty still just thought she was Mum.

'Let's go back to the beach for our breakfast,' she said.

'Just me and my gal,' Kitty sang.

It was lunchtime. The sun was hot and high. The little café was deserted and their truant game was an interlude of suspended childhood, enhanced by the dolls' cups of coffee and tiny rocklike pastries. It was Harriet's compensation that there was still some childhood left in Kitty, hidden deep under womanly foliage.

'What will we do now?' Harriet said, when they had finished breakfast.

'We'll have lunch!' the greedy child said. 'It's lunchtime.'

'Of course,' Harriet smiled. 'What would you like? We'll have anything you like. There's peaches and figs and we could get some of those little . . .'

'Chips!'

'. . . shellfish things.'

'CHIPS.'

'Yes, darling. Yes, little lamb.'

When they got back to the cottage and let themselves in, the little kitchen was crowded and shadowed by the three enormous

49

teenagers and the heavy breath of their moods. It was a relief to see Lulu and Roger on their feet and fully dressed but Harriet got the feeling that something was wrong. They did not seem radiant, nor even as content as she and Kitty looked, having held hands and sung songs on the way back up the track. They were making lunch and moved clumsily and gloomily about their preparations. Lulu looked up, her eyes huge with the responsibility of sexual freedom. 'You don't mind, Mummy, do you? Say you don't.'

Harriet put an arm around her and kissed her. 'There,' she said, withholding forgiveness.

'We're making lunch,' Roger said. 'A thing with aubergines.'

Something about the high and low hollowness of Roger's voice filled her with compassion. It sounded as if it was held up with braces.

'You children go out and play,' she said. 'I'm making lunch. It's chips.'

'Chips! Oh, Mum! Cosmic!' Lulu hugged her emotionally. There was a noisy racing about, a scramble for swimwear and towels, and the four teenagers streamed out into the sunlight on the grace of her release.

There was a moment after they had gone when she felt the sneering emptiness of the cottage, a desolate preview of her future. Her hand shook as she picked up the first potato and began to peel it. 'Peace,' she said aloud and defiantly. 'Perfect peace.'

FIVE

In ways Roger's arrival was an advantage. For some reason the children looked up to him and they behaved. He was fastidious. His pale eyes and sharp nose ferreted out bad smells or hints of untidiness. He marshalled meals and led expeditions to the beach. Although he had streaks in his hair, although he cursed and drank and liked to wave his bony little behind about when they passed the café in the village with its emanations of old pop music, he was really a different sort of man from a different generation. Harriet knew and he knew that she knew. Roger. It was a name for a hamster.

All the same it was amazing the difference it made, having a man in the house. No one slept late. The teenage forces of chaos and resistance had been replaced by a light mixture of apprehension and anticipation. There was a sense of authority. There was even a feeling of security.

On the first day of Roger's arrival when Harriet had braced herself for shocking scenes of amorous display, she was surprised to find him up and dressed before she was; well, dressed after his own fashion, which was after the victims of shipwreck. He wore tattered espadrilles and jeans torn off below the knees and a frayed tee shirt.

He was leaning over the kitchen table on which he had spread out a map.

'Good morning, Roger.' She forced herself to be pleasant, was careful not to ask if he had slept well. 'What is that?'

'That, Madam, is a map.' He smiled with one side of his mouth and bowed a little. 'A map of Keptos.'

'Where did you get it?' It had never occurred to her that Keptos might have been charted.

'The souvenir shop. I've been for a walk. Look!' He tapped an area with a bitten hand. 'There are caves. One could take a boat from the harbour. I thought we might have a picnic.'

The relief she felt was enormous. At last someone had come who

51

would take time off their hands. 'I'll get the children up,' she said. 'I'll see about some food.'

'The children have been dispatched.' He smiled at her with a complicity that was only in regard to their shared seniority. She felt confused and had to go and check the rooms for herself.

She went into Kitty's room, Timmy's, the one Lulu shared with Roger. It was like visiting the past. The rooms were empty, ghostly clean. Windows had been flung open and the curtains, drifting free against the metallic blue sky, flung out the vapours of the night.

All at once she was excited. A picnic! She washed and dressed quickly and put a lace blouse over her jeans. She was glad Roger had come. They could none of them cope on their own. They needed someone to take charge. Through the window of her room she saw her children coming back up the track with bread and milk and fruit and cheese, and experienced the same sense of happiness as when they were small and had locked out the outside world. She felt a child's happiness at the prospect of the boat.

When she came back into the kitchen the four teenagers formed a phalanx and she thought she detected an uneasy shifting as she stood expectantly, fluffing out the frills of her collar. She smiled at them. Lulu caught Roger's eye and looked away. It was Kitty who broke the silence. '*We're* going to the *caves*, Mum,' she beamed. She leaped forward and a kiss bounced off Harriet's cheek. She understood. She was excluded.

'Bye bye. Have fun.' She fluttered a pale hand at the lush fog of the window's lace. Nobody saw. The house was empty of children. She could see them far down the track, but they could not see her. Her own three had a clumsy eagerness like overgrown Enid Blyton characters. Roger, his skinny legs scampering and his little claws slicing the air in bullying command, was an old rat.

Her own instinct, after the initial disappointment, was to do something mildly bad to dissipate the feeling she had of being an insect on its back. She had often eased herself out of the pit of vulnerability by dredging up bad thoughts and putting her fingers where Reggie Lantern had. But she now was like a child let down and had no recourse to adult consolation. Once, when she was very small, her mother had delayed so long in talking to a neighbour in the street that Harriet had been unable to hold out on nature's call and had let out a great hot stream like a horse. The two women had laughed at her while she screamed and danced in humiliation. Afterwards she stole a shilling from her mother's purse and put it under the runner of the carpet in the hall. She could never spend it. She went to look at it from time to time and it glimmered like a trout under a pink silt of floor polish.

She had not planned to steal the shilling. She was led to it by a redemptive instinct. It was the same instinct that took her presently from the house by the back door. She stood a moment in the garden in bewilderment clutching an implement, the skinny little legs of which poked out under her arm in the manner of an intransigent lamb carried by a farmer. She clambered over the fence and strode quite purposefully up the field. When she had reached the top of the second field she erected her telescope and screwed up her eye to spy on Psiros.

At first, when she found her field of vision, the contents were microbes, floundering on a painted coin, but she expertly manipulated a little ring and bright, separate colours asserted themselves and the tiny creatures that strutted or squatted or swam were people.

She did not return to the cottage until lunchtime. She had a headache from unhatted hours beneath the hot morning sun. She made herself some coffee and sat on the entrance step to drink it. She closed her eyes to ease her aching head and there she found the callipered grey giant, the hotel, swarmed by Lilliputian peasants, like a hateful doll's house invented by Hawna Maroyle for her to play with.

The children did not return until late in the afternoon and this is how they found her; the cold coffee clenched in her hand, her eyes shut tight and her lips slightly parted with the effort of peering inward. They were dismayed. They had had a very good time and the emptiness of her day yawned in comparison.

'Mum?' Lulu touched her shoulder nervously.

Harriet opened her eyes. 'Children,' she said, disappointed.

'We've had a smashing time, Mum,' Kitty apologized.

'And now, Madam, we are at your service.' Roger gave his hateful little bow.

She remained silent when they brought her indoors. She was not sulking, as they feared, but thinking. In the early part of the day when she had been properly spying on the new hotel, she had trained the lens of the telescope experimentally away from the building to see if any of the tourists had escaped and was taking a walk around the lovely green hills, settling down to a picnic, perhaps, or sketching the sea – or if the hotel was really more prison than holiday camp. She had been astonished to see a couple making love. They were in a field that was studded with flowers – a long pink form like a side of bacon in a butcher's shop (and at first she tried wildly to convince herself that it might be such – anything rather than real, warm-fleshed beings who offered each other the love of their bodies in the beauty of the earth and the air). Even though it was at a great distance there was no mistaking it; sexual celebration. Delectable flagrante! It was not a part of the scheme of things for her third-class travellers. She would allow them a sex life but in its proper place, in a squeaky mass-produced bed, upon a raft of booze.

She accepted the glass of wine Roger brought her and watched him kicking logs into the grate and striking fire. Her own children, sawing skins off potatoes with as much squeamishness as if the vegetables were alive and screaming, played at house but Roger took over with ease.

She did not speak again until they were seated at the table and scooping ravenously at the vegetables and some mince which Kitty had cooked into mud pies. 'They have orgies on Psiros,' she said in a low voice.

'Mother!' Tim had a new tone which was indulgent and assured.

'Don't argue with me,' she said. 'I know what I've seen.'

Roger stood to replenish her glass. She noticed how near he stood – to ingratiate? to intimidate? 'Madam,' he said, 'if you have seen then you have seen. But how could you have seen?'

Harriet opened her mouth to speak, but it shook slightly so she lifted her glass carefully and dipped her tongue into the cooling liquid.

'We've got a telescope,' Kitty said.

'And used at this range – a microscope?'

54

Harriet looked at him sadly. She left the table and went to her room. She lay down on the bed and sighed with relief, pulling a blanket like a shawl over her clothes. She closed her eyes and, after a brief skirmish with trepidation, she entered the Paradise Hotel.

In the days that followed the children worried. Harriet was not herself. She neglected to coax them. She did not care if the bread ran out. Her loneliness ceased to clank like the medals of a mutilated soldier. Most of her time was spent on top of the hill. She watched a lawn unroll like a giant Swiss roll over bumpy ground. Smartie-sized flowering shrubs were heaped up on cowpats of peat. The pink human grubs gathered round to watch the installation of an upturned mushroom in the centre of the garden and then the joke mushroom squirted water at them. A fountain! Another lawn unravelled and was studded with sandwich flags for mini-golf. A bar with coloured awning, like a flower stall, was established by the swimming pool. Squealing children were soon contained in a concrete playground where they played in a sandpit instead of on the beach and, for grown-up children who liked to romp within safe distance of the concrete parent, little plastic boats bounced by the shore. She did not see the lovers again, but she remained suspicious in regard to a figure in yellow swimming trunks who languished by the pool all day (presumably to save lives) and was lapped by a tide of female tribute. Astonishing the depths to which some women sank, flinging themselves at a foreign gigolo with crowns on this teeth and a broom-handle in his swimwear!

The children brushed Harriet's hair and brought her breakfast in bed. It was the first time she had ever been treated in such a manner but she did not protest. She was like a Victorian wife, cosseted and bewildered. She accepted their attention as the price they were prepared to pay for keeping her in the dark.

At first she was only mildly put out that she was not included in their excursions. She forced herself to be glad for them. They were having such a nice time. Roger made energetic use of their days. They climbed rocks, swam, watched birds, sought impossible ingredients for outlandish meals. Kitty blossomed. She made enormous attempts at seriousness, discussing Freud and Timothy Leary, describing everything as the *epitome*, attempting the names of Latin

55

American novelists and occasionally forgetting and running about after Roger like a large dog with slippers in its teeth. Tim, in the atmosphere of Roger's funny-smelling cigarettes, his whinnying laugh punctured with swearwords, had matured and sharpened.

It was Lulu who concerned her. She had none of the joyousness of a young woman in love. She had instead the faintly harassed air of a woman married for years but still unable to anticipate the expectations of her partner. She reminded Harriet of herself when married, and her heart ached for her.

There was a more practical aspect to her concern. She lay awake in the night straining her ears for sounds of activity and trying to recall the date of Lulu's last raid on her box of tampons. She could no more interrogate this adult about birth control than she could make her wash her neck.

Once she attempted a heart to heart. 'Orgasms,' she pronounced casually when Lulu was drying her hair and the others had gone out to look for firewood.

'You what?' Lulu said.

'What makes you think every woman wants orgasms? Tell me the truth now, have you ever had an orgasm that shook the earth?'

There was a pause in the towelling rasp.

'You don't like me asking that sort of thing,' Harriet said quickly. 'Never mind. Carry on. Well, nod anyway, if you agree with me.'

Women are often accused by their teenage offspring of forgetting what it was like to be young. Harriet remembered perfectly but the information was not useful to herself or anyone else.

She had been a chalky, stick-like figure, gauchely ornamented with little hats and bags and pins. A false mouth, sticky as a wound, was crayoned over narrow lips. Even at that age she had longed for love and laughter but she was an only child, she did not know how to respond and her mother was a grim warden of her own experience. She hovered about the adults begging for clues. She knew from the way her father skulked in the toolshed and punished the cat that he had done some unforgivable thing and was in disgrace. 'What will I say?' she would whisper to her mother in the besieged teenage years when violent youths tore at her undergarments and bullied her to yield up the natural substance beneath the defensive layers of clothing. 'Least said, soonest mended,' her mother would smile mysteriously. It was fear of the unknown, the necessity to make it known, that had spurred her to marry Martin when she was nineteen.

Stricken, Harriet realized that she was becoming like her mother. She never really talked to the children. Defending them from the facts of her life, she made herself a closed book to them. She never told them what to do. She let them do as they liked and hoped for the best. She imagined that by shielding them from the discomforts of her life she freed them from the tie of guilt. Instead, she had loosed them in the wilderness.

There was nothing she could do. She no longer knew right from wrong, even from the powerful position of parent. The world was changing too fast. The treadmill had become nuclear-powered and it beat back at her clutching limbs as she endeavoured to keep hold. Young women had such big feet and bottoms now, compared with when she was young. Perhaps their hearts were different too – not dizzy with longing and eggshell-thin. She knew nothing really, except that she could not bear to look on Lulu's unhappy face and listen to her suppressed sighs. She preferred to take herself off to her hilltop where the real or imagined excesses of the invaders caused her only the indigestion of irritation and not the helpless burning of the heart.

SIX

She developed names for the people on Psiros, and faces: Bertie and Sheba, Dotty and Mare. Darren, Cliff, Clint, Majella. Hawna. She filled in their features from quiz shows on television or faces in the Sunday tabloids.

Other people – builders and painters and gardeners – composed new features for the hotel's face. The building was now complete but the scaffolding remained for a decorator's maquillage of geisha-white. A black hole in a field became a tennis court. Harriet's eye narrowed when she noted this development. She used to enjoy a game of tennis.

She became so familiar with the pursuits and pairings in the miniature world that she sometimes felt she only needed a magic potion to alter her size and then she could squeeze into the narrow tunnel of the telescope and from there enter directly the Paradise Hotel.

There wasn't a getting-to-know-you party for Harriet as there undoubtedly was for the tourists on Psiros but it was surprising how much could be deduced at a distance from simple cell formations. With a few exceptions the visitors moved in groups. Her first positive identification was the honeymooners. She was pleased, although it was hardly a triumph. There is no disguise for that clumsy three-legged creature, showing off the scars of its welding, antennae painfully probing for clues to contentment.

Other units moved in groups of three and could be distinguished by their foliage as female. They executed a curious advance-retreat manoeuvre upon the opposite sex. She frowned over this puzzle until, watching them one evening at the terrace dance, she noticed, at the point of contact, a flash of white light which left rings of blue on the night and she sighed with relief. Office girls! (She nicknamed them the Teasemaids.) They rarely succumbed to sex until the second half of a fortnight abroad. At first they only lured waiters into Polaroids and brought them back home for showing to other office girls.

The least interesting groups were the families, and the most interesting, the solitaries. Many of them were women and as yet Harriet had been unable to place them.

They had all of them come halfway round the world for a change, picked lovely Psiros out of a brochure (how had it been described? she wondered. 'A jewel of the Aegean where you can make as much noise as you like without disturbing the natives'?). Better than the telly, they probably thought, stewing in the sun and the cheap drink, ogling the better-assembled members of the opposite sex in their brief swimwear through eyes rosy with retsina and then bouncing on the bed with whatever unappealing creature they had been coupled. She shuddered in her superiority. None of them ever experienced the exquisite drop of walking out of the sunshine and into a cold and shady little church where golden-ringed saints on stone walls calmly perpetuated their torment or ecstasy and the smell of incense evoked temporal rapture. None would climb to the top of Psiros and discover its crumbling wedding-cake temple, or look out over the sea on the bright, humble Cinderella beauty of Keptos.

On one of her vigils she ran out of cigarettes and had to dash down to the village to buy a pack. She was in high spirits. A unit identified as Office Girls had emerged this morning with a missing limb. There were only two of them, arm in arm, stiff with worry, seething with jealousy. Their friend was missing. She must have made a conquest. She took a deep, excited intake of breath and almost fainted when this gust of fresh air hit her lungs. She reached automatically for a cigarette and, finding only the empty pack, hurried off to the shops. Halfway down the track she became aware of an extraordinary sensation. She had not experienced anything so odd, so irresistible, since she had been betrayed by her bladder while her mother gossiped with a neighbour. Long, fine needles wove intricately through her nerve endings. She doubled over this delicate pain and put a hand on her stomach to repress it but when she did this her body throbbed boldly.

'Oh, golly,' she cried out in a panic. She wanted (her body wanted) a man.

To Harriet this unprecipitated cry of the entrails was as alarming as if her car had broken down on a motorway. There were certain things she did not understand (and did not wish to understand) but she expected all mechanical systems to be governed by their own laws of discipline. 'It's my nerves,' she told herself. 'I just need something to steady my nerves.'

She moved along peculiarly, stiff in the grip of her little hormonal ache. She prescribed a drink for herself at the bar on the beach. From past experience she knew that sexual greed has little staying power. If she could once snap shut the yawning jaws of her body the pangs would fade away and she would be able to go about her business.

She felt it was unfair that this need should have been sprung upon her from nowhere. In the past week she had not once thought about sex. Yet she had imagined it constantly, in the squirming dots of the despoilers of Psiros and later in the enlarging frame of her imagination. Before that she had been radiantly lustful for Joe Fisher. There had been days and days of sunshine to wreak feckless-ness in her limbs, and long nights of rest.

When she got to the bar she ordered brandy and drank it down in a gulp. She felt better immediately. The ache thawed to a pleasant rasp. She bought cigarettes at the bar and smoked one, turning her back on the shed to watch the sea. A scorching breeze brought smells of herbs and flowers – and the scent of just-dead fishes. 'You will please have one more,' came a gentle inquiry, and she turned, smiling, to the lovely serious face and perfect pouting mouth of the fisherman Apollo. 'Yes, please, I will,' she smiled, and she offered him a cigarette.

He told her about his boat, describing it as a little boy would boast of a toy to float in his bath. She was amused by his solemn swaggering. She wondered how she had been so unnerved on the earlier occasion when he had admired her hair and touched it. She accepted another drink. She did not really want it but she liked watching his lips and his tongue on the glass. She would not mind if he touched her hair now. She stretched out her arms in relaxa-tion and noticed how brown they had grown and spangled with little soft orange and gold hairs. He too observed this gesture with eyes as huge and puzzled as a puppy pursuing a rat down a hole. Instinct and experience told her she need do nothing now except retreat sufficiently to allow him to catch her.

She finished her drink. 'I must go.'

'When will I see you?' he begged.

'Soon, I expect.'

'Tonight.'

She nodded as one under duress.

She did not return to her viewing post. Instead she went to the cottage. She felt larky and agitated and needed to be out of the sun for a while.

Lulu sat on the front step of the cottage, feebly scraping the potatoes.

'Where's Roger?' Harriet said.

Lulu shrugged. 'Tim's room.'

'Where's Kitty?'

'In Poxy Music probably. She's been hanging around there, you know.' It was the name the children had adopted for the Keptos coffee bar.

'With boys?' It gave her a disagreeable sensation, as if her tights were on back to front. Guilt flared in her but she beat it out. 'What can Roger have been thinking of, letting a little girl like that go off on her own?'

Lulu's look was wry and elderly. 'What indeed can Roger have been thinking of?'

Harriet was dismayed by the change in her. Lovely impudent rosy Lulu seemed pinched and diminished. She even looked pale despite the sunshine. She took Lulu's hand and it stayed in hers, cool and unresponsive as the subdued paw of a little tutored poodle. 'Are you all right, darling? Are you happy?' Harriet said against her better judgement. Lulu shrugged but huge tears swelled up in her eyes. 'I wish it was like it used to be when there was just us,' she said.

'It's all right, sweet.' Harriet patted her. 'I'll make Roger go.' For some reason the prospect gave her no satisfaction. She did not want to have her family to herself. She wanted a man to herself. It was awful, but visions of Apollo's strong, stupid jaw and glistening throat kept coming at her, sounding in her like a gong. Lulu burst into tears. 'Don't you say anything to Roger.'

'Hush now.' Harriet wiped Lulu's face with her thumbs. 'If you don't want Roger to go, what do you want?'

'It's not just Rog. It's you, Mum – everything's changed.'

'I'm sorry. I thought you young people wanted to be on your own. I'll fold up my telescope and come down right now. I'll make chips.'

Lulu's narrowed eyes considered forgiveness. She gave a gravelly sniff. 'What about your bloke?'

'I haven't got a bloke,' Harriet said cautiously.

'What about Joe Fisher?'

'You know very well. He never came.'

'Well, he's coming now, isn't he?'

'What?' In fright Harriet dropped the child. Her hands shrank back from her progeny and Lulu snivelled afresh. 'You see, Mum. You see for yourself. We're just not number one any more.'

'Who told you? What are you talking about?'

Harriet had to bunch her hands to stop herself from hitting the wretched girl but in a moment she felt sorry. 'Please, darling,' she wheedled. 'Tell me why you said that?'

Lulu said nothing, observed her knees with a constipated gaze. Harriet touched the soft, muddy cheek. 'Look, we're all in the same boat in regard to men. I could tell you otherwise, but that would only be excusing myself. And it never changes. We never get sense. We don't really learn from experience. You know just as much as I do except you haven't the proof. Not that proof makes a difference. It's always the exception for us that's going to prove the rule. Proof is like galoshes, it's an insulation but it isn't attractive. Have you ever noticed, darling, that only despairing women wear galoshes?'

'What proof?' Lulu cried out, despairing. 'What are you talking about?'

'Proof that no one is ever going to come and rescue us from ourselves.'

There was a long silence in which Lulu's wounded snuffling subsided to sighs and Harriet imagined her ear licked by the tip of Apollo's tongue.

'Melina said he was coming,' Lulu whispered. 'She came over this afternoon and she said he was coming.'

'I don't believe you.' Harriet was confused. She could not cope. The tubes of her heart had been ligated. How could she stand a fresh insurgence? But she could. Already a silly twittering had begun and a half of her lip took flight in a faint leer. 'What did she say? Tell me what she said.'

'Look at you, Mum!' Lulu yelped. 'Just look at you. You're hopeless.'

'What did she say?'

'Oh, just the usual bloody annunciation. "He is coming! Tell your mother he is coming." '

'It isn't him.' Harriet let herself down with her little tight pronouncement.

'Well, who the hell else then?' Lulu said.

'I don't know, dear. I'm going to find out.'

She went indoors and rapped bonily on Tim's door. 'Can I come in?'

There was a degree of furtive noise. 'No!' Tim's voice sounded adolescent again in indignation. Harriet knocked once more. 'I want to talk to you.' The door opened and it was Roger who stood there, in his dressing gown. 'At your service, Madam.' He gave his little bow.

'I want to know, Tim,' Harriet shouted past Roger's shoulders, 'if you have invited anyone, however informally, to join us here on Keptos?'

'Get out, Mum. I'm having a private conversation with Rog.' Tim, seated on the bed, kept his bare back to her.

'Have you?'

'No.'

'There.' Roger smiled at her. Hateful as he was she could do nothing but grin at him complicitly. Her lover was coming. There was scarcely any doubting it now. Just to be certain she would run over to the farm and question Melina very precisely. She left the house again, almost stepping on the irritatingly dirty and droopy Lulu. She wished the girl would pull herself together. She had every advantage – foreign holidays, an uncritical mother, a tempting appearance. Why should she be so ready to give in to misery when Harriet scarcely ever complained? What they lacked was a real man around the place. They needed Joe, Roger had failed them. He had given them no sense of security at all, only tried to turn her children against her.

63

When she found Melina, Harriet came to the point immediately. 'You have been talking to my daughter,' she said, 'about a visitor.' Melina nodded and then shook her head. 'We did not know. He is coming.'

'Who is coming?' Harriet said patiently. 'My friend Mr Fisher?'

Melina was amused. She had to throw a hand over her mouth to hide a gasp of laughter. A lewd eye kept happy watch over the fan of reddened fingertips. 'Mr fisherman!' she cackled.

Harriet laughed too and nodded wildly although she hated the woman and would have liked to kick her. 'Yes, yes,' she said. 'My friend is coming?'

The woman touched her mouth again, this time in stupefaction. 'No, no. Not possible,' she protested. 'Stefan, the son of my uncle, he comes.'

'You mean . . .' Harriet stooped and shook a finger at the window. '. . . The man who owns the cottage? He is coming back?'

'Soon.'

'But he's been gone for twenty years.'

Melina nodded.

They faced each other, exhausted after this massive translation and then after a while Harriet rose again in a rage.

'When's he coming back?'

'Soon. He write.'

'Well, you jolly well write back and tell him the villa has been rented out and we've paid good money. He can have his cottage after we've gone.'

Melina sank down in misery. 'He comes,' she said stubbornly.

'We'll see.' Harriet left, feeling angry and defeated. Melina had only been holding on to her own hopeless dream, as she had to hers. Vengefully she cast out the loved substance and invited in the lean form of Apollo.

Lulu was still hunched on the step when she got back. A limp hand caught Harriet's leg. 'Mum . . . I want to talk to you.' Harriet reached down and ruffled her hair. She was surprised to find it still felt soft and springy. 'I know. You've got troubles. I understand,' she said.

She had troubles of her own; how to get an innocent and unspoiled creature like Apollo into her bed. He would feel obliged to woo her and tell lies to her. He might even imagine they would have to get engaged before they could make love. 'Me bad woman,' she might say, but then he would think he was making fun of her. She would have to dress like a bad woman, or like Apollo's idea of a bad woman, to license him to make free with her. Her mind rummaged through her sparse wardrobe. Her few remnants of Oxfam bohemiana would probably fill him with fear. There were her nice new summer dresses, bought for Joe Fisher with a view to permanence; definitely, no. She had a black dress with no sleeves. Black was a widow's colour on Keptos but if she took up the hem and had high heels and pearls and a reddened mouth he must surely grasp her meaning. She stepped quickly into the house to begin preparation but found that Lulu's hand still apprehended her leg. She looked back in irritation. Lulu had assumed a grey and whining aspect like a horrible child with worms. 'Behave, dear,' she begged. 'Mummy's in a hurry. We'll sort out your troubles later.'

'Not my troubles, Mummy.' Lulu let go of her leg listlessly. 'It's Tim. I think Tim's in trouble.'

Harriet dressed carefully. She washed in a big basin of hot, scented water and then rubbed her body with a cream to counteract toughness. She sprayed perfume on her thighs and her chest and in the pits of her arms. As she anointed herself she looked at her limbs with a puzzled frown. Her legs and her arms had been roasted to a deep golden brown. It made for a curious effect against the whiteness of her body and the pallor of her face which had shielded itself over the telescope. She never used to go brown. She used to prefer the shaded places from where she could spy on the children playing their solemn games or sunbathing, plump and bare as sausages. Now and again she would emerge from her shade to turn them over, or round, so that they would tan evenly and not get burnt. They used to brown so beautifully, like golden trees. Now, when they ought to be like Coca Cola ads, they were driven into shadow by their preoccupations and were pink or grey, according to the swing of their hearts. While she smoothed pale beige make-up on to her white face the irritation of Lulu cut in on her thoughts. It was as if she had caught greyness, like an unwholesome infection, from Roger.

She sat in her slip and stitched impatiently at the hem of the black dress. Every so often she would pause with a considering look and she was taking stock, asking her body if it was still really intent on the ridiculous escapade. It was. Best to carry on and get it over with.

The dress was put on, the pearls added and a bright slice of lipstick. She sat on the edge of the bed, like a girl before a dance. Her tragic eyes observed, unamused, the white-masked, gypsy-limbed harlot in the dressing-table mirror. She smoked a cigarette, her lips clinging greasily on the paper and imparting an impression of poppies. Now and again one of the children opened the door and lurked there silently, studying her, before going away: Timmy, who looked to her like a child that had been stretched on a last, and her faded Lulu; Kitty, golden, with her new slice-of-knowledge eyes; Kitty looked her over, frowning slightly. 'The bluidie tryste,' she commented. She felt like a prisoner in her new disguise. She could not even ask them for a glass of water. After a while she amused herself by making come-hither eyes at herself in the mirror. Her mouth fell down like a clown's but, if she kept a cigarette in it, it held a better shape. This passed the time quite quickly.

When it was night she slipped out of her room. She smelled food. The door to the kitchen was open. She stood against the wall and peered in. The candles were lit and the children sat at the table eating stew and bread and drinking wine. They were smiling and talking. Harriet sniffed. She was hungry. If one of them had asked her in to eat she would have forgotten about Apollo. 'They won't want me any more,' she thought resentfully. 'They don't need me any more,' she thought then, and felt a bit better.

Outside she grew frightened and embarrassed. She felt as a child dressed up on Hallowe'en night. Trick or treat? One never quite gave oneself permission to grow up. Sex was always naughty. It was why marriage was best in the end. It was a magic suit. Married, you were grown up. No one questioned it. You could even feel your partner's leg under the dinner table, so long as you let everyone know it was a joke.

She clicked and stumbled in her highest heels on the pitted track. Underneath everything she was very excited, short of breath and charged with tension. A compensation for the punishment of guilt one imposed on oneself was that the boldness became its brilliance. Sex and circumstance, they were the real star team. She slowed down and took deep breaths as she entered the village and click-clacked behind the wharf. The village was full of people. It was very gay and exciting. Boys were drinking in the coffee bar and an argumentative youth bellowed out of the juke box. People were gathered in separate little groups in the street, idling men and chortling widows. She wondered why she had never joined in. Had she been imprisoned on her hill as the visitors to Psiros were on theirs?

When she arrived on the beach it was silent, the noises of the village captive in their distance like bees in a shrub, the sea a twisting ribbon of tin on a black sky.

The front of the bar faced the sea so she had to negotiate the soupy expanse of the strand to see if he was there. She stepped on to the beach and waded with determination, her high heels swallowed by sand. He was waiting, exquisite in the silky moonlight. Her throat felt as if a ballcock constricted it. She could not speak or swallow. She pushed back her hair and smiled at him sheepishly as she plunged the last few engulfing yards.

He had bought her a drink and now he helped her on to the stool and watched her as she lifted the glass. She shivered with pleasure. She had not enjoyed this kind of attention from a man since she was a very young girl and then she had not enjoyed it at all for fear and misery. For once she knew she had done everything right. She had only to stay quiet in case she came out with something confusing or clever, and Apollo would handle everything.

Harriet enjoyed her drink and kept her gaze, not too bold, on the boy. His face was full of angry workings. His eyebrows writhed, his nostrils flared, his lips compressed and inflated. Once, he threw back his head in the manner of a horse and a gleaming stretch of gold throat showed like a lovely little piece of a lake. She longed to touch his skin but contented herself with catching his excitement and feeding it tiny titbits by crossing her legs and fingering the pearls that rested on her breast.

'I live,' he recited tensely, 'in a small flat close to here. I have a radio.'

She smiled encouragement and she nodded.

'Do you like to listen to the radio?'

'No,' she said idly and then cursed to have been so treacherously overtaken by honesty. 'I mean, yes. Sometimes I do.'

It would not do. His disappointment was menacing. They sat in gloomy silence for a minute and then he said, 'This is not good brandy.'

'It is.' She gulped it down like a good girl. 'It's lovely.'

'At home I have some very good retsina,' he went on determinedly.

'Lovely,' she said, understanding.

'Very special. I think you like.'

'I love,' she said eagerly.

'Only for you,' he said and delivered his hand in a most casual manner to her thigh. It was a hopeful move and she thought she might now seize his thigh too but he said patiently, 'Hold my hand.' He helped her from the stool and they went off together, he tall and straight and striding and she stalking and sinking in the sand.

He took her to a part of the village where she had never been before; down a wet little lane (wet from what, since there was no rain?) between the cake-icing shops and through several other alleys until they came to a series of ugly concrete buildings with washing lines strung in between. Every so often she paused, shocked by laments, and rough, ringing voices and the bright blue glare of television. The buildings looked like gun emplacements, stitched together and placed end to end or one on top of the other. Odd that she had never noticed them before, for they projected above the pretty roof-line of the village centre and were, in their way, far more obtrusive than the hotel on Psiros.

She was so interested in this that she almost lost sight of the focus of their errand. When the boy pulled her roughly into a doorway and kissed her she gave a muffled moan of dismay and struggled away from the pressure of his body. His gaze in the shadows was as beautiful and uncomprehending as a sheep. She could tell it was no longer her that he saw but a saintly creature, the saviour of his fantasies.

'Here,' he said, proudly indicating with his hand a gaunt concrete passage winking with puddles; 'I have a furnished apartment.'

'I am a respectable woman,' Harriet longed to cry out as she followed him up a stone stairway, her heels picking their fastidious path through the smelly pools and small heaps of refuse. But she was not. Nor was she, at the moment, in the grip of a ruling passion. Her lower regions had lost her attention. She was at the mercy of her prudish nose. She kept her eyes on Apollo's back and wished that they could have made love on some sheltered part of the beach, with a nice nip of brandy on hand to bolster them and the pounding of God's good ocean to absorb the eye and improve the imagination.

He stopped on a squalid landing and let them into a little room. He shut the door, excluding the smell of the public area. Fingers touched her in the dark. His breathing was cut from him like wood shavings. 'Lovely red-hair lady,' he gasped. He seized a fistful of her hair. Sparks flew out of her and she smiled. Full of badness, she kissed him. She was filled with the sense of her own power, more aroused by his desire than by any want of her own. She opened the buttons of her blouse and drew his hand to her. 'I must look at you,' he said. He switched on the light.

There was a double bed on an iron frame, a tiny table with a plastic top and two chairs. A dirty sink and some toy cooking arrangement cowered in a corner. Clothing hung from nails on the wall. A piece of linoleum, patterned with grease and holes, covered a section of the floor. Before she had time to observe more the boy dived upon her, pushing her back on the bed. The perfection of his body, the simplicity of his desire, were a summons to pleasure. If only she had not smelled the hateful hallway and witnessed the wretchedness of the room! A portion of her mind worried that the sheets might be dirty. She could not tolerate dirty sheets. Her simple desire for domestic order now brought her further away from the lovely boy. Her own household was in a different kind of chaos. She suffered a memory of Lulu's whinging plea: 'Tim's in trouble.' At the time she had been distracted and the words did not sink in. Now they enlarged and settled in a blinking, migrainous neon.

What was he doing locked up in a room with Roger when he should be out enjoying the sunshine? Had it something to do with Lulu's misery? Tim's face when it peered around the door as she sat on the bed in her finery earlier in the evening, had it been haunted or happy? Was her son gay?

Somewhere underneath this nightmare enlargement of thought there was the sensation of a conjuror at work, trying to remove her underwear while observing the proprieties of leaving her dress in place. In another moment or two it would all be over and her mind had gone miles away. She pulled herself together and pushed at the boy firmly. He gave her a glazed and disinterested glance. 'Too soon!' she said sternly. 'I can no longer wait,' he complained, moving back slightly and holding on to the waistband of his trousers as if it would explode.

'Behave,' she commanded, taking advantage of this interval to sit up and get her clothes back in place.

He watched her sullenly and fanned his fly with his fingertips. 'You no like to love?' he said.

'In my country we don't talk about such things,' she said. 'If it happens, it happens – if one gets carried away.'

Apollo picked her up and ran about the room with her in a passion. 'I carry you!'

'Put me down,' she commanded. He dropped her sadly back on the bed. 'Now,' she said sternly. 'Let us start again with a little less feeling. Give me a drink and tell me about yourself.'

He looked terribly confused and hurt but he brought the yellow retsina and poured it into a mug and handed it to her. She nodded her approval and took the drink. 'Now, talk to me.' He sat stiffly down beside her, his hands between his knees. He turned to her and touched his chest with his long fingers. 'I talk about myself?' She nodded, smiling.

'I was not born on this island, no. My brother and I, we come from another island, Verico. There are many, many sisters. We are poor, very poor.'

She pulled back an edge of the scrappy blanket that covered the bed and noted with relief that the sheets, though yellowing, looked fairly clean. She smiled at him and nodded.

'When I am six years old, my father, he is dying, "My son," he say, "I am dying. You must promise me, your father, that always you look after your mother, your brother and your five sisters." I say yes. He die.'

'How sad,' Harriet said dreamily. She drank some retsina and lay back, waving the mug about to imaginary music. Her legs dangled like tulips. Apollo put a hand on her knee for sympathy. 'Delicious, darling,' she said. 'Do carry on.'

'Then my mother, she is sick. I am a good scholar but school I must leave to tend my mother and my brother and the girls. One of the little girls, she is also sick. All night I sit up, but she die.'

'Dear boy!' Harriet sat up again and kissed him with feeling. She tried to draw him to her but he was grimly hunched into his memoirs.

'My brother and I, we have a boat in the harbour. We catch fish. We feed the family. We are very proud. One by one my sisters grow up. They want husbands and my mother, who is dying, she say: "Promise me that you will see the girls to marry safe – and look after your brother." I say yes. She die.'

Harriet drank the rest of the retsina. Later, she thought she might be ill but in the meantime the effect of the drink was imperative. She clacked her tingling heels together and massaged the base of Apollo's spine.

'My little boat, which I love but which makes only enough for our food, I must sell. I must leave my home and my sisters, taking only my brother and come to live on Keptos to send home money to my sisters until each is married. I have no wife of my own. I am so poor. I have no woman. My sisters, they are kind, they send me clothes but I am all alone. You are a kind and beautiful lady.'

'Think nothing of it,' Harriet sat up and flung a motherly arm around him. She pushed his head down on her bosom and kept it there, stroking his hair, until their original intention had been resumed. He raised his stricken face to her and their lips and their tongues met and they wove their limbs together. She gazed at him boldly. 'Now,' she said to let him know that she was ready.

'Now,' he sat up again, 'my eldest sister she is married, two babies. Her husband he is sick and he say to me: "Apollo, take care of your sister and her babies."'

'Take off your clothes!' Harriet said through clenched teeth.

Miserably, he began to unbutton his shirt. 'My next sister she come to me and she say, "I bring shame to the family. Apollo, take care of me and my baby." Now my brother, his girl, she is also with child.'

Harriet took over the job of undressing. She did it roughly and deftly.

'My youngest sister, she have a crooked eye, she say, "Apollo, take care of my eye or I get no husband."''

She had taken off his shirt. She held it aloft with triumph and cried out with horror. Underneath it, he wore the strangest garment that was ever made. It was a vest cut from rough cotton and resembling a housemaid's night-dress. She did not think it had ever been washed.

'What is this?' she cried.

'It is my vest.' He was defensive. 'I also suffer with my chest. One lung, it is spotted. My sister, she make this for me. "Apollo," she say. "Take care of your chest. If you die, who will take care of us until we have husbands, and Christina's eye and the babies and your brother?"'' Pity and horror and revulsion attacked her. Her hands shrank back from his yellowing underclothes, his spotted lung. Her face too, she knew, was wrought with disgust. She stood up abruptly. 'I must go.'

'Oh, no.' he pleaded. 'You must not. Oh, how cruel! Oh, I burst with love!'

She stood stiffly in her crumpled dress. 'I'm so sorry. I hadn't noticed the time.'

He fell from the bed on to his knees and clutched the hem of her dress. 'I love you. I talk to you. I give you drink. What I do wrong?'

'Oh, no!' Her cry came out flour-coated. 'It's been lovely. I've enjoyed myself – really. Thank you so much.'

Retrieving her dress with a little jerk she fled. All the way down the stairs she could hear, as a backdrop to the festive castanets of her heels, his cries of rage. 'Bloody cruel lady. What I do wrong? I love you.' This was punctuated by a series of bashes, caused by his head or his heel or his hand, against the wooden door of his apartment. She had to pause to catch her breath when she got to the front entrance and then when she came out into the blessed cool and clean air she heard a rattle of high-pitched laughter, like Macbeth's witches. There was a flurry of black across the road –

72

one of the widows; no, two – three! 'Mr Fisherman!' cried out a
voice which she knew well, though never before in such a dreadful,
mocking mirth. 'Oh golly!' she said as she put her head down and
hurried past Melina, and she ran and she ran.

SEVEN

For some reason she found herself thinking about her mother. What else was there to do? The growth of the children had gone awry in the self-devouring manner of a cancer. Tim was turning into a homosexual and Lulu into a drudge. Little Kitty had not come home until dawn when she was returned by a primal-looking youth. 'Where have you been?' Harriet cried out, stretched as a catapult, for attack. 'Walking,' Kitty said dreamily. 'Walking on the beach.'

It was a small beach. One could walk its length and return in a space of fifteen minutes. To promenade it all night would be an up-and-down procedure like prisoners exercising in a yard. Kitty looked innocent enough. Oh, it was hopeless. Women did not cease to look like virgins until they developed an appetite for their despoilers which showed as a greed in the eye. Harriet had no wish to fight with Kitty. She was so tired and so sorry for herself. She wanted to put her arms around the child and weep. Instead she turned her anger on the enormously satisfied-looking boy.

'Walking? Just walking?' she demanded.

'Ah, yes,' he said with a smirk.

'I suppose you spend all of your nights walking on the beach?'

He considered this. 'Ah, no. My friends and I, we are walking on the beach many days with the sunrise.'

'Your friends?' Harriet was genuinely caught. 'You mean boys.'

'The boys!' The youth was boasting.

'What for?' She was intrigued.

'We come to kick the queers.'

She gave a lopsided grin and it froze there as a boom of terror struck her chest. Bothersome little memories connected violently. She thought of Lulu's hopeless hand on her ankle; the shame in Timmy's angry voice when she glimpsed his silvery back on the bed behind Roger.

'Go home now,' she said to the boy. Kitty and the youth clung

74

together, their eyes dark and quivery as port wine jelly. The boy went away. Harriet brooded after his swanking figure. Kitty came then and clung to her just as she had hung on to the boy. 'Bed now,' Harriet said, patting her shoulder.

She followed the same prescription herself, lying stiffly in the double bed, all passion fled and hope of sleep faded. Her mind was neon-bright and the train of her thoughts was ghostly.

She kept hearing the cries of the fisherman Apollo as she clattered down the stairs and they rang in her head like the cries of a person in a burning house. She had condemned him and his life and his underwear. In the morning she would write him a note. 'Dear Apollo, I am heartily sorry for having offended thee ...' Her mind was drifting, drifting more with boredom now than tiredness, but she snapped back with a snort.

'Dear Apollo, I am so sorry about last night. I could not be yours because I am a mother. At the last minute I remembered my children and my duty to them to remain pure. Thank you for a wonderful evening.'

She thought he would be critical of 'at the last minute ...' A proper mother would not admit the children as an afterthought, but it was his pride she was out to save, not hers.

A proper mother. The minute her mind had formed the thought it presented her with a picture of her own mother. The word 'mother' was quite a different word used in connection to Harriet and her mother than to herself and her own children. Harriet's mother seemed to have no unifying point with her. She was round and soft as a baker's white loaf. Out of this softness Harriet had come, bony as a chop. Her mother had had a fine contempt for men as long as Harriet could remember (and it was odd to think that she must have married young, as Harriet herself had done and been less than thirty when Harriet was old enough to judge her). Harriet looked automatically in the arms of men for love as a small boy searches gutters for money. Yet for all their strangeness they had a common bond. They were on their own. No one wanted them.

Her mother lived in a room in Finchley with a dangerous dog to protect her. Harriet lived alone with the creatures of the new world, the parasitic aliens that had once been her babies. 'Mummy!' she cried out alone in the dark, experimentally. There was no responsive echo from her heart but she thought she heard in answer her mother's call for help.

How could she expect anything from her own children if she neglected her mother? In the morning she would turn a new leaf. She would write her mother a letter. When she posted Apollo's note there would be one for her mother too. The prospect pleased her. 'Dear Mummy,' she wrote in her head. 'I am so sorry . . .' Her mind slipped away, decades away. '. . . I have not been a good girl.'

What had she done to displease everyone so? For a haunting second she saw her mother's face before her, hewn with displeasure like Mount Rushmore, and there was her handsome husband too, his teeth bared in a rage, and she saw Lulu's pinched greyness, telling her of her failure. It was very tiring and soon she fell asleep.

She was woken by the blare of morning. It sliced through her sleep, crackling blue and boiling hot. She writhed and curled up like an insect on a hotplate. There was no escape from the pert hand that pulled back her blanket and she was forced to look at the other bright and burning blue of Kitty's eyes. 'Morning, Mama!' (and a kiss). This morning Kitty was Pollyanna.

'I've made you coffee. Aren't I good?'

'Hmm,' Harriet took the cup and drank from it cautiously. It was horrible. Kitty was not domesticated. She blundered from time to time at the chores designated as female, effecting great chaos and demanding huge emotional ransom. She would make some man a most confusing wife.

'You're dreaming,' Kitty said. It was a provocation to think of Harriet's attention anywhere other than on herself.

'I was thinking.'

'What about?'

'My mother. Your grandma.'

'Thinking what?'

'I don't know. Something about a corset.'

'Poor Mum. Dotty old thing.' Kitty came and put her arms around Harriet. She smelled of Harriet's scent. 'Aren't you my best girl?'

She was looking for forgiveness. Harriet gave her a gloomy look and patted her. 'My own worst enemy, more like.' She remembered

76

her mother saying something similar when a neighbour who had fallen on hard times implored her to buy a corset; scarcely worn. Her mother bought the corset too and she wore it loyally for years, although she carefully removed all its bones first.

'Mu-um!' Kitty pulled her hair quite hard. Harriet turned to look at her. At a later stage in life Kitty would be the kind of woman who would need to wear a corset unless she opted for the alternative discomfort of aerobics.

'Yes, dear.'

'I don't know. What are you doing today?'

'I have some letters to write. And I might pop up the hill to keep an eye on Psiros.'

'Oh, don't go, Mummee, don't leave us again,' the child cried, flinging herself about. 'You're our Mummy and you're never, never there.'

Harriet felt the old pleasurable tug of responsibility, the reward of the indispensable. 'I'm here, little love. I won't go anywhere. I'll stay right here. What would you like to do? Come into bed with me like you used to and we'll tell stories, we'll talk and shut out the world.' She put down her coffee cup to hug her child and felt the strange foaminess of another woman's breast against her own. She sensed also the current of resistance in the child. 'Where will we go, little precious pigeon?' she persisted. 'Where would you like to go?'

'I'm going out, actually,' Kitty said in the manner of a disaffected husband, withdrawing herself neatly. 'I'm meeting Manolis.'

Harriet's arms ached with emptiness. She beat them up and down to get back their normal feeling. 'I see.'

For a minute Kitty looked uneasy but then sullenness brewed up in her cheeks and she flew into a rage. 'Oh no, you don't see! You don't see at all. You're meant to stay here because you're the mother. That's what proper mothers do. It doesn't mean we have to hang around too. You're the one that had us – we had no choice in the matter. Now you have to look after us.'

She thinks it's a choice, Harriet thought. She thinks people actually choose to have children, but she just cried out helplessly; 'Oh, you bully!'

Kitty's dazzling stare was righteous. 'I'll be gone for good soon enough, don't you worry about that. I won't tie you down for long.

In the meantime I'm going to see to it that we resemble a normal family, however odd it may seem to you.'

She did a little dance then, with her arms held high, a twirl like a victorious warrior dancing on the corpse of the vanquished, and Harriet cringed in fear; but she was only checking her appearance. 'Do I look all right – my bum isn't hanging out or anything?' Harriet nodded. 'You look fine.' Her buttocks twitched in the manner of an impertinent man winking as she strode out of the door.

'Oh!' Harriet clenched the hem of her blanket and sank down weakly in the bed. 'I hate you, I hate you, I hate you. Hate, hate, hate. Oh, you horrible, horrible, little fiend. You think I'm going to cry. I'm not crying, not on your life, not for you.' She blubbered violently at her pillow. She cried loudly and stickily for a long time and although the house was full of people, no one came. 'Blast and blast,' she sighed. 'I need a friend.' She searched like a madwoman in her mind and in her memory, raiding the head's faded picture library for smiling faces seen across crowded rooms or a sympathetic eye fleetingly poised at a bus window. She had hardly any women friends. She liked them but they did not much like her. She lacked the home-making facility that is common to her sex whereby women in strange and uncomfortable places can, by the rearrangement of an ashtray, or the sugaring of a cup of tea, suggest permanence and security. Her natural facility was for dispersal so that even in a proper home the way she dropped her ash, or neglected to put the milk into a pretty container, hinted at urgency and imminent flight. She wasn't a refuge. She thought that perhaps she was not even a comfortable woman to enter, that her interior had not the artistic arrangement of cushioning of the proper woman, so that lovers did not yearn to return.

'I need a friend,' she said stubbornly; and there was a friend. 'Joe,' she said quietly and in great relief. He was there, quite solid in her head. She did not even feel the need to have him with her in person. She knew what he would do. He would touch with his hand the place where her panic-stricken heart was captive until she was calm. His presence always made her feel all right. He liked her because she was as she was. He had never tried to change her. It was she who had attempted to rearrange the order of things, trying to divest him of his wife and involve him in a complicated deceit.

78

It was against his nature. If she changed him she would no longer love him.

In a little while she felt perfectly calm and was able to get up and make herself a proper cup of coffee and she enjoyed it, sitting in the front garden on a little broken piece of wall which was studded with pink flowers that looked like the buttons on babies' clothes. She had a friend. It had never occurred to her that she could claim Joe as a friend. It would have seemed like a liberty. But she knew that whatever the governing emotions, or the circumstances overriding those, she liked him and he liked her.

It was a beautiful day. There was a slight breeze to sweeten the air and it was the kind that would sweeten tempers too. Distant goats swam in a haze. Prickly shrubs, ruffled by insects from within, quivered pleasurably and from the town came the faint snarl of its few old motorbikes. Far below the sea played quietly with its toys.

The day invited pleasure. There was nothing to stop Harriet running down to the sea and splashing about in the warm and shallow part of the shore. She would not even consider this. She never did. There was something in her nature that locked her off from a free indulgence in the elements. She was like a child that had never learnt how to play. For an instant she was tempted to feel sorry for herself, but then she saw two women swathed in black trudging up the track and she came to her senses and realized that most of us who live on the surface of this spinning planet are suspicious of it and inhibited in regard to its favours. Quite right too. There is quick death in the sea and slow death in the sun – and premature ageing. In any case she was a naturally modest woman and did not like going around with bits of her body exposed. She was in a good mood and would enjoy herself in her own way. She would write her letters and post them and then take her telescope up to the hill.

She walked to the village and bought notepaper and a postcard in the shop that sold souvenirs. There was a good supply. It surprised her until she remembered Apollo's sad story of scattered sisters with crooked eyes and fatherless children. Keptos was a place of loss. Everyone had mislaid someone. Children crossed the sea to Athens or America. Brothers and husbands sank to its bottom. All over the island were women of Harriet's age who would never see their grandchildren, except in the demonic red glare of a Polaroid snapshot. How they must envy her. Or did they? They all wore black. It was natural to them to accept their losses instead of fighting them as she did.

She sat on the rocks where in earlier years she had watched the children as they swam and staggered and paddled.

'Dear Apollo ...'

Silly. A boy half her age. By the time he got her note he would have all but forgotten the incident. Best that she should forget it too, except that would be bad manners. A brief impersonal note of apology – that would do.

'Dear Apollo, I am sorry about last night but I was concerned about the children.'

She left the letter at the bar with the barman for delivery and ordered coffee while she considered the composition of a card for her mother. She smoked two cigarettes and studied the card. It was a view of Keptos, a wan depiction many years old and it pleased her for nothing had changed. One could even see their cottage. She drew a ring around it and penned a note on the blue sky; 'I am here!' – with an arrow pointing to the villa.

She had nothing to say. 'I am well. The children are well.' It was awful to have so little to say to the woman who had gone to all that bother with a man in order to have her. She wanted to say something meaningful, to trace the birth cord that joined their hearts. Dearest mother, yesterday I wanted a man. I found one but his underwear made me ill. My daughter is a monster, her brother's turning queer, goodness, gracious, I am mad with fear.

In the end she just made a sketch on the open page, of a dog on the beach with his legs all at odds like a broken chair and a trail of bloody paper in his teeth and a look of boredom to his bad eye. She got bored too. She left some money for the coffee and went off to take a peek at Psiros.

On the way back through the village she bought bread and butter and milk and fruit. She brought them back to the villa as evidence of her position there as mother. She wanted to put them properly in presses where they would come as a surprise and cause pangs of remorse, but the kitchen was crammed with slovenly young adults banging and slopping about the business of breakfast.

'Morning, dears,' she called to them from the hall, dropping her groceries there in the shade. The children squinted and scowled. Her telescope was folded up behind the coats. She took it quickly and went away.

From the top of the hill she made an astonishing discovery. She felt like Galileo finding out that the very earth is on a universal treadmill. She learnt that there were women like herself on Psiros – not just wives and office girls but women alone; women who wore their loneliness at a jaunty angle, women plunging awkwardly into middle age; women who said too much and drank too much. Harriet guessed that in addition to single women there were separated ones and widows and even some wives whose husbands, having spent sleepless years trying to tame them, like goshawks, were now catching up on their sleep while the wives stalked off, alone and full of energetic despair.

She had not noticed these women up to now because she had been identifying character types by their patterns of behaviour and women alone do not form part of a pattern. Curiously, although she identified with them immediately, she did not relate their situation directly to her own. She saw them as women who had not found their niche in life or who, having found it, failed to accommodate themselves to its space. She pictured them faced with the unpleasant disposal problem of the holidays, tactfully taking their ill-fitting lives out of the range of others' concern.

She herself had a very full life, quite adequate of purpose and lacking nothing essential except love.

She made another interesting observation. Every morning when the bar opened by the pool a line of what looked like exotic flowering plants was arranged under its awning. One by one these would be claimed and it was always the same – it was Harriet's ladies who made off with them. After a time a bout of erratic behaviour would follow – tossing of deckchairs into the pool and once or twice with their occupants still inside. It occurred to her suddenly that these bright arrangements were not plants but drinks, probably the hotel's special cocktail. It was served in some sort of Grecian pottery vase and rendered deceptive with flowers and cherries and bits of orange stuck on top. Foreign waiters were notorious for their cocktails. A girlfriend of hers had been ill in Spain with a period and had asked the barman for something for her stomach. He mixed up brandy and Cointreau and crème de menthe with an egg and she drank it and had to be carried to bed, screaming at the management to send her up a man or a banana. 'I ought to warn them,' she thought. 'Someone ought to warn them.' They were probably perfectly respectable women in their own way, not used to a tipple and attracted to the bright colours of the cocktail. The young waiters would sneer at them afterwards, and so would the young women, sober and limber with their purpose of mating. The older men would feel at liberty to register their natural sexual disillusion.

Harriet began to feel an exciting tremor of virtuous purpose. She would take the boat to Psiros. What would she do when she got there? She could hardly advise them against drink entirely, not without being a hypocrite. She could give them tips on how to hold intoxicants, or pace their drinking. She would reveal to them that she herself had been abandoned in marriage at an early age and had not succumbed but had brought up three children single-handed, negotiated Greece without the aid of travel agents or supplementary benefits; that she had survived.

Her thoughts were disturbed by one of the women on Psiros who, having finished her morning cocktail and flung the vase away, was now being followed by a man. This was so unexpected that Harriet fiddled urgently with the ring on the telescope as if it were possible to arrange a close-up view. The woman rocked someone's deckchair and the man ran towards her, full of desire, his arms stretched out like Rupert Bear in quest of butterflies. Good Lord! She did a little dance in excitement and peered again. It was Delbert – Delbert J. Mallard from America – who had comforted her when Joe Fisher failed to turn up. It was Delbert as sure as eggs, and the woman must be Betsy, for whose bad health Delbert had apologized. Betsy was a soak. Poor Delbert had been trying to cover up for her. Harriet felt sure that she could help. Her life had its gaps but her experience had few or none. Whatever Betsy's problem was, Harriet was confident she could come up with a corresponding trauma to share and halve.

Her thin arms prickled pleasurably. She must go to Psiros. She must warn the single women against mixed drinks and restore a dry-cleaned Betsy to Delbert.

She gave one of her lop-sided smiles, all of the terrors of the night banished and her whole self open to let the sun soak into her soul for she knew that without the slightest doubt her happiness was at hand. Not a mile away she was wanted and she was needed.

EIGHT

The children were still at breakfast when a man came to the door.
He was holding a bunch of fainting flowers and looked, himself, as
fatigued as if he had raided them from the Lost Ark. The youths
glanced out with bulging jaws and gave him brief and hostile review.
'Scouts' sodding honour,' Roger swore softly over the intrusion
and the man's clothing which was a kind of boy-scout outfit
fashioned in the plastic-based fabrics favoured by middle-aged
freaks who should be put down painfully. He wore a short-sleeved
knitted shirt and shorts in a khaki shade. His white limbs projected
bravely.

'Villa Anna?' The man consulted a piece of paper in his free hand.
The children lowered their gaze and returned to tearing up oranges
and bread. If he wanted something, there was no one stopping him
from asking. If not, he could go away.

'I am Joe Fisher,' he said. There was no response until Lulu
looked up, her face dazed and only one eye showing alertness. 'Joe
Fisher? He's Mum's geezer.'

'Where is your mother?' The man spoke wearily but politely.
Lulu shrugged. 'Up the top most likely. Take the track to the right –
quarter of a mile or so, but steep. You can't miss it.'

'A quarter of a mile?' The man sighed. 'If you don't mind I'll
leave these here.' He vanished for a moment and returned with two
large canvas cases.

'He's not going to stay?' Tim asked of Lulu.

'Naw,' Roger snorted. 'Just look at those cases. He's a travelling
salesman. Patent all-purpose remedy – hair loss to herpes.'

The roses made him think of Harriet, their unwise use of scent,
their beauty blown to bits by the dry heat.

If it hadn't been for that he didn't think he would have made it
up the last hundred yards of the track. It would have been easier
and safer to stumble back down to the harbour and sit there
drinking until the boat was ready to take him away.

He saw her bending over the telescope, her brown legs planted like a child's in their flat sandals, and he remembered that she was a guileless woman and that nothing was expected of him. He felt a weight drop away from him, as if he had only now put down his cases. He came up behind her. 'Good morning,' he said.

She turned and squinted into the sun, her hand over her eyes. She was puzzled to hear an English voice, and so polite. There was a white man, very white, in shorts, with close-cut hair and a pleased expression. He had flowers in a little paper cone. 'What a beautiful man,' she thought. He came over and put his arms around her and held her very closely and it was only then, when his figure blocked out the sun and she had struggled from his grasp to take a look at him, that she was able to say, 'Hello Joe.' She mangled him in a hug. 'Oh, Christ, Joe, hello.'

They had to collapse on to the creaking bank to touch and smell each other, to kiss and inspect. 'I never thought . . .' she kept saying. She kept touching him as a woman would an infant that has escaped death.

'You're here! How did you get here?'

'By deceit. By plane. By hydrofoil. By caique. It was hell.' He shook his head and laughed. He wasn't blaming her. 'I came on the boat this morning. I called first to your villa.'

'You met the children! Aren't they sweet? Did they give you coffee?' Harriet said.

'They told me where I could find you.' He avoided her search for truth. Mention of coffee reminded him of how weary he was and how disappointed he had been to find the cottage full of teenagers. She had not mentioned them when they made their plans. He had imagined they would have the villa to themselves. He wanted to sleep with her and get drunk and then lie out in the sun.

'What did you tell your wife?' Harriet said.

'I couldn't think of anything,' he said. Her face fell and it made him laugh. 'I told her I was going to Brighton. To a conference.'

'Brighton?' She began to giggle nervously. 'Oh, you couldn't! Did she pack your suitcase? Did she put in vests and Argyle socks and a lumber jacket? I'll bet it's raining in Brighton.'

'Cats and dogs,' he said. 'Pissing.'

She laughed so much she grew weak and had to hang on to his neck and he laughed too and then they settled down and lay on each other's shoulders and stroked one another's backs.

'It's bloody hot here,' he said happily. 'Do you know what I'd like? I'd like a wallow in the blue stuff down there. Let's do that. Let's go for a swim.'

'I can't.' Harriet shook her head.

'Why not, pet? Aren't you well?'

'Oh, I'm fine. I haven't a swimsuit.'

'You came out here without a swimsuit. What's in your case? Argyle socks?'

'I gave my swimsuit to Kitty.' Harriet was getting her guilty look.

'Well, take it back, then.' His voice got an edge of impatience and she winced.

'I can't.'

'Why not?'

'I'm too tired.'

'Tired? You're on holiday. Tired from what?'

She turned away. She dared to say it now that she was safe but she did not dare look at him. 'Tired of pulling myself together. Tired of whistling in the dark. The children are growing up all wrong, Joe. I'm afraid for them. I'm afraid *of* them.'

She had never spoken like this before, to him or anyone. It was his fault. The relief was too sudden. She gave him a bashful glance. He came and stroked her, her hair, her back, her arms. He put his hands between her legs and stroked her there, not in the frantic and furtive manner of a schoolboy trying to rub out a mistake but in a contemplative way, as if happiness was a leisurely experiment. It went on like this until both of them grew greedy. 'Is it all right here?' Joe Fisher said.

'No,' she said. 'I know a place.'

'I'll take you there.'

'Wait a minute.' She bent to rescue the little cornet of his flowers.

He picked her up and carried her. She said nothing but lay back and pointed with her flowers – where he should turn, which hedge surpass, in which group of trees to seek cover. She led them to the place she had plotted out for their loving.

He put her down gently and felt the ground. 'It's rough here,' he said. 'I've nothing to put you on. You'll get scratched.'

'I want to get scratched,' she said. 'I want to feel.'

'Yes, but not pain.' He drew back the neck of her dress to kiss her shoulder. The dress put up no argument. At the determination of her hands his own schoolboy clothes fell off sheepishly. She saw his white bottom gleaming in the sun and felt an intense happiness, only faintly tarnished by the intrusion of a little crowing contempt for the mad, the common, the desolate women of Psiros. 'I love you,' she said, holding his face; 'love, love.' There was no time any more, for talk, and he went into her and massaged her and held her together and soothed her in that little interval before gratification.

There was a legend on Keptos that a Venetian prince once sailed there and was overcome by its modest beauty. He planned to conquer the island and start a rich and ornate settlement. When he arrived with his troops he saw a very young and beautiful girl and he fell in love with her. He came to her house and was surprised that her family did not try to hide her but brought her forward and entertained the prince with music and cakes. They told him that they would prepare a feast for the evening and that afterwards the girl would be ready for him. All day he was on fire with thoughts of her and when evening came his curiosity was inflamed by the fact that she was not at his table. He could not eat or speak but merely moistened his throat with wine and yearned for the creamy skin, the brilliant hair, the luminous eyes of the radiant flowering bud whom no man had touched before. When the meal was over they led her to him – a common, stinking little parody of womanhood. Her face had been painted, her hair greased and curled, her little body was exposed through crudely slit robes ornamented with coins and beads. She reeked of scented water. With tears of anger and disappointment the prince threw his wine cup on the floor and shouted angrily, 'Take her away. You have destroyed her. You have turned her into a whore.'

'No, your highness,' said her father with a grave bow, 'we have merely adorned her with fine ornament, as you propose to honour our island.'

It was the turn of the prince to bow to the cunning old man. He was powerless to take the girl. He realized that simplicity is the warden of beauty, that to disarm the first is to destroy the second. He left the house and went away from the island.

Joe Fisher was asleep and snoring. Harriet watched over him. She was ablaze with happiness. Life now was still and simple. Joe Fisher was an ordinary man and his simplicity was his beauty. He wanted to be with her so he came across the world – by lies, by plane, by steamer, by caique. He wanted to make love to her. His sleeping face showed pleasure in this achievement. Impossible to tell if he had any greater ambition in her regard! Hopeless to predict whether she could settle for simple pleasure, should this be his wish. She prayed, anyway, let it not be spoilt.

He lay in the sun. Already little fingers of pink were stalking the bones of his back. She moved into the shade of the tree thinking with enjoyment how she would rub his back with balm in the night as she used to do with the children. She was on her holidays. Love was the only holiday. Any other kind of freedom was just loneliness with a brave face.

Her flowers had fallen again. She fetched them and freed them from their cellophane cone. They were suffocated yellow rosebuds, limp as dead birds.

After an instant's grieving, she crumbled them into petals and scattered them over the sleeping body of her friend.

The feathery shower woke him. She came and crouched over him, gaping in anxiety. He would forget where he was and call for his wife. He would think she looked scrawny without her clothes, without his lust. He would be exasperated by her skittishness. He smiled. She quickly adjusted her expression.

'I smell roses,' he said. 'I must be in heaven.'

'You are,' she said. 'I am.'

He drew her to him and stroked her but she pulled away in case he would think she expected him to make love to her again. She did not want to make any demands. 'What would you like now?' she said. 'Would you like to come back to the cottage? Would you like a wash? Some food?' She was proud that there was food in the cottage – not just tinned tomatoes and instant coffee but proper food – good bread and milk and eggs.

'Any of those things,' he smiled happily. 'All of them.' His smile dropped off quite suddenly and she backed away and watched him as a dog watches an unpredictable owner. He had remembered the crowding of sullen teenagers in the kitchen. It made him feel queasy, like going home to unmade beds or dirty dishes.

'What's up, pet?' she said fearfully.

'It's nothing.' He reached for her hand and forced a smile. 'If you don't mind I'd rather not go back yet.'

She swung her hair over her face. He did want to love her again. 'Why not?' she said coyly.

'I don't like your children.'

It was a mortal blow. 'Oh,' she yelped. She scuttled away from him, reaching out a claw to snap up her dress. She crawled to the highest point of the field, regardless of who might see her and struggled into her clothing.

'I'm sorry,' he said.

'My kids! They're my kids,' she protested.

'I can't pretend,' he said. 'I don't much like my own kids either. I don't like teenagers. I thought we were going to be alone.'

'I always bring them,' she said. 'We've been coming here years and years. Long before I met you,' she added defiantly.

There was a brooding pause. She felt his determination in it. 'Harriet, they're rude,' he said.

She put her arms around herself and rocked back and forth. 'I know,' she said quietly. 'The worst of them isn't mine.'

Now that she hated him he came to her and she accepted his comfort because she needed it.

'They need to be taken in hand,' he said. 'They're too bloody big to ignore.'

'They're at a difficult age.'

'They're a menace,' Joe Fisher said with deadly accuracy. 'They need a firm hand.'

'I haven't got a firm hand,' Harriet whispered. 'I just haven't.'

'I know. I know.' He kissed her sodden eyes and cheeks. 'Never mind. We'll sort them out. First things first; I need some food. Is there a caff around here where we can get a drink and something to eat?'

'There's a restaurant on the beach. It has fresh lobster,' Harriet boasted, remembering a rotted sign outside the taverna which showed a pink crustacean which appeared to be dancing.

'Good girl,' he said. 'Let's go and have a lobster.'

He put on his awful clothes and smoothed down his hair with his hands. With his eyes red-rimmed from tiredness in his pale skin and a faint reddish fuzz making his businessman's jaw disreputable, he looked terribly handsome, Harriet thought. He held on to her hand very tightly, for safety, as if she was a child, and she smiled up at him. It was remarkable, the relief she found in treachery. Now that she had pretty well admitted that her own children were abominable and beyond her control, she had shed the daunting piggy-back burden of their responsibility. 'White wine and lobster,' she thought joyfully. She doubted the restaurant's capacity to produce a lobster, but it scarcely mattered. Why had she never thought to go down and have a lobster on her own or to bring Kitty? Because lobster-eating was a reckless business. One needed a man to collude in such extravagance. One needed a man. Joe Fisher had an arm around her waist, a hand under her breast massaging her, always stroking and massaging in that lovely way he had. One needed a man not just to solve the problem of one's children but to solve the problem of oneself. She stopped quite suddenly on the track and had to pretend that she had a stone in her shoe. She had remembered something – the day after Roger's arrival, when she had felt the same light-hearted joy, the same sense of relief in acceding to masculine will. He had not taken anything over as she had hoped. Instead he had taken everything from her. Joe Fisher would deal him a firm hand. She grasped that hand and held on to it for dear life.

There was no one in the taverna except the family that owned it, eating in a dark corner off oilcloth. Harriet and Joe were glad of the dark and the desertedness. They picked a different angle of gloom and Joe lit the candle which had congealed into the table's surface. He studied her in the dusty bloom of light. 'You've gone brown,' he said. 'Your hair's gone gold. You look like a girl.'

'I didn't think you'd come,' she said.

'I thought of you alone on your island,' he said; 'not caring about danger or company or – anything.'

'Is that how you see me?'

'It's how you are. You like to be held but not *held*. You're a free spirit, Harriet. It's maddening. I couldn't bear to be excluded.'

She shook her head and was about to protest when the proprietor arrived and planted two stubby glasses and a bottle on the table.

'Krasi,' he commented with a smile and rubbed his fingers on his vest.

He waited until they had poured out the wine and tasted it and attested to its goodness with vigorous nods of the head and then he departed with a contemptuous noise.

He came back with plates and cutlery and a bowl of oil-sodden greens which harboured mince. 'We'd like a lobster,' Joe said indignantly. He turned on Harriet. 'Tell him we'd like a lobster.'

She didn't know the word for lobster. It hadn't cropped up in ordinary conversation. 'Lobster,' she said with a most polite look. The proprietor grinned and pointed to the dish. 'Lobster,' she insisted. She indicated the door and made stabbing motions to the left to locate the sign. 'Aah,' he said. His eyebrows waggled.

They drank some of the wine and wedged their legs together beneath the table. 'It tastes all right,' Joe said in surprise.

'It always does when you're here, in the sun,' Harriet said. 'Here, try one of these.' She held out a dolmade to him on a fork. He ate it.

A woman brought a nicely glistening salad and some flat, warm bread. The proprietor came with lobsters, pebble-coloured, dripping and gnashing the air with irritable pincers. 'Stella and Irina,' he introduced, grinning proudly. He held them out, one each to the diners, within fighting distance of their faces.

Joe Fisher looked delighted. He nodded approval. The proprietor was gratified. He kissed each of the lobsters on their stony heads. Only Harriet sat rigid and appalled. She could never understand what was so wonderful about being introduced to the creature that was about to be boiled alive for one's dinner.

'They look marvellous,' Joe said; 'don't they, darling?'

She shook her head fractionally. She hated disappointing him again but her throat had seized. 'They have *names*,' she said. 'You can't eat lobsters with names.'

'Eat?' The proprietor uttered a roar of rage and pulled back the lobsters, tucking them under his arm. 'Eat Stella and Irina? Crazy foreign fuckers.' He turned marginally sideways and spat. Harriet ducked.

91

'What are they for if not for eating?' Joe was disgruntled.

Harriet translated into clumsy Greek for the restaurateur.

'For dancing,' the man replied sulkily.

'They are ... for dancing.' She addressed Joe in English, in a reasonable tone, avoiding his eye.

'You want for them to dance?' the proprietor wished to know. Harriet nodded solemnly. He watched them with hostility for a while but he was appeased by the amorous scratching of his armpits through his vest by Stella and Irina. 'Okay, okay.'

He settled the lobsters in a terracotta pot for safety and went away. When he came back he had donned a red-braided jacket and he carried a bouzouki and some bells. The lobsters were taken from their playpen and the bells, on small garters, were attached to their claws. The man began a Greek folk tune on his bouzouki. The lobsters lumbered around, their bells clattering. Joe seemed genuinely impressed. He applauded loudly until one of the crustaceans took fright and scuttled away to hide behind the pottery.

The other one remained to complete a lonely and dignified prowl.

When the tune and the dance had come to an end the proprietor bowed low. Harriet and Joe applauded wildly. The proprietor picked up his lobsters and bowed again, sweeping them with him. Harriet took a pile of notes from her handbag and handed them over. She did not look at Joe until the man had retreated after several more bows. His face was strained with the effort of suppression. The moment she caught his eye he emitted a great snort of laughter. They laughed until they could only squeal. 'Oh,' Harriet cried, 'I've never really enjoyed lobster before.'

A woman brought more dishes – pieces of tough meat, stuffed peppers, chips. Their senses distorted by love and the wine, they found the food delicious. They ate one-handed, their other hands clasped beneath the table.

When they had finished and were drinking little pools of muddy coffee and small glasses of bright fierce grappa, Joe said gently, 'Tell me.'

'Tell you what?'

'Your troubles.'

She told him about Lulu and Tim and how they had been affected by the arrival of Roger. She told him of Kitty's nocturnal wandering and of her bullying. She even confessed her guilty concern for her own mother. She recounted it all calmly, as if it was quite a natural thing, and not a calamity to have one's family falling down around one's ears and tearing one's hair out in their descent.

He listened in his relaxed, almost indifferent way, rubbing her hand as she spoke and saying at intervals, 'Well, that's no problem.'

When she had finished she fell quite silent. The inn was empty now. A child stole out from its back regions and put, as an afterthought, a plate of figs in front of them and went away.

'There's not much you can do for them, you know,' he said at last.

'I'm all they've got,' she said.

'No. They've got themselves.'

'But they're not grown up,' she protested. 'They look big but they've no sense.'

'That's true,' he said; 'not fully grown – but fully formed. They are the kind of people they're going to be. A newborn child comes complete with its perfect genetic pattern – individual, unchangeable. Teenagers have much more – everything except experience. Once they're big enough to make their own decisions they have to make them, just as we have to live with ours.'

'No!' she cried. 'People get second chances! We could have a baby!' He had given her hope with his talk of new life. She could see their child (their bond) with its perfectly executed pattern of him and her.

'Harriet!' He was exasperated. 'You're not listening. For God's sake, we've enough on our plates.' He sighed with love and pity. 'No, there's nothing you can do for them now. Except pay for them. And keep them in order.'

'But Kitty!' She hung on desperately. 'Kitty is only fourteen.'

'Ah, Kitty,' he said. 'Yes, she's a different matter.'

'What shall I do with her?'

'She'll be all right. It's yourself you have to look out for with her. She's turned the tables on you. When a child stays out all night, what do you do? You lock her up until she learns some sense, that's what. She turned the key on you before you could do it to her. She tried to lock you up, Harriet.'

'Oh, it's true,' Harriet cried out in horror, 'She did.'

'We'll sort her out, don't you worry.'

She got a feeling of foreboding. She knew she was no good with the children but at least she loved them. Joe Fisher had admitted he did not even like them. But he loved her. And she was desperate for help.

'What about my mother?' she said weakly.

'Write to her. Write to her now.'

She took the postcard and pen from her bag and placed them on the table. 'I can't,' she said. 'I don't know what to say.'

'Go on now, put her address on it,' Joe urged. She did as she was told.

'Put your address too so she'll know where you are. Now –' he dictated. 'It is so lovely here. Harriet.'

She scribbled his message and added a triumphant signature. 'Good girl,' he said. 'That's all she'll need to know – that you're safe and in a nice place; and you're thinking of her.'

She licked her stamp and put it on the card. She no longer had to worry. She was in his hands and she was safe.

After they had posted the card they went for a walk along the water's edge. Joe wanted to swim. 'Stuff your dress in your knickers,' he advised. 'There's no one around to see.' He tore off his tee shirt and shoes and dropped them in the sand. They looked quite awful lying there, limp and twisted; like cats' majocklins, as Hawna Maroyle used to say when they were nine or ten and had been presented with something they did not like such as braised kidneys or brown wool tights. Why did she suddenly feel like a bold schoolgirl? It was because Joe Fisher had told her to put her dress in her knickers, had asserted that no one was around to see. Was he taking over her children and her island? 'God sees!' she wanted to shout after him to put him in his place but already he was on his belly in the waves and striking the ocean with pale arms. She tucked the skirt of her dress into her knickers. The thin silky white stuff bulged and crumpled. She looked like a supermarket bag full of rubbish. She pulled the skirt out again and smoothed it down and contented herself with opening some of the buttons near the hem. She ran into the sea, after the cleaving arms, fearful of being left behind.

The sea at the edge of the shore was warm and it rushed at her

94

legs blind and thick; like blood, she thought, her eyes clenched tight. The water sucked at her hem and seeped upwards in dark clinging blots. At school Harriet had been quite a good swimmer, not from enthusiasm but from a fear of criticism. Now she could not move. The water swayed back and forth teasingly and an occasional playful wave splashed her crotch. She knew she must look a sight with her eyes and mouth squeezed tight and her arms folded over her body as if she stood out in the Arctic sea instead of the steamy Aegean. She couldn't help it. Blind panic had leaped upon her again and left her in the dark. She wanted to cry. It was the fear of everything going right, she thought. A part of her was pulling against it. She had a sudden memory of a book she had read once in which a female character was likened to a boat – 'crafted for pleasure'. 'What have I been crafted for?' Harriet wondered, shuddering in the sun. 'Shipwreck!' Hawna Maroyle said viciously.

Arms came around her, wet and warm, wet hair and mouth; a wet body with a thumping heart. 'What happened to you? There's something wrong. I thought you'd follow. What is it?'

'I thought I'd lost you,' she said. For the moment that was part of the truth.

'You've got a suspicious mind.'

'You didn't wait for me. I don't like to swim.'

'Why not?'

'I look better in clothes. I'm too thin.'

'But you've got all your clothes on,' he said.

'Well, dry, I mean, and fluffed out.'

'Nonsense. You look like a goddess.'

'Venus sinking into the waves.'

'Give me your hand now.'

He led her until they were waist deep and the water was ice cold, clean and green. There was no possibility of aloofness here. It was a fluid world and land was only the bony bits sticking up. It was like stepping into a painting. She looked down. Already the bottom halves of them were changing into sea creatures. Their feet, tinged with verdigris, rippled and swelled, developing back to bonelessness.

He lifted her up and tucked her legs around his waist and she clung on to his neck. 'What's that for?' she whispered.

'Take the weight off your feet.'

She kissed him. His mouth had a lovely post-lunch wine-barrel rustiness and she gave it long licks like a child with a wooden spoon. She hitched herself up on him and felt his body tightening against hers. She experienced real desire now, not the needy relief as when he first came and put his arms around her but that demanding twinge that had only yesterday driven her in search of a man, any man. In a moment their clothes would miraculously melt away and his fingers would prepare his path and then . . .

She moaned in a happy daze of heat and drink and the mouth's moist promise of bodily delight.

Quite suddenly Joe slid backwards and she was completely submerged in water. She had to struggle free from him to gain some air. 'Oh, you cruel sod,' she howled, and then she was swimming.

The first surprise was the weightlessness. The sea held her. She no longer needed his support. Then she felt curious and had to swim vigorously to keep in the wake of the blanched flippers of his feet. She loved it under the water. It wasn't dangerous, as she had imagined, but refreshing and supportive and prettily-tinted. Every few seconds she put her head up for breath and the world above water now looked quite strange to her, the gritty little beach and rotting taverna receding into parched stillness, like baked bones in a desert.

They swam around by the rocks. She called after him several times for she was not used to swimming and imagined that her arms and lungs would give out and she would sink down in a little horn of bubbles and he would not notice. Eventually she saw his legs flutter and climb the water and she struggled up after him. He was pulling himself on to a flat rock. She lunged at a sharp projection of stone and a small gauzy streamer of blood was softly released from the palm of her hand. She felt heavy and clumsy now and her wet hair and clothes were a rubber sheet around her.

'Help me,' she mewed at Joe. He put out his hands and hauled her up on the rock, pulling her back on top of him. Water spewed from them, dangerously enlivening the placid grey of the rock. 'You left me,' she accused piteously, pulling slimy strands of hair from her mouth. 'You went off again. What for?'

'I had to,' he growled. 'Look at the state you have me in.'

He collapsed back on the rock hopelessly. Well, he did look a show with his damp hair and his stubble and his streaming eyes. She glanced away, ashamed. Any other woman would have had a hot bath ready on his arrival, and handed him a pile of towels. She would have pressed his shorts and organized his socks and had something steaming on the stove so he would scarcely know he was away from home. She knew there was something missing in her presentation of herself as well. She should have perfume behind her ears and carmine paint glistening on her toes. A proper woman would have swum with her head well above water to keep her mascara in its place and her hair dry.

She put out a hand and patted him. 'You miss your suits,' she sympathized.

'Ha!' He gave a despairing laugh. 'I don't think they'd help.'

'You miss your wife,' she thought, but the words were too dangerous to voice.

He took her grazed and abject palm and placed it on his sodden shorts. He projected hot and monumental from the schoolboy garment. She touched his soft tip first as if instinctively to reassure herself that he was vulnerable but he took her hand and wrapped it firmly around his erection.

She felt absurdly proud and sentimental to have effected this sculpture. He shivered in her grip. 'I can't wait,' he apologized. 'I really can't.'

'Could I just have a look at you first?' she asked. There was never time to look at each other at home. Their rushed assignations, in which to undress fully seemed a dangerous indulgence, were more like handshakes than lovemaking. She knew his body but she did not have a picture of it for her mind. She recalled the fear she felt, looking for him amid the crowds at the harbour when the boat had come in, tugging at the clothes of strange men to see if any of them might be him. She was resolved that she would acquaint herself with every bone and feature of him so that if ever they were separated again she would know him instantly in a crowd, by a freckle on his knee or the pucker of his elbow or even by some intimate part of him in the unlikely event that that was all there was to see.

'You want to look at me?' Joe Fisher said. 'My wife never looks. She makes me feel ashamed of myself.'

She felt a little stab of triumph as she pulled off his shorts. She caressed him briefly to soothe and tease him and then she sighed with satisfaction.

His body was all of a piece.

Unlike so many men who appeared to have been thrown together from odd pieces of rough lumber with genitals projecting like an evil clump of fungus from the torso's root, he seemed to have been made from a single piece of some smooth material. She was enchanted by him. She ran her hands over his smooth body. He closed his eyes and rumbled with happiness. 'You're beautiful,' she said to him.

He opened dazed eyes. 'Look at you,' he said. 'There's beauty.'

She looked down on herself, crouched over him, her knees striated by the rocks' cracked skin. Steam rose in a halo around her from her wet clothes and her breasts showed bold little pink buttons of desire through damp fabric. He leaned over and opened the front of her clothes and caressed her, returning her spirit to the water, absorbing her in ripples and circles until she was engulfed.

They joined their bodies and rolled around the hard surface of the rock, sometimes connecting with baked stone, sometimes with the little lukewarm puddles they made with their dripping clothes. Some of the pools were spangled hellish black and in others were held little upturned skies, blue as birds' eggs. Rupturing one of these with wild fingers, Harriet experienced a mad, momentary fancy that it was not merely the water that trembled, but the earth.

It was the first time she had properly experienced sexual pleasure. Up to now her climaxes had been knocked back quickly, like a gin and tonic, to take the sting out of life. Even with Joe the fear of failing to please him or being found out by his wife had compelled her to contain her joy, as if it might leave a mark and betray her. Now she delighted in her ruined appearance, in her aching backside, in the discomfort of the burning sun on her body. 'I'm happy, Joe,' she cried out. She was proud of this. It was a new achievement. Happiness, she was finding out, was not wanting anything. It was the digestion of the residue of sweet surfeit.

'Look at that!' Joe said.

She pulled herself up on painful elbows. The first thing she saw was how tender and disarmoured his body looked now. 'Cover up,' she said, protectively. 'You'll burn.'

He struggled into his salt-stiffened shorts indifferently. She worried about the rest of his body.

The rock was a sun snare. His flesh was too delicate a meat for grilling. She feared the sound of her own nagging voice so she kept quiet.

'Don't fuss,' he said. 'Look!'

He was demonstrating Psiros. He had not noticed it up to now. From the beach it just looked like a projecting finger of Keptos but from here it could be seen for what it was, solitary, sumptuous, disfigured.

She told him about the islet and its place in the scheme of her dreams when the children were small. 'Now, look what they've done,' she complained.

He stood up and walked to the edge of the rock, shading his eyes for a better view. 'It's a bloody great hotel!' he confirmed.

'The Paradise Hotel,' she said bitterly. She could afford to resent it again now she did not have to depend on it.

'Great!' Joe Fisher said.

'What did you say?' She swung her head around.

'It's great, Harriet? Why didn't you tell me? You could get there in twenty minutes by boat. I can tell you now I wasn't all that keen on this Godforsaken place, but we don't have to stay here.'

'Joe, Joe!' she cried out, stumbling over to trap his face with her hands. 'Don't say you want to go there. It's ugly there, it's ... common. It's lovely here. We're alone.'

'Of course it is, love,' he said solidly. 'I just like to keep one eye on the civilized world, that's all.'

'Civilized?' she said with scorn. 'You call that civilized? It's indecent what they've done to the island, and you should see the carry-on of those people.'

'Ah, you've been there, then.'

'Never.'

'Then how do you know?'

'I've seen them.'

'From here?'

'Yes.'

'You can see nothing from here. Just a grey matchbox.'

'Magnified. In a telescope.'

Joe Fisher looked uneasy. He speculated doubtfully on her mascara-stained face and patchily-tanned body and grinned anxiously.

'Harriet? A telescope? What is this – some sort of game?'

She was embarrassed. She crossed her hands over her body to cover it from his critical gaze and then turned her back to put on her dress. 'Yes. A game. We used to play it when the children were young. Silly.' She threw her shoulders up in a treacherous shrug. 'Kitty still likes to play.'

When she had put on her dress she turned a wary eye on him to see how he had judged her. To her relief he was smiling. Ladies' games!

'A game – that's right, pet. That's all I meant. Let's go to Psiros for a few days by ourselves and have some fun. Think of it, darling – steaming hot baths, ice cold gin, *lobster*. I know this island means a lot to you. I know it's the real thing, but enough's enough. You need a bit of pampering. You need to get away from those children.'

She shrank back from him. 'No, Joe. You go if you want.'

There was silence. She could feel it drifting in like a fog. She could see his burning back wrestling with love and common sense, his hand twitching for want of a cigarette or a steering wheel. 'You must have been a bitch of a child,' he said. 'I won't go.'

She came and clung to him. 'You won't be sorry,' she said.

He still had his civilized eye on the island. 'All the same we might just drop over for lunch sometime. I'd like to have a look at the place.'

'All right, then,' she conceded.

A strange flutter of excitement arose in her at the prospect of this brief visit. She began to feel there was something bracing about the reverses of fate. However you shook the bottle the quintessential sediment of destiny remained. She was fated to visit Psiros. The sun was going down behind the island. She could see the blue scrap of the bar's awning convulsing in a little wind. Already the guests were at the warmer bar indoors or in their rooms, soaping off sun-protective unguents under a boiling shower (she suffered a small contraction of longing at the thought of a boiling shower and a warm, floor-length towel, but it passed), preparing for the evening's unexciting entertainments. For a moment they would stop and sigh and wonder what was the point of day after day after day in which nothing changed except the colour of their skin.

But she was coming to change all that.

She had been frightened by the thought of going to Psiros alone – frightened that they would think she was one of them.

She knew she looked nothing special. Her individuality was all in her head. It was different when she was with Joe Fisher. His love for her was a mystery which even a fool would fail to understand. To have intrigued a man so beautifully ordinary, she was clearly an unusual woman.

She thought she would go all in white – a white dress and Lulu's fingerless white lace gloves; her straw hat with a wilting rose pinned to its brim. She hoped Joe Fisher had proper clothes in his luggage, a blazer, she imagined, and linen slacks.

She saw them coming ashore on the boat (she pictured a pristine motor launch and not the perilous fishing caique which was the day-to-day transport) and strolling up the narrow path to the hotel, arm in arm through its artificial gardens and the concrete slabs of its verandah. She could feel speculation rise among the guests in a cumbersome buzz as they entered the glass curve of the à la carte grill room, where the wet feet of the pre-paid guests were prohibited, where each morning stiff carnations were rushed in to supplant the limp and disappointed predecessors. Lobsters, executing a bored backstroke in their tank, would wave with rude contempt at the chef when he came to cook them.

Out under the brave awning of the bar, in the television lounge with its video games and vending machine, around the toothpaste-blue swimming pool, nervous whisper and giggle from holiday-makers who would have assumed themselves securely penned.

Office girls, abandoning their dreams of masterful suitors, would shove each other forward with scraps of paper for autographs in case she was someone famous. Children would finger the edge of the table wistfully and she might throw them a lobster claw.

And what would she do for them, poor children of Eve, weeping and gnashing! She would eat her lobster and go back to Keptos with Joe Fisher, brimming over with exhilaration and proteinous lust. She would show them that life gave you back what you put into it. She would demonstrate the way. When the boat came to take them back to Keptos the guests of the Paradise Hotel would line up on the pier to wave. She saw herself sailing away on just such a plum-coloured evening as this one, and the serried rows of small eyes piercing the dusk for a last look.

'Come home,' came the worn-out plea of Joe Fisher.

'Yes, love,' she cried, turning guiltily from her fantasy. When she saw his drawn face, so much more harrowed by sun and sea than by a day of bonds and securities, she knew that the cry of 'home' was a cry for a warm flat with a little fire, the sounds of sherry being poured, and Schubert, the scent of blood from the oven. Seeing his longing then, so plain and unadaptable, she loved him, really loved him, and she longed to cherish him. She took his hand and led him over the rocks on to the flint track so that they would not have to swim in the dark. She made him wait there while she raced down to the beach and retrieved his clothes and her shoes. She brought him home then, all the while comforting him with the promise of treats. 'I'll heat up gallons of water and you'll have a nice hot bath – a real treat here. I'll make you a lovely meal. I'll rinse out those clothes and press the rest of your things for tomorrow.'

'And please God,' she prayed to herself as she spoke; 'let me be like other women.' She found, now that she had a decent stretch of happiness to herself for the first time, she did not wish to expend it in service. She wanted the bath for herself. She wanted to bring him to bed, and a bottle of wine, and fling her feckless body down on his. She knew that between what was necessary to him and what was tempting to her stretched the great grinning gulf called freedom.

Joe Fisher paused on his stony pilgrim path and bent, very seriously, to kiss her. Her arms flew around him and she gabbled confessions of love. She only wanted to please him. She wanted to *want* to please him.

'And please God,' she whispered, as they came in sight of the cottage, with its glut of roses blue in the moonlight, its tremulous eggs of golden light within, its lace curtains lashing feathery snow against the warty white walls of the little villa; 'let the children be good.'

NINE

The children were drunk. In the split second after she saw that it was so she told herself no, it wasn't possible, it was a trick of the light.

'Children!' she cried out. She threw her hands over her heart, over her mouth, waiting for the box in her chest to dissolve and the scene to return to normal. Grotesque shadows rolled on the wall as the teenagers tried to force the new arrivals into focus.

'Crazy!' Tim said, raising a bottle of wine which fell from his boneless fingers and spewed red on the wooden table.

'Krasi!' Harriet turned with awful cheer to Joe. 'It's Greek for wine. The children call it crazy.

'Sorry,' she mumbled then, seeing the expression on his face – aghast, unforgiving. Bottles stood and lay in puddles on the table and there was broken glass on the floor. The children laboured over the disarray, their coarse baby faces sinister with unanchored leers. They were all there, Lulu, Tim, Kitty, Roger, Kitty's Greek boyfriend, Manolis. Except for Roger, they were out of control and there was an edge of weeping to their laughter.

'What the hell's going on?' Joe Fisher said.

'Bit of a party, it looks like,' she gibbered.

'Let them answer. What's going on?'

'Like the lady said,' Tim jeered; 'we're having a party.'

'Harriet, where did they get the money for this?'

'Don't fret, Fred – no bread,' said Roger in his hateful whine. 'Kitty's friend works in a wine factory.' He gestured at the stupefied Manolis. 'The gin, sir, is courtesy of your kind self.'

Harriet now noticed that two empty gin bottles stood squatly among the slender wine vessels. 'You bloody little swine!' Joe Fisher advanced. 'You've drunk my duty free.' He dealt Roger a stinging slap on the ear. The children shrank back. They gazed with blurred astonishment. Kitty belched and her eyes popped and she scuttled past them looking alarmed to throw up horribly in the yard.

Joe came back to Harriet. His hand was still rigid for attack. She flinched, ready for her punishment. 'I'm going to bed,' he said. The disgust in his voice was more painful than any physical assault.

He went to bed without unpacking, pulled off his shorts as if they too disgusted him and flung himself into the narrow cot. Instantly he was asleep.

Harriet stood in front of her mirror. Her burnt and gritty face was that of a bomb victim. Dislocated mascara made muddy channels under her eyes and her nose was shiny and tattered. 'I stink,' she whispered and sniffed with self-pity. She could not even bear to enter the kitchen to heat water for a wash, with the children in that condition. She scraped the dirt off her face with some lotion on cotton wool and shrugged out of her dress. Weeping quietly she slipped into bed beside him.

He had left hardly any room. She had to wind herself around him very cautiously to balance her body on the mattress. 'He stinks too,' she noted with interest as her rigid neck relaxed on the pillow. For some reason the thought comforted her and allowed her to insinuate herself a little closer. First she eased her legs up under his legs, with his bottom to her belly and then she pressed her breasts into his back. He had not woken so she comforted herself by stroking, very softly, the back of his head, rubbing the blunt hairs at his nape with a finger. The hot night soldered them and after a while she flung caution to the winds and laid a brazen hand on his chest. She started nervously when he picked up her hand quite sharply but he only pressed it to his lips and then guided it down and pressed it to his sleeping penis.

'Thou art all fair, my beloved,' she thought, happiness rising chokingly in her throat. From the kitchen came the sodden shrieks of the children. She tried to shut them out, to bar her heart against them so that it would be neat and free for Joe Fisher. But they were all fair too, just young and high-spirited. It was only life, bloody life (she thought indulgently), that was unfair.

It was Harriet's dilemma that she could tolerate almost anything so long as she was loved. This tolerance could be very taxing to those friends whose behaviour did not require it for it embroiled them in her provocations and often impotent irritation dealt the love a mortal blow. She found the children a thorn in her side, but she considered this due to a lack of spontaneity in herself and imagined that others must find their youthful exuberance infectious. Joe Fisher seemed ruthlessly determined to defend his environment against this infection. Pest control or Endorat would not be out of the question. It was too late for her to start fighting with the children. Their indifference to her wishes would incite Joe further. She saw the answer as a game for six or seven players, in which she, leaping and scurrying and occasionally ducking, must make all the moves. If she made meals and heated baths for Joe Fisher; if she marshalled the children, gave them money for outings and cleared up their dirt; if she discreetly managed the shopping and a reasonable presentation of herself, she believed she could deter her lover from desertion or destruction. The thought tired her but she calculated it as the price of love and she knew she had to pay.

She had been awake most of the night. Love and loyalty kept her from moving out of the cramping position that bound her to the revered form. Worry and discomfort detained her against sleep. The little room seemed quite transformed by the presence of a man. His shorts on the floor, his body in the bed, both quite lifeless yet entirely compelling, sucked up the pure still air of celibate cell and returned it as a turmoil of unidentifiable spinning fragments, *quarks*. She was delighted and disturbed by him. His coming had damaged the peace of their lives in which trouble had been properly confined within the accepting walls of family. His coming had brought her the peace of the womb.

She strained her ears to the sound of merriment from the other room. Hours after she had gone to bed the noises guttered into heavy silence. Someone was weeping quietly. She thought she heard a cry but so altered by its preoccupation that she could not tell if it was one of her family nor even if it was a male or a female cry.

She slept briefly and was awake at dawn. She prised herself out of bed and forced herself to face the kitchen. 'Water!' her soul cried out. '*Boiling* water.' The table was littered with bottles, spilt drink, cigarette ends and some open and empty tins with forks in them from which someone had, for convenience, eaten directly. Her feet skittered to avoid winking arrows of broken glass. She dragged out from cupboards all the large metal containers she could find and filled them with water. She staggered from sink to stove with her slopping burden. While the water was heating she cleared the table, put the dishes in the sink, the tins and bottles in the bin, and swept the ashes on to the floor. With groaning arms she swept the floor. She longed for coffee but feared its aroma would wake the household and bring its members into the kitchen and she needed to be alone for her Herculean chores. Instead she lit a cigarette but she gagged on it and had to put it out.

When the water was hot she emptied three potsful into a tin bath, reserving a fourth for the sink, and refilled them again. She washed the dishes and dried them and then ferried a basin of the still-warm soapy water to the kitchen and she scrubbed the floor.

The cottage was beginning to look quite normal. Harriet filled a pretty piece of pottery with water and put it on the table. She went out into the garden, where night still hovered in one half of the sky, and gathered an armload of damp roses which she brought back and arranged in the bowl. She looked for some pretty lace mats, but when she found them they were filthy and crumpled and she shoved them back out of sight. She set the table with the freshly washed cups and glasses and squeezed oranges into a blue jug. The bread bin yielded a clutch of stale bread rolls and she damped these with milk and put them in the oven to warm. When this work was completed she lugged the newly heated pots of water into the bathroom and emptied their contents in on top of the already cooling pool. She then refilled the pots and put them back on the stove. After that she found herself a towel and a great big bar of soap and she eased her stiff and weary body into the water.

It seemed years since Joe's arrival. She could not remember their hours of leisure and laughter. She could only think of the work that having a man around necessitated. She longed to sleep. Desperately pulling herself together, she scrubbed her face, her body and her hair. She creamed her hair and rinsed it and then she creamed her body and powdered it. She sneaked into her room and slipped on her prettiest dress, an entirely innocent-looking shift with faggoting on the neck and sleeves.

When she glanced at herself in the dressing-table mirror she thought that her skin suggested one of those compressed sausages of luncheon meat, sometimes with a bright yellow boil of egg in the centre, that glare at one from the cold slab of English delicatessen display counters, but she did not suppose anyone would notice. Joe looked rosy and rejuvenated in his rest and this reward restored her to her sense of purpose. She went back to the kitchen. With legs splayed and feet braced she lugged one more load of water to the bath and set another load on to boil. Then she put on the coffee.

There was coffee and fruit juice and egg and warm rolls. There was a wonderfully hot bath for Joe infused with scented essence; warm towels and fresh clothes, pressed by Harriet with the mouldering little flat iron, which she heated on the stove. He was delighted. He bounded out of his bath and into the garden, paced about, snorting in the hot, exciting air, with its skittery little herbal winds, and then charged back into the kitchen, ravenous for breakfast.

'It's beautiful, darling, it really is.' He kissed her. 'I'm sorry I didn't appreciate it yesterday, but I was exhausted. Today will be different.' He gulped back juice and coffee and ate several eggs. 'The light!' he exclaimed. 'It's quite wonderful. I hope you've done some paintings.'

After several cups of coffee Harriet was able to face a cigarette. She left it in the corner of her mouth where its smoke discreetly veiled her bruised complexion. She placed one hand on Joe's warm and surging leg and used the other to prop up her face which smiled and made faint and agreeable murmurings at his virile enthusiasms.

She felt better. She could not look on his hair, which was sweet and crunchy as wheat after his bath, nor on his restored face (restored not only from the rigours of yesterday but from the required set sternness of the business world), and fail to exult. Tears of emotion were in her eyes, swelled by a natural watering of exhaustion and a faint irritation from the smoke. Joe wore a blue short-sleeved shirt and pale baggy trousers which she had selected from his packing and his pink-tinged cheeks beamed out a blameless David Attenborough kind of sexuality.

He had started to talk about himself. The island, he said, put him in touch with his dreams, evoked memories of early childhood; his first holiday on a farm where a labourer called Grant had brought him, for a treat, to watch some kittens being drowned in a bag. Later he had gone back on his own to save them, but they were stiff and sodden; his first sexual experience, also on a farm, with a sly fat girl four years older than himself; romantic voyages on student fares, his honeymoon. All of his dream memories were veined with disappointment and Harriet serenely accepted that this was her doing, she had become a part of his dreaming and those dreams that did not contain her were deficient.

She was jolted when he came back to the present and offered her a set of vigorous plans for the day – a walk to the top of the island and then around its upper rim to admire the view from all its aspects; a boat trip to look at the caves, a visit to Psiros. 'You choose,' he urged. 'What would you like?'

'I'd like to go back to bed with you.' She crept over to him and climbed on to his knee, surreptitiously sneaking away her cigarette in order to rub her mouth against his neck. 'You're a randy little baggage,' he admired cautiously.

But no! It was tiredness. She was used up, drained, squandered, and he was telling her that she must start all over again. His proposal of fresh activity exhausted her to the point where real tears – the liquefaction, perhaps, of her furred brain – dripped down her face and she needed a bed, a comforter, a mother.

How often in the past had she gone to bed with men from sheer tiredness? Unable to sit up any longer and listen to their legends of income tax, adventure and romance, she had boldly called for bed. She was admired and feared for her directness. She developed a reputation. It was different with Joe. Love ruled out coercion or submission and complicated the business of bed.

He did not sweep her up in his arms and bear her masterfully to rest. She was resigned to this. When she failed to laugh at her own audacity she felt him grow angular with unease. 'What's the matter?' he said kindly. 'Are you all right?'

'I'm a bit tired,' she admitted.

'Tired?' His voice got an edge of exasperation. 'I don't understand you, Harriet. Why are you always so tired on your holidays?'

She rubbed away her tears surreptitiously and gave a noiseless sniff. 'Did I say tired?' she sobbed brightly. 'Happy, I meant. I'm so happy.'

'That's my girl.' He turned her round to face him. 'I want you happy. You're going to have a wonderful time. Don't think I don't want to make love to you every minute of the day but we can't go to bed right now.'

Of course not. The room was airless and disordered. She had to open the windows and make the bed, polish the surfaces, put fresh flowers on the dressing-table, wash out his shorts. She gave a huge sigh, leaning on it to make it sound like a low one, of contentment.

'There are the animals,' Joe went on. 'They're bound to come barging in any second.'

'Animals?' she giggled nervously. 'What animals?'

'The children. Those filthy little beasts who stole my gin.'

The children! She had forgotten them. She could not bear to think of them. She slid bumpily from Joe's knee and tried to think of an excuse to escape. Shopping? She couldn't face a confrontation between Joe and the children. There was no avoiding it but it could be evaded. Let them all kill each other. At least she could go back to bed.

The animals came in two by two; first Lulu with Roger. Kitty hung sheepishly behind Tim; after the horror of being cornered by them there was the slight relief that Manolis had not stayed the night.

They looked appalling; her lovely rosy children whom she had brought boastfully to Keptos to display her powers of reproduction were like a clutch of the little grey boiling fowl the village housewives haggled over at the midweek market.

'We smelled coffee,' Kitty said.

'Sorry, Mum' – Lulu's head dropped – 'about last night.'

'Sorry –' Roger bowed and his diluted blue eyes slid upwards to connect with hers – 'to have interfered with your pleasure.'

She could see Joe's hand twitching. She moved over to him and took hold of it to prevent an incident but he snatched his fingers away and brought his palm crashing down on the table. The roses shed a litter of pink petals into the butter.

'Whose idea was the party?' he bellowed.

They shuffled and pointed at one another.

'Aw, Mum, are you going to let him go on?' Kitty groaned. 'I need a cup of coffee.'

'Yes, well, I don't see why not,' Harriet murmured faintly in favour of each point. She moved to the coffee pot but Joe shook his head at her so fiercely that she put her hands behind her back.

Kitty stuck her tongue out at him and smiled defiantly at her mother.

'Who stole my booze?' Joe said.

Roger stuck his hands out in an exaggerated gesture of self-defence. 'Borrowed, man!' he said.

'So it was you, you rat-faced little fart,' Joe said humourlessly. 'That's ten pounds you owe me.'

The children sniggered. 'I haven't got ten pounds,' Roger said. 'Blow me, I haven't got a bean. Tell you what, old man, put it on my account.'

Joe glanced at Harriet, possibly to see how far he could go before she would fling herself at his feet and intervene for clemency, but she gave him a tremulous smile and looked away, biting her lip to control her giddiness. She was enjoying herself. The thumping of her heart came not from fear but from a tiredness that transported her to some remote and irresponsible region. All of the men she had known in her life up to now were sensitive creatures, kind to the whole world, gentle with animals and children and only brutal to a person in particular – to her. She was excited by his mastery and felt a queer detached sort of vindictiveness towards the children. Bereft of their beauty she could see that their attraction had all along been superficial.

'Ten pounds, you little fucker!' Joe lunged forwards and picked Roger up, murderously, by the pink scarf knotted at his throat. Roger gagged and his face paled with terror. When Joe set him down he backed off into a corner and panted, with his hand to his skinny throat. Then he looked up again and his bleached face was full of spite.

'I haven't got the money, mate,' he said. 'What are you going to do about it?'

They all watched Joe to see how he would rise to the challenge. Lulu and Tim had the stupefied look of children in a classroom witnessing one of their peers being punished.

Kitty ran melodramatically into Harriet's arms and Harriet, out of tiredness, hung on to the big, fleshy luxuriance.

Now that he had been dared, Joe had surely no option but to finish off the youth. Joe was much bigger than Roger and he belonged to a military generation for whom ordinary codes of social behaviour were a matter of life and death, and death itself a trifling issue. Already she could hear the snap of Roger's meagre bones, could picture his dull complexion enlivened with a loop of blood. She glanced around to gauge the children's anticipation of violence. They were like herself. They were looking forward to it. Roger's death was the relief they all needed. Lulu and Tim, trapped in the complexities of their emotional entanglements; Kitty, bullied into sexual flirtation by the recent blood of her womanhood, needed the sharper, thinner blood of male against male. Harriet had to have her honour restored. It had been robbed by Roger in his various seductions. She wanted her children back.

They were disappointed when Joe walked past them in a calm and rather cowardly fashion towards the front door.

Roger could not resist the provocation. 'So what are you going to do about it, you ageing snot-rag?' he taunted.

Joe turned at the door, mild and agreeable. 'I'm going to the police,' he said.

Harriet thought she detected a flicker of fear on Tim's face. All the young people hated the police. Pigs, they called them. She could never understand where pigs had got their poor reputation. She always thought them private and endearing animals. When she was small and her grandmother had called her her little hen, she had said, 'Don't call me a little hen – call me a little pig.' Even then she could see that hens were a vulgar lot, squawking and dropping eggs from their bottoms.

In any case, it was Roger who reacted. His pink scarf clawed the air like a drowning hand as he fled past them, past the astonished paleness of Lulu, past the middle-aged immutability of Joe. He paused in the brilliant stillness of the yard, seeming dazed, and then scurried back and forth around Joe as if to deter his exit.

'Aw no, mate, don't do it – give us a break.' His hands grovelled in space. 'Have a heart, dad – not the cops.'

Joe was watching him with interest. He wagged a reproachful finger at him, as if it was a naughty child in the nursery. 'You've got a little secret, haven't you, my lad? You're scared shitless, you little creep, and that isn't over my gin. You've been in trouble before – what was it? Funny-smelling cigarettes? Breaking and entry? Worse?'

Roger seemed on the verge of tears. It fascinated and exhilarated Harriet. 'They lock you up here,' Roger pleaded. 'They throw away the key. They keep bloody prisoners in bloody chains.'

'That's not very nice, is it?' Joe condoled. 'You ought to have thought about that before you nicked my gin.'

'Don't go,' Roger snivelled.

'Don't go.' It was Harriet's voice. She had no idea why she had said it. Murder was one thing but captivity was another. She had a vague uneasy feeling that a brush with the law might infect her own offspring.

Joe gave her a hard look but it softened almost on impact. 'All right then,' he sighed, 'what are we going to do with him? I want my ten pounds.'

'I'll get it for you, honest I will,' Roger promised.

'Steal it, you mean – no, thank you.'

'I'll do anything,' Roger promised.

'Right,' Joe said. 'Work for it.'

'What?'

'That's right – you're going to work off your debt and you're going to do it today.'

Roger looked relieved but wary. 'What do you want me to do?'

'Go down to the beach. Search the fields. Get sticks and drift-wood. I want enough wood to keep the stove going for a week.'

Joe stepped back into the house and they all moved aside. He seemed huge in his authority. He was looking around for some suitable implement, some stick-carrier or hod. He found the tin bath and thrust it at Roger. 'Take this and don't come back until it's full. Proper sticks mind – no twigs!'

Lulu sidled past Joe and stood beside Roger. 'I'll go with him,' she said. 'It's my fault too. It's all our fault. We all drank your gin.'

'Good girl,' Harriet encouraged.

'You stay,' Joe said sharply. 'You're going to shop for your mother and cook us a nice meal. Tonight we'll have a civilized dinner.'

To Harriet's surprise the atmosphere in the cottage lightened. Joe's authority was a charge of negative ions. It made her think of the day they had cleaned the cottage and hung the curtains, how

112

much the children had loved being organized, how uncomplicated they had been.

'I'll need money,' Lulu said. The children watched in awe as he carelessly handed over some notes with a value of about ten pounds.

'What shall I cook?' Lulu said.

'Ordinary stuff,' Joe said. 'Roast lamb and roast potatoes. Could you make an apricot and almond tart? That would be nice.'

'Sure.' Lulu was delighted with herself. 'I can make pastry.'

'Good. Splendid. Breakfast for all and then work.'

Joe poured orange juice for them and spouted coffee into mugs. They fell upon the table, gulping the juice, colour flooding their cheeks as they recovered instantly from their hangovers. Harriet sat weakly down and allowed herself a satisfied smirk. Her man had taken charge. Even without Roger's death, her honour and her family were being restored to her.

'What shall I do?' Tim said, his mouth full of bread.

'You?' Joe speculated. 'You can guard Kitty.'

'Guard wha . . . ?' Tim spluttered.

They all giggled cheerfully. Even Harriet could see it was a joke. Only Kitty, who still lounged against her mother as she slurped from her mug, was stiffening for a fit.

'Watch it, fuckface,' she murmured at Joe.

'You I'll watch,' Joe said. 'You've given your mother a very rough time and a lot of worry. As from now I'm taking over. You're to go to your room and stay there all day.'

'In a pig's eye,' she spat. 'Mum?' she yelped, seeing real hostility in his face.

'Please, dear,' Harriet wheedled. 'Do as he says. It's best in the long run. I'll buy you something nice.'

'There's a law against locking people up,' Kitty screamed at Joe. 'I'll tell the police on you.'

'Call it citizen's arrest,' Joe said. 'You tried to do it to your mother. Now see how it feels to be confined to quarters. You can go to the police tomorrow. Today you're going to your room.'

'Tell-tale,' Kitty breathed malignly at Harriet, who quailed.

'Look here,' Tim struck out recklessly. 'I'm not doing it. I'm not Kitty's guardian. I'm going stick-picking with Roger. Come on,

Rog.' He gave Joe a feeble glare of confrontation but Joe merely nodded solemnly and the boy stalked nervously past. They all watched until Tim had made his exit and whooped with loud triumph as if his escape had been a hazardous thing. Indoors Kitty added an encouraging war cry to the two youths retreating with their tin bath. Joe turned to look on her with an amiable concern. 'Well, if Tim won't look after you I'm afraid I shall have to lock you in,' he said.

'Lock me in?' Kitty gasped. 'Mum, you're not going to let him?'

'Don't interfere, Harriet,' Joe said.

Harriet started to clear the table. She collected plates and glasses noisily and brought them to the sink. She left the tap fully running to lessen the volume of Kitty's howls.

'I'll tell the newspapers! I'll tell my father.'

The sound faded as she was removed from the room and interred securely in her own quarters.

Harriet found that she was smiling. Joe was a kind man. He would not hurt the children. Nor would he give them any quarter. His harshness in dealing with them was due to a lack of complexity rather than a lack of sympathy. All through their lives Harriet had felt compelled to issue the children special treats and treatment because her clumsiness in love had lost them their Dad, their figurehead. Now they had Joe. He suffered no confusions in his patriarchal role. He made a blackguard of a Dad.

A great tranquillity enveloped her. She no longer felt confused by tiredness. She suffered rather the pleasant weariness of accomplishment, and was carried by bright ambition. She no longer wanted to go back to bed, either for sleep or sex. She was ready to start work on Joe. Falling in love with a married man, she reflected, was like seeing a lovely sweater in a sale. Although perfect in its own way, it was bound to be a wrong size. One had to unravel a bit and knit it up on new needles and then, when it had been re-fashioned for one's own fit, it was fit for no one else.

She put wine into a wicker basket and apples and bread. She found a piece of tolerable cheese, pared off its horny skin and tucked it in underneath. A small sharp knife, corkscrew and glasses were added and she padded the food with the folded pink tablecloth.

When Joe came out she was preparing a second picnic, on a prettily ordered tray, for Kitty.

She looked at him in query to see how he had fared and he hung his head in distaste at his action. This small gesture appeased them both.

'How is she?' Harriet asked, as of a patient.

'She's at a difficult age,' Joe said.

'Aren't we all?' said Harriet, seeking his eyes with hers where barbs of mirth united them. She looked busily back at her tray. 'I'll just take her in a bit of lunch. Poor little thing.'

Before entering Kitty's room she set the tray down on a table in the hall. She felt that the child might have an eye on the door and might charge it like a rhinoceros when she heard the key turn. The room seemed unhealthily quiet. 'Kitty,' Harriet knocked. 'It's Mum.' In the perturbing silence the key made a brutal little crunch like the breaking of a tooth. She waited a second in case Kitty was crouched for ambush but nothing happened so she picked up her tray and stepped into the room in brisk relief.

The relief died. Kitty, her big sleek kitten, was crouched on the bed like a fat, unlovable child in disgrace.

She faced her with the dull eyes of despair and her chin shook. 'Sorry, Mum,' she whimpered.

Harriet put the tray down and went to hold her. 'It's all right,' she said. 'It will be all right this evening. We'll have a lovely night tonight, all of us together like a family.' She soothed Kitty's hair with a hand. 'Why don't you get back into bed and have a little sleep? You need your sleep after last night. You're still my baby.'

'We're not a family.' Kitty held up her arms to have her dress removed. 'He's not our Dad.'

Harriet stood on her toes to drag off the dress and then she held the abundant girl by her arms, forcing her to look at her. 'I need him,' she said. 'I do.'

'It isn't fair,' Kitty said. 'I need someone too.'

'It's fair in a way. We all have to live our lives.'

'All's fair in love and that sort of thing?'

'That sort of thing.'

Harriet got Kitty's nightie on and settled her down and drew the

115

blankets over her. Her face loomed over the sheet, tearful and trusting. It was like when Kitty was a baby and Harriet had to abandon her to a babysitter while she went out to work. 'I'll bring you back something nice,' she promised, just as she used to do in the old days. 'What would you like?'

'A bowl of Rice Krispies and Adam Ant.' She staggered a smile.

Harriet fled from the room, her heart streaming behind her in shreds.

'Joe,' she cried. Her hands wrung from the wretchedness of their jailor's role. 'Joe, she's only a baby.'

Joe had vanished. The kitchen was empty. Even Lulu had gone off with her shopping basket and the provocative wad of Joe Fisher's money. The little villa was haunted by Kitty's silence. Harriet was about to go back and release her when Joe reappeared, looking pleased with himself. 'Look what I've found.' He had brought out a canvas carrier which contained her survival kit of harsher years – her paints, her paper, her brushes. 'I was looking in the wardrobe for a sweater and I came across these. They're coming with us. I want to watch you painting.'

Harriet wasn't listening. She let out a little moan and held aloft the key to Kitty's door. She felt like Lady Macbeth.

'You locked the door? Good girl.' His tone was rewarding.

'She said she's sorry, Joe. She's just a child. Couldn't we bring her with us?'

He took the key from her and put it in his pocket. Then he took her hands in his. 'No. It isn't fair to her. Believe me, dear. She's gone through the worst already. To let her out now would be to say we just wanted to make an example of her. She'll sleep most of the day and in the evening she'll have forgotten all about it.'

'Oh, no,' Harriet said knowingly; 'she won't.'

'Besides ...' Joe damped her hair with little persuasive kisses; 'I've got a grown-up programme organized for us.'

'What?' Harriet relented. There was a faint and hopeful hammering on the inside of Kitty's door as the child heard her mother pleading her case.

'I'm going to see if I can rent a boat and some fishing tackle. We'll row round to the other side of the island. Such limited mention as the guide books make of Keptos suggests that there's a really good deserted beach on the far side. I'll fish. You'll paint. We may even get around to some light carpentry.'

'Carpentry?' Harriet murmured, showing her teeth to him in total trust, quite oblivious to the murderous thuds that now afflicted Kitty's door.

He swept her up to his body and as always his warmth and the tension of his bones, his quick response to her own unremarkable flesh, made her giddy and dizzy and feckless. 'Screwing,' he whispered into her bold, delighted ear.

TEN

She painted a sea of hyacinth blue. Orchid pinks, duck-egg blues rose off its surface like notes of music. Her sky had the tantalizing pink of raspberry ice-cream. It touched the tongue as well as the eye. Joe, in his boat, stripped to the waist and magnolia-white with the same faint blush warming his skin, was not a man but a sexual flower. An outcrop of rock was seen as luxuriously in an act of self-reproduction, sprouting ledge out of crag out of boulder.

She had painted all day and was absorbed in her work. She had gone through her exhaustion and she was exhilarated now. It was nearly evening and it was her fourth painting. She thought she had never done anything so good before, so fertile. Up to now there was no predominantly female quality in her work. Her London landscapes were meticulous and strong. They had bone structure. Here, with Joe Fisher, she flowed. Alone with her, he too developed this fluid quality, without schedules or children to annoy. He was aimless and content. He fished. He even caught a fish and made a little fire with sticks to roast it, like a boy scout. It was some local mongrel, soggy of flesh and robust of bone, but the burnt skin tasted delicious and afterwards they licked each other's fingers and then quickly made love.

When she was painting she paused every so often to look at him, so limp and amiably available in his drifting rowboat. She ought to be talking to him. She ought to be letting him know of her needs and her financial stability. Other women used days and settings such as this to extract promises and cement relationships. It made sense. Even later, if the relationship went bad, the man could hardly fail to look back on its beginning with sentiment. She should be subtly assisting him in the undermining of his marriage; telling him of her nightmares, her sexual fantasies: but she held her tongue.

Much as she needed him, she wanted this day. It was so perfect that there was no place in it for change and Harriet had lived long enough to know that nothing alters romance so much as the suggestion that it might be made to last.

118

The beach at the back of the island was a little sandy bay with a deserted chapel inhabited by a thin white cat. Harriet's pleasure had not been merely in the discovery of so enchanting a place but in the manner in which Joe had carried her off and installed her there as though already making a spiritual home for her. Another discovery was the grace they derived from one another's company. They did not have to say anything important or stimulate compatibility with touches and glances. They hadn't to put themselves out to please. Companionability rose off them like steam.

It was this too that put Harriet off her plan to make use of the time to secure him for herself. Joe brought her not only happiness but self-containment so that she enjoyed her work and built upon her limited self-esteem. After yesterday's demanding lovemaking they required only the smallest tokens today. Their lovemaking after lunch had been a refreshment more than a slaking, and they had gone briskly back to their separate pursuits. Only once in the afternoon – distracted from the parma-violets and marshmallow-pinks of her third painting – had she been overwhelmed and had to drop her brushes and wade out into the deep water to be near him.

'What is it?' He looked up from his pipe and his line.

'I love you,' she blurted; then feeling slightly ashamed she said playfully: 'We could live here. We could make a home in the church with the cat. We could live on fish and row round to the village for wine and fruit and coffee.'

'What about the children?' He smiled around the stem of his smoking piece.

'Oh,' she said; 'yes.'

'You're a lovely soft woman,' he said.

Now the day was gone. For a time the sky was all heavenly light and then it became bloodily streaked with night. Quite suddenly the sun was gulped down and Harriet found herself looking at mauvish hands and paper the colour of post-war sugar bags. 'Joe!' she called out. She packed away her paints and her finished paintings and waved the most recent one to dry its surface. 'Jo-oe!' She slung the canvas carrier over her shoulder and collected the picnic basket, picking her way carefully through a group of oval-shaped rocks that projected like curious moles.

When she got to the water she could see the boat at a distance sulkily slapping the waves, but even in the evening gloom she could tell it was empty. Joe was gone. He must have fallen overboard. Perhaps he had tried to trap a fish with his hands and slipped in.

'Joe!' She let loose an eerie wail.

'Yes, my love,' said a quiet voice at her side.

She turned on a scared half-swivel and she was in his arms.

'I'm always losing you,' she yelped.

'No, no.' He patted her back. 'I came around by the rocks. I didn't want you stumbling about in the dark. You'll never lose me.'

Harriet became rigidly alert. She wanted to make him write it down. She would find witnesses. 'Have you been happy today?' she asked him quickly, her sharp gaze slicing the dark to read his expression.

'I've never been happier.'

'You'll stay with me? Won't you, Joe?'

'Look,' he enfolded her. 'I'm with you.'

On the way back, in the boat, she made up for lost time. She questioned him in close and practical detail about his home, his family and securities. He had two children, boys. He did not think them very clever. One was apprenticed to a plumber and the other successfully installed in computers. His wife had her own car and was always talking about going back to work now that the boys were big, although he couldn't remember whether or how she had earned a living before they married. His house, which was in their joint names, was paid for, and he felt lately that he had more money than he could spend, though you could never afford to feel smug in a recession.

'Do you still love your wife?' she asked with a thumping heart. 'Do you make love to her?'

There was a pause in the purple shadows. She could hear the sucking of the water on the boat's oars and a tiny imitative sucking as he sought contemplative refuge in his pipe. He reached out for her. 'Steady, love,' he said, his hand firm on hers as if only this limb was in need of steadying. 'I don't feel right talking about old Georgy behind her back.'

'None of it feels right, my dear,' she said. She could not possibly speak like this if it was daylight and he could see her. 'The numbers are wrong. It can only be wrong for all of us or right for some of us. I know that you respect your wife and I'm sure she's fond of you but the thing is, I really love you. The thing is, you have to choose.' Her quaking teeth gleamed in the muffled light of the moon to demonstrate friendly intent.

There was a silence so long that Harriet thought he had been afflicted by shock and had lost the use of speech, but when at last he spoke his voice was quite clear and solid. 'You have to show trust,' he said.

At last they reached the cottage, its melon-coloured beacons of light giving tidings of welcome and dread. They both grew tense as they climbed the last yards of the track. What if the children had been drinking again, or if Lulu had met up with the boys and forgotten about dinner? Joe was a person whose sense of balance depended on a certain sequence of domestic order.

The scene that met them when they entered the kitchen was like a sentimental representation of the Last Supper. The children, sun-burnished from their day out of doors, recently washed and wearing those faded cottons that look so wholesome when they are not filthy, stood expectantly around the table, their faces bright and good by the light of candles. The table had been set with bread and salad, olives, wine and water. Apricots, almonds and green leaves were arranged in a large, flat dish and beside this was Lulu's triumphal tart, a little fire-damaged, but with apricots huddling with almonds under a great gloss of melted jam.

'Oh, my darlings, how lovely!' Harriet exclaimed; and Joe, stepping forward, solemnly offered his approval in the form of an adult acceptance of them. 'Let me give you all a drink,' he said.

'What about Kitty?' Tim said.

'Oh, golly, yes – the key?' She held out a hand to Joe who dug about in his trouser pocket and produced it for her.

She experienced only an acceptable level of trepidation as she entered Kitty's room. Everything else had gone so well in the day that it would merely be a leveller if the child should spring forward in the dark and bite her throat or call her 'fuckface' or 'flatarse'. All the same, as seconds passed in the dark, there was an involuntary

121

stiffening of the hairs on her neck, so she quickly switched on the light.

Kitty was asleep. Plump and harmless, rosiness restored, she gave Harriet a lovely moment of joy, as when she first held Lulu in her arms. She came and crouched beside the bed and put a hand on the warm and heavy brow. 'We're home, sweetie,' she whispered. Kitty opened an eye.

'What did you bring me?'

'Oh, pigeon! There wasn't time. I'll buy you something very nice very soon.'

'How do I know?'

'You have to show trust,' Harriet said.

They were all seated around the table.

'He was in the war,' Tim said.

'No, no. He was in the movies. He was in movies about the war.'

Wine foamed into tumblers. Meat was apportioned. The pallid green wings of lettuce fluttered over candle flame on impaling forks.

'Who?'

'The baldy goof. Four marriages – regular tit and bum man.'

'I heard he had more unusual tastes,' Roger said.

'A bit and tum man,' Kitty shrieked with joy.

Harriet had no idea what they were talking about. Conversation blew about like weather. She chewed serenely on wads of Lulu's hard meat. She was so contented she almost wished they would leave her alone for a little while to inspect this unknown quality. She was a woman of substance. She had a family. 'And look!' she kept exclaiming to herself as a child who has defied death and his parents' warnings shows off his hinged limbs; 'there is no damage! I feel no pang of unresolved personal ambition, no twinge of elderly resentment for past afflictions of the heart.'

She had gone into the kitchen earlier to serve the dinner. Joe was at the table having a civilized drink with the children and Kitty was getting dressed in Harriet's white lace blouse and her fringed Indian skirt. Harriet thought she ought to get the meal on the table before hunger provoked hostile passions. While she was putting meat on the plates and allotting the scorched potatoes, Lulu had come in.

'It's all right, Mum,' she said softly.

'What?' Harriet leaped guiltily aside, assuming she meant it was her dinner and she would do the honours. 'Sorry darling,' she said automatically.

Her elder daughter came and stood beside her. She looked healthier. Her hair was washed and her eyes less dull. 'I mean,' she said. 'It's all right about you and him.'

'Do you think so?' Harriet said doubtfully.

'Yeah. We all do. Cheers.' Lulu gulped from her glass and then thrust it, tilted, at Harriet's face, where it fell into her wondering mouth and down her chin. 'How do you know,' she said, 'what the others think?'

'We had a rap session after Tim got back.'

'Kitty?'

'We shouted at her through the door and she shouted back.'

'And . . .?'

'He's mean – but not to you. He's a shit but in a funny way he's fair. He knows how to get things done. We reckon he's not too bad at a distance.'

'So . . .?'

Lulu kissed the top of Harriet's head, delighting her out of all proportion. 'Marry him, Mum. You're cracked on the sod, aren't you?'

She forebore to mention that the sod was already married. It seemed at this point a minor detail. Within a week or so he would have grown used to waking up beside her; his lips would be attuned to her firm and narrow ones, his body comfortable against her angles. His wife (photographed flatly in his mind against the costly burden of their home) would be just the fire of his guilt, the frost on his sexuality. Harriet was beginning to see herself as he described her: a lovely soft woman, a great curvaceous heart upon which a boy could bounce. Compared to her his wife was . . .

His wife was what?

He had never described Georgina and although she did not wish to demand an identikit picture she had questioned him cunningly about her tastes in magazines and music, the meals she put on the table, to try and fill in her own composite. She pictured Georgy as a wrinkled and boyish woman with wiry hair and a hearty laugh, somehow deprecative. She saw her in dark, plain jersey wools, worn a little too short, with leathery tights and sensible shoes. From what clues had she assembled this image? It was partly, she thought, because of his intimation of her as a good sport. It suggested mirth and hockey. There was also the undeniable fact that this was the kind of wife men like Joe tended to have – not from desire or conscious selection, but from an early shyness which prohibited for them the softer and more incendiary female types.

And there was this; the Georgina Harriet had invented for Joe would never die of a broken heart. She would fill her life with dogs and the garden and wait cheerfully for grandchildren. She would probably be quite relieved that there was no more giving in to the dear boy's naughty streak.

She always saw her as a little older than Joe. She might well be approaching the menopause and could even be trying to subdue a hot flush when Joe stood before her, pale and grave as a thirties movie star in his putty-coloured suit, and told her he would always be grateful to her. Suddenly Harriet saw herself in the same scene, an older drama – a lifetime ago – with a struggling baby on her knee. Martin with his hands in his pockets, his dark and stern head (mean, if looked at in a good light) drooping in a disaffected manner when he said, 'Look, there's something I have to tell you. I'll always be grateful to you, you know . . .'

And then the horror, the truth – not that she considered his falling in love with someone else a betrayal but the terrible turning up of all that had gone before, digging and scooping like the monster machines on Psiros so that the soft and fertile pastures where they loved and made babies became an endless expanse of hard grey, overshooting her present into her precious past.

She could recall the exact feeling inside herself – a lift going out of control; somewhere inside her chest the cables snapped and her whole centre went plummeting down, killing all the foolish tender things that lived inside, pulling her mouth down and open like a sugar scoop, so that she couldn't speak. She looked so stupid, sitting there, that Martin had laughed. 'Don't do that, old pal, you look like a trout.' He chucked her chin to close it. And she laughed too, her teeth clacking when her jaw snapped.

Halfway through the happy dinner Harriet's eyes filled with tears

124

and her salty spit enrobed the piece of meat that was in her mouth. After a few minutes Tim's rough, loose laughter stopped and they all paid attention to her. 'Look at Mum! What's the matter with Mum?' She shook her head and smiled bleakly at them, guiltily swallowing the lump of meat, which made her cough and gave her an excuse for the tears. She beat her chest. 'I swallowed something the wrong way.' After that she thought she'd better stop her dreaming and pay attention to the dinner. How on earth could she explain to them that she was trying out another woman's pain?

They were talking about the future. For the young people it was a topic of charm. In spite of the bomb and the lack of jobs their eyes glowed. It was all theirs – a place without footprints or fingerprints, where no one had ever been. Harriet had not heard them talk like this before. She hadn't liked to ask; they were still so young. She did not wish to pressure them. Coming from Joe it was something other than pressure. He only prompted their hopes.

Kitty wanted to be a dress designer, which was shrewd enough. Already she had a clever talent for dressing (in Harriet's clothes) and on the rare occasions when she exerted herself to draw she displayed a strength of line which imitated Harriet's established style.

Tim wanted to be an accountant. She felt her mouth drop open into its sugar shovel shape. She gawped in fuzzy indignation at the overgrown, loutish, rebellious youth. Of course he was not really rebellious. The unconventional defied the tribal trends of their peers. The ones like Tim and Roger who sought refuge in a special identity, they were the conventional ones. She could see him in years to come, a meaner, stiffer version of Martin. Already he was a large boy and might well run to sufficient weight to wear a waistcoat and intimidate the bankrupt. She felt shocked and let down. She had imagined that when the rudeness of his teenage years had worn off, the languor might remain and he would become an amiable friend. She now thought that the rudeness would remain and he would grow out of all the rest.

Lulu said she wanted to teach and to get married and to have babies. Apart from the momentary relief that she did not look at Roger when she said this, Harriet experienced the same sense of a stone dropping into a well causing ever-widening circles of dismay.

They were not, after all, gods and goddesses. They were ordinary people. All the years of expense and understanding had gone to make accountants and teachers. Kitty was really too young to make up her mind. She might yet decide to become a traffic warden.

She fixed her eyes on the sticky orange wheel of Lulu's tart. It wasn't just that the brilliant path to the children's future had turned out, after all, to be black utility tiling. Her own future, which half an hour ago had been so dazzlingly clear, was now smeared with those victims she must destroy to proceed on its path.

She ought to be relieved to know the children were not aiming for extramarital pregnancies or drug addiction, especially with Roger in the house. She loved Joe precisely because he was ordinary. But ordinary with Joe meant reassuring and accessible. With the children it just meant they were growing up and going to go away. It was this evidence that upset her, that they really would grow up into people and her table would be filled, not with the awful, half-grown creatures who still sometimes called her Mummy, but with little obliging ghosts, aged six or seven, who spoke with their mouths full, who had trouble with buttons and bootlaces, who trusted her utterly; and then the teenage Tim and Lulu and Kitty who looked at her now with such pink belligerence would have disappeared and be gone forever.

Their pinkness tonight was due to drink. Joe poured for them quite liberally, though judiciously. For Harriet he poured with love, without measure, and she had drunk far too much. She felt swamped in a fairly unpleasant sea of emotion. 'Oh, Joe!' she sighed. She no longer had to defend herself against the children. Already they were trying to shield her, trying to get her settled with a steady man so that they could slip off into their own calm adult waters. Joe kissed her hair and hung on to her with a comforting fervour.

'What about your future, Mum?' Lulu teased. There was a rustling of knees and napkins, and glances. Harriet kept her head hidden against Joe's chest until she was certain he was not going to speak and then said, 'I'm going to Psiros dressed as the Queen of Sheba. I'm going to drink White Ladies with umbrellas in them and eat a lobster.'

'What else?' said Kitty, who was too young to know better.

Harriet plucked at a button on Joe's shirt until it came away in her hand. 'That will have to do for now.'

There was a brief silence, a slight feeling of judgement around the table, and then Lulu stood up abruptly. 'Right, then. We're off to the village to have some fun. All right if we leave the washing-up to darkness and to you?'

'Now look here!' Joe said.

'It's all right,' Harriet said.

'I'll put the dishes in the sink.' Lulu started clearing the table. 'I'll do them in the morning.' She gave Harriet a curious lewd smile as she stacked plates and gathered glasses and moved them to the sink. Kitty followed with cutlery and then wiped the table and rearranged the remaining items to make them look more like a setting than the remnants of a meal.

When Lulu came back she had brought a tray with coffee, but only for two. The boys stood up abruptly and Kitty followed them to the door. They were all grinning. Even Roger had looped his mouth into a cordial twist.

Joe glanced from Harriet to the children and back, half rising from his chair, as if he was the victim of a trick. 'Now, wait a minute . . .'

'Have fun.' Lulu went to join the others. 'Don't wait up.'

'What about Kitty?'

'She's coming with us.' Lulu and Tim spoke together. They flanked the youngest child defensively.

'Where are you going?' Joe said.

Lulu looked beseechingly at her mother but Harriet was hopeless. 'Just. Out,' she said in a quiet tone.

Joe was equally, icily reasonable. 'As far as I know you haven't any money. It's dark outside. Your only source of free entertainment is that unspeakable greasy Greek, Manolis, and if he fits anywhere into your plans then Kitty isn't going.'

'Mum, she's all right!' Lulu seized Kitty roughly like a hostage. 'She's with us.'

'You go,' Joe said. 'Kitty stays.'

'It's no use going without her,' Tim argued. 'It's Kitty Manolis is waiting for.'

'I see,' Joe said. 'Kitty's your bait. Manolis is your source of free booze and Kitty's your bait.'

Kitty lunged forward, still part restrained by Lulu's grip, and she spat in Joe's direction. 'And that's too nice for you,' she said. 'You leave me alone or I'll ... I'll fix you. If it wasn't for Mum ...' She shot Harriet a filthy glance.

'You're not going out,' Joe said.

'Try and stop me.'

'If I have to.' He advanced.

'Ow! Ow! Ow!' Kitty screamed in brief, frightened barks as Joe detached her from Lulu and thrust her towards her room.

'No, Joe!' Harriet was really shocked this time.

'He's going to lock her up again! Do something, Tim,' Lulu cried.

Tim and Roger approached Joe together. Harriet wondered whom she should hit and with what if it came to actual violence. She knew that she could stop Joe if she really wanted to and she knew she should, but he was doing his best, he was taking responsibility and that was the first step. Earlier in the evening, when he had been properly in charge, he had been friendly and persuasive with them and for a brief time they had liked him and it even seemed as if he had liked them. In another little while he would be legally in charge, almost their father. She had to show trust.

Although Roger was short and skinny he was malevolent enough and, with Tim as aide, made up a quite dangerous-looking team. Harriet thought it would be all right if they unnerved Joe just for the moment, just enough to make him release little Kitty who was genuinely scared. Joe didn't seem at all perturbed. As the youths neared he reviewed them coldly and mentioned indifferently, 'Police?'

The two boys looked uneasy and backed away.

'Naoo!' Kitty howled as she was removed to her room. 'Mu-um!' came a muffled screech and she pounded on her door.

Harriet knew she must have looked exactly as her mother had done on an occasion when Marlborough, their dog, after some spring excursion, rushed into a room full of people with a gamey look in his eye and his unacknowledged organ burst forth from its furry pouch. It was the look of the whistler.

'Mum!' Lulu demanded her attention. 'She's going to hate you

for this. She's going to resent you all her life and serve you right.'
There were tears in Lulu's eyes as she stamped off after the others
and slammed the door.

Bit by bit the screams and the banging from Kitty's room died
and there was peace. Joe enjoyed a hearty helping of Lulu's tart
and poured the coffee. His glance had softened again. 'She makes
good coffee,' he smiled. 'It would go well with a brandy.'

She nodded but would not look at him; not that she was angry
with him but she felt unworthy of his gaze. She had probably
murdered Kitty's love and was about to do the same to his wife's
affection. She moved from the table quickly to get the brandy,
wiping her eyes and her nose covertly with the back of her hand.
When she came back with the bottle he caught her hand and
kissed it.

She squirmed with embarrassment in case it was sticky with snot
or tears but he didn't seem to notice. 'I love you, you know,' he
said. It was the first time he had said it with all his clothes on. She
dumped the bottle on the table and went away again to get the
glasses, feeling weary with all the shocks. When she poured the
drinks, her hand was trembling.

'What's the matter?' he said. 'Are you cold?'

She nodded. There was only the tiniest breeze coming from the
open windows, like that roused by a woman's hankie in tepid
farewell.

'What would you like?'

'I'd like a fire.'

He did not argue. He put her sitting in a chair and arranged
around her her cigarettes, a cup of coffee and a drink. He fetched
papers and the tin bath full of wooden sticks and crouched over the
hearth. He began to organize his materials into complicated layer
and lattice. He was skilled at it. He was used to it. For Harriet it
was as a legend unfolding. There lived in her heart a belief in men
as firemakers. She had no evidence of this, but she had faith. She
believed grimly in old values and the promises of tradition. She was
fervently attentive to the myth that was about to be realised. In a
little while she would sit with her lover by a flickering fire, wordless
but content.

Everything went according to plan except the wordlessness. Joe wanted to talk. At first he crouched mutely like her around the struggling flames but he was only trying to get his thoughts into words.

'Poor kid.' He shook his head.

'Who?' She moved against him into the general arena of his sympathy.

He jerked his head in the direction of the door. 'Kitty. I hope I didn't really frighten her. Do you want to go and see if she's all right?'

'No.' Harriet said it too quickly. Kitty would have been brooding for half an hour and would be ready for physical assault. 'No, she'll be asleep by now,' she added more gently and forcing a smile.

'I like your kids,' Joe said slowly. 'They support each other and they've got some spark. Mine are a bit dull.'

'Perhaps you've been severe with them,' Harriet suggested.

'Only later. Only after . . .' He gave a very long sigh. 'I learned the hard way. Deep in your heart you always know what's right and you get used to the fact that it's never what they want for themselves.'

So Joe had had trouble with his children too. Was it the plumber or the computer? When he first told her his son was a plumber she had felt a twinge of disapproval. It seemed as if he didn't care but it was clear that he worried just as she did. Perhaps the boy wanted to be a plumber and Joe had swallowed his dismay. Maybe he liked to join and bend pipes down among the scummy twists of hair and ghostly bandages of tissue. Plumbing was profitable.

'Kitty's such a pretty child,' he said and sighed again. 'In a year or two she'll be able to look out for herself but anything's better than letting them loose at that age.'

She thought he worried more than was necessary. Time and again it had been proved to her that youthful injuries are subject to miraculous healing but the blows dealt in middle age turn rank and septic. She knelt beside Joe and patted his knee.

'It's all right,' she said. 'She's a tough little girl. She plays at being a baby because she knows I like it and she gets away with murder but she's no porcelain doll. I know her, Joe.'

'Yes,' he said quickly. 'I do understand. I know what you mean. You're lucky in a way. Few people ever get to know any others

130

really well. You! I realise now I scarcely knew you at all. You formed part of a fantasy for me. I had quite a different picture of how it would be. At home you seemed a butterfly. Here, with your children around you, you make me feel the butterfly – sometimes on the outside of the window. I never knew you. I never knew how beautiful you were.'

He lifted her hair and let it fall through his fingers. She watched this and felt she had never even known herself. Her hair looked quite a good colour in the light of the fire.

'What did you think of me then,' she said with her crooked smile, 'when we met?'

He gave her a curious look, a gaze filtered through broken glass and at first her heart skipped sideways and she thought, 'I know that look. He's in love with me.' But then she saw that his mouth was set in misery and she was confused. 'I thought you were a little girl. You reminded me of a little girl.'

'Lying bastard,' she said. 'I look a hundred in the cold grey city light.'

'It was the way you stood and your long hair. You have artless feet.'

'You said I had Botticelli toes.'

'I couldn't see your toes then.'

'So who was this ghastly child I reminded you of?'

Silence. She thought he had lost interest. 'My daughter,' he whispered into the fire.

'But you only have sons!' she protested loudly, as if she was a child and had caught him cheating in a board game.

'Yes, yes,' he said obediently.

'Oh,' she moaned. 'Oh, no. Oh, Joe.' She held his face with her hands. She pressed his head to her breast. 'You had a little girl,' she said, to be certain, 'and she died.' He nodded into her chest.

There was a hideous moment of glee. 'I have him now,' said a devil inside her. But she beat the devil out and concentrated on the child. She pictured her with Joe's paleness and his sandy hair, verging on red. She saw her like Ophelia, floating in the water with blossoms around her waxy cheeks.

'What happened?' she said, squeezing him fiercely. 'Was she only little? Did she miss a vaccination?'

131

'She was fourteen,' Joe said. His voice sounded dulled by revulsion. 'She was full of vodka and she fell under a bus.'

'How long ago?' She stroked his bent head.

'Five years ago.'

'You mustn't blame yourself,' Harriet said. 'These things happen.'

He detached himself from her and resumed his role of protector, putting his arms around her. 'I don't,' he said. 'I didn't believe she was gone. I kept looking for her. I found you.'

Harriet shook her head. 'It's no good,' she said with trepidation. 'I'm not a little girl.'

'No,' he agreed.

'I'm a calculating old bag. I can't take her place.'

'No,' he denied and assented.

She sat stiff with selflessness and misery until he touched her very gently. 'You don't have to take her place. It's what I'm trying to tell you. I can let her go now that I've got you.'

She looked at him in mild surprise and then yawned. There was a curious sense of anti-climax to the moment of resolution, but then she remembered that she had not slept all the previous night and that her brain was bouncing lightly inside her skull, blurring and overlapping its undigested contents.

'Say something,' Joe Fisher said.

'Come to bed,' she said, and then turned away and gave a little tipsy grin of joy as she registered what must amount to a proposal.

In the middle of the night she was woken by the sound of breaking glass.

'Joe! Joe!' She pulled at his torpid shoulder. He gave a grunt of contented familiarity.

'Joe! Someone's broken a window. There's burglars.'

He eased himself around to face her and nuzzled at her mouth. 'Burglars on Keptos? Come on, love, we're not in the civilized world now.'

'What then?' He was right, of course. Crime was unheard-of on the island. She rubbed herself against him sleepily.

'Those bloody clowns who call you mother. They went out without a key.'

Afterwards she could not get back to sleep. She was haunted by thoughts of the little red-haired girl, a greedy child guzzling vodka as if it was milk and then stepping blithely under a bus and out of life. Thank God Kitty was safely locked in. Goodness only knows what state the others were in if they had to break windows to get in. They might at least have knocked first. Awful, unthinkable, unbearable that anything should ever happen to Kitty. She drifted off.

Just over the precipice of sleep she found herself hooked by the claws of an eagle and she woke again wrestling with it, with an awful sense of alarm. What was the matter? Kitty? She had been thinking about Kitty? No, Kitty was all right – it was the other little girl; Joe's dotty, drunken Ophelia. Ophelia had been a daughter – not just to Joe, who could swap her after a suitable period for a woman with artless feet. Ophelia was Georgy's daughter.

Her pleasant picture of Georgy-in-the-garden vanished. There were some things you couldn't be a good sport about. Harriet had often thought about the death of her children. She had gone over each of their deaths in turn, sometimes choosing gruesome methods, sometimes mundane, in order to be able to accept the unthinkable should it occur. But always, like a dream, the horror film she ran through her head stopped before the ending. She couldn't face that. Inasmuch as she thought about it, she thought the death of a child was the death of the heart.

She had that sense of urgency that succeeds calamity. She sat bolt upright, her hands clasped about her knees. 'What shall I do? Oh, what shall I do?' she thought. She was in the centre of a rising bridge. She was caught, legs splayed and trembling between dividing lives and each half belonged in its own secure harbour. If only Joe Fisher did not love his wife; in that case she would be simply putting him first. But she knew he did and she knew why. She knew now the kind of woman Georgy was. She had consumed the entire helping of guilt which accompanied the child's death, to spare her husband. Someone has to take the guilt.

For all that he loved her, Joe Fisher was a happily married man.

She lay down and carefully turned herself into him. His body eased against hers. Their faces joined. They had learnt each other's bodies though perhaps not each other's minds. 'I'll have to let him

133

go,' she thought, holding on so tight that it did not seem probable. But she had two weeks with him first. She would put a whole lifetime's love into those weeks and after that life could look after itself.

ELEVEN

In the morning there was a series of screams; first Lulu – that little-girl siren she still assumed when something dreadful had happened that was beyond her scorn. 'Mum! Oh, quick, Mum!'

Harriet flung herself from the bed. She hammered at Joe in case the crisis called for a man and then fled out of doors, following her daughter's cry.

She was standing in the garden with Lulu (shaking hand to quivering jaw) assessing the evidence of disaster and its grim possibilities, when she heard the second shout.

'Good Christ!'

They angled their heads and listened, as if to a rare bird. It was Joe, a strangled cry from the sanctuary of his room.

Harriet was outside the window of Kitty's room. The glass was broken and Kitty was gone. She had no idea what to do until the sound of Joe's voice reminded her that she was not alone. 'Joe, Joe!' she cried out in fear, little morsels of shattered glass crunching beneath her bare feet as she ran for his help.

He had got out of bed. He stood by the mirror with no clothes on but his look was the look of a man in a suit. It was a look of frightened indignation. 'For heaven's sake, Harriet,' he said.

Her garment of guilt, so readily assumed, fell over her head, obscuring for a moment, dreadful images of Kitty. 'What, love?'

'I've gone brown.'

She felt the little pink spots of confusion. 'It seems, my dear,' her hands wafted, brainless as sea anemones, 'perfectly normal under the circ . . .'

'Use your head, Harriet. I'm supposed to be in Brighton. It's raining in Brighton.'

She stared at him in astonishment, her cut feet squelching blood on to the bald pink rug. If she lived to be a thousand – which she felt she had – she would never understand men. Tears filled her eyes. 'But you said . . .'

'Said what? Said I was going to Brighton!' His look was challenging.

'Nothing.' It was the truth. He had said nothing except that he loved her and what was the declaration without bonds and securities?

'Kitty's missing, Joe,' she said. 'She broke the window and got out.'

He was running his hands over his radiant skin, down his body, over the delicate yellowish bikini line with its drooping pink stem. He looked as if he was fitting himself for a new, pale, blameless skin. Not that he blamed himself; it was Harriet he held responsible for his adulterer's hide. She ought to have had more sense than to suggest an assignation in so searing a location; she should have warned him about the strength of the sun or made him cover up, like a mum. It occurred to her that since he did not blame himself for the death of his daughter, he probably blamed his wife.

'What are we going to do?' she persisted.

'Look, I'm dreadfully sorry, darling. I shall have to go. You do understand? My wife thinks I'm in Brighton. If I leave immediately, there's a chance I'll have lost this blasted burn by the time I'm due to go home. I'll see if I can get a boat out of here this morning.' He eased himself into trousers, his eye on the mirror. 'Then I'll just hang around for the hydrofoil and hope to Christ there's a flight the same day. With any luck I can be in Brighton by tomorrow night.'

She viewed him with despair and admiration. 'I meant,' she said, 'what are we going to do about Kitty?'

'To hell with Kitty.' He began taking clothes from the wardrobe and folding them carefully for his cases. 'I'm only sorry our holiday has been ruined. You do see, don't you? My wife's no fool, she'd catch on immediately.'

'Don't go.'

'I can't let my wife down.'

'You've let me down.'

'I've never promised you anything.'

'Two weeks! I was counting on that – only that. I need that, Joe. I need your help to find Kitty.'

'I've done all I can for that child. You've spoilt her, Harriet.'

136

'If anything has happened to her it will be all your fault!' she said meanly and slammed out of the room and into the gloomy passage where she stood bleeding and shaking and making little noisy breaths. The children were there, ghostly with guilt. Even Roger looked more like some miserable laboratory rat than his usual scampering self.

'What does he say, Mum?' Lulu wanted to know.

'He says he's going home. To his wife.'

'Oh, the horrible shit!'

'He says he's gone brown.' In spite of herself Harriet's mouth began to twitch. 'He's going back to Brighton . . . to fade.'

Her voice died on the last purgative note. She stifled a giggle which was half a sob. There was a silence and then the children began to grumble uneasily.

'Moralizing bastard. Taking it out on Rog.'

'Yeah, the prick.'

The bedroom door burst open and the prick came through. He was dressed in a business suit, packed by his wife. Harriet could not help glancing at his ankles for a bulky ridge of Argyle sock. None of them looked at his face. His brilliance offended them.

'Look! Darling . . .' he appealed.

She turned resolutely towards her children.

'These things take time . . .'

'Finding Kitty could take a long time,' Tim said with truculence.

'Kitty!' Harriet was horrified. For moments she had forgotten.

'Harriet, I'll get in touch as soon as I can,' Joe said.

'Kitty!' She cried more forcefully to focus her thoughts and to blot out the tweedy ghost of her happiness, who hovered, a woolly vacuum, substantial only in his clothes.

'Harriet . . .' Joe's voice begged her but he said no more. A little silence gripped them and held them quite securely until they heard the banging of the door. Harriet felt it as if some trailing part of herself had been caught in the slammed door, and she jerked and winced.

'Mu-um?' Lulu recalled her warningly.

'Darling.' She managed a wretched little smile. Pain was all around her, sharp and bright as the light splinters in the sea, and alarm glared her blindingly in the eye. Joe was gone. Kitty was gone. The children watched her with the oppressed and wary eyes of thieving cats.

What would she do? What would a man do? Martin had once told her that truth was best achieved by a process of elimination, casting out the perished half-truths, discounting swollen and blackened boasts so that a crisp, refreshing honesty was revealed. Her own experience of reality – the reality he had left her with, for instance – had been less appetizing than that but at least a commanding approach to the crisis would help bear her through the children's reproach.

'Put the coffee on, Lulu. Tim, set the table. Roger, get me some paper and a pen. Everybody get dressed very quickly and sit down.'

She went to her room to put her clothes on and get hold of herself. She was unnerved to see that Joe had left all his summer things, his shorts and tee shirt, the pale-blue short-sleeved shirt, in a furtive pile in the wardrobe. She avoided these as she reached in for a pair of jeans and a black tee shirt. When she was dressed she fetched the key and let herself into Kitty's room.

At first she thought she might find a note. Kitty liked to cause chaos but she did not like there to be confusion as to its meaning. She looked, but there was nothing, just the mix of coarse and delicate disorder that pursues the adolescent female. Clothes were piled on a chair. A ripped magazine picture of an obscenely painted young man was speared to the wall on a nail.

A filthy teddy, paws flung up in imprecation, was visible beneath the bed. A chair lay sideways on the floor, presumably after its exertion of window-breaking. Broken glass was everywhere and the frame was a wickedly grinning mouth of sharp transparent teeth, except along the sill where Kitty had fastidiously picked free the glass to allow herself a safe exit. Dropped beneath the wall mirror was a delicate little snake of blue satin ribbon. She picked this up and stroked it. It was the ribbon Kitty had bought to go with Harriet's swimsuit.

'Coffee's ready,' Lulu called from the kitchen.

'Coming.' She tied back her hair absent-mindedly with the ribbon and went to join the children.

She wrote a list of questions on a page and the answers went underneath in brackets.

What time did the older children get home?

(Dunno?)

Did anyone hear the glass breaking?

(Yeah.)

But why didn't you ...?

(Why didn't *you?*)

About what time was the window broken?

(Four o'clock – Roger was quite precise.)

Where might Kitty conceivably go – friends, favourite hiding places?

(Manolis was her friend. If she had a hiding place, she would hardly tell anyone, would she, *stupid?*)

Might she have gone somewhere other than Keptos?

(Psiros?)

How would she get there in the middle of the night?

(Grunts, dazed blank stares, soft squalid expletives.)

'All right,' she said, without feeling that it was so. 'We must search the island. You children concentrate on the village. Find Manolis. Search any places that are sheltered but unlocked. Ask everyone you see, particularly anyone who might have been up early – farmers or fishermen. I'll take a taxi to cover the rest of the island, or as far as she might have travelled. We'll meet back here in an hour.'

The taxi rank was situated in the village where a dented lollipop sign announced the service and two lustreless antique heaps comprised the fleet. These were the only cars on the island. They were used mainly to jolt ingenuous tourists around the hills and occasionally for the transport of sick animals. In fact the island was not suited to motor conveyance, its roads were mere tracks, and the suspension of the cars that of a family mattress. Harriet would not have considered using a taxi except in an emergency and for such contingencies the drivers could be summoned by vigorous use of a monastery bell, erected over a well in the village square.

Harriet hung from the bell rope until Yannis, buttoning a jacket over his vest and trousers, made a leisurely exit from the black interior of his snow-white house.

'Quickly,' she begged him.

'Where?'

139

'Everywhere.'

He shook his head and blew out his lips to indicate the difficulty of such a venture and its likely expense.

'Please hurry,' Harriet said.

They got into the car and he turned the ignition and the taxi began rolling and pitching at a pace so slow that it seemed not motivated by an engine but, like an ox or a donkey, by some slumbrous will. Harriet sat electrified in the festering rear. The vehicle swayed serenely along. 'Which way, which way?' Yannis' hand came off the steering wheel to await direction. 'Never mind, carry on,' Harriet said with an equally lofty and useless wave of her hand.

They left the village and began a painful assault on the hills. She kept her window open. 'Have you seen a young girl? Have you seen my daughter?' she shouted in Greek at the old farmers and ancient, leathery shepherdesses. Some of them smiled and nodded placatingly. Others backed away as if a young girl was a blood-sucking revenant. There were quite long periods when they saw no one and were hurled aimlessly about beneath the baking tin roof. In such intervals she grew resigned and reflective and peered down at the darkening sea or at the hills around her. In a Greek guide book she had once seen a brief commendation for Keptos, which proclaimed; 'Its green is astonishing for it grows over its beautiful green valleys making a contrast with its nude hills.' Now, after months of summer, its green was not astonishing. It was the bitter yellow green of pickles. The hills did not strike her as nude at any time. Nude was the pearly skin of naked women. The hills of Keptos were grey and bristled like old men's chests. She glimpsed a little house, like a cube of Camembert, daintily placed in the rocks, and two huge oxen, of biblical evocation, which dragged an iron plough around a field of dust and stones. 'Men and women live there,' she thought. 'They don't know anything about the butter mountain or the oil crisis. They probably don't even know about the bomb. But they know all the things that matter – how to make love, how to make food.' As usual these thoughts in her head were addressed to Joe. It was a shock to find that he was not there. It was her first intimation of the quality of real loneliness – the deserted imagination – and it brought her sharply back to the present. They had travelled four

140

or five miles from the village. Kitty would not have come so far. 'Turn round,' she said to Yannis. 'Go back.'

Just then she heard the noise. It was a horrific sound, more a moan than a shout, dull with terror and with a strangled quality as if the victim was gagged. 'It's Kitty! She's been kidnapped,' Harriet thought and clawed at the shoulder of the taxi-driver, gesturing to make him follow the cries. He grumbled and wrenched the car about in the direction she demonstrated. The cries were low and monotonous, but still female and full of fright. Was the victim drugged or exhausted? Who would have taken her? Were there bandits in the hills of Keptos who might seize a young girl for ransom? She sat rigid as a fork, making rash promises to God as the cries grew louder.

It was a little black-eared sheep, tethered near a grass-heap to a stake in a yard, wild with terror of the long thin cat, lumpy with kittens, which with nose and paw made a gourmet's perusal of the garden's rubbish tip.

'Sheep,' Yannis said in English, as to a very small child. 'Cat!' He thumped his steering wheel for emphasis. He turned to her then with a wild grin.

'Thank you,' Harriet said. 'Take me home.'

'Home!' he said with a delighted cackle at the defectiveness of tourists and the elderly car was coerced around once again and pointed down the hill. 'England?'

'Villa Anna,' she said wearily.

'Villa Anna, eh? Stefan? Stefan come home.'

'Please hurry,' Harriet said.

Instead of increasing speed the vehicle rolled gently into a grassy bank and came to a halt. Yannis opened the door and called out to an elderly woman who was descending the hill on foot, carrying a big box of eggs and followed by a hen. She turned, her crumpled features mild and diffident, and he spoke to her rapidly in Greek. After a moment's hesitation the woman came back to the car. Yannis opened the door and she laid the eggs carefully on to the front passenger seat, then, with a shy smile at Harriet, she picked up the hen and pitched it on top of her in the rear of the taxi. With great dignity she inserted herself into the front, lifting the eggs on to her lap with care.

Harriet did not question this procedure and took no notice of the hen. It was a disarming sin of the local business people to take advantage of the reckless spending of tourists to benefit impoverished islanders. She was glad of the company. Yannis and the woman now talked to each other in intense low voices in Greek. Harriet settled back as comfortably as she could in the violent motor. She was suddenly very tired. When she closed her eyes she experienced vivid flashes in which Joe, pink-tinged and fired by passion, made love to her, caught food for her, talked to her. Her body indulged itself with restless memory of his touch. Within moments fickle imagination had given way to a painful reality of need. She burned like an addict wanting his arms around her, his kiss on her forehead – no matter that his heart was hollow, anything to keep the emergency at bay. But then she pulled herself together and told herself he was right to be alarmed when he went brown. He was right to flee. Joe Fisher was a thoroughly white man. Already, after just a day or two in her company, he had been marked and contaminated by her. A little longer and he might turn into a swarthy savage. Who would believe his soothing talk of bonds and securities then? All the same, when the car pitched to a halt in the centre of the village, provoking a flood of timid profanities from the hen and its owner, Harriet found that her resolute eyes had leaked; her face was full of tears.

The children were waiting in front of the house. She gave the taxi-driver the modest sum he requested and ran to meet them.

'We've found her!' they cried. 'We know where she is.'

'Oh, thank God,' Harriet breathed. 'Where is she?'

'On Psiros.'

'Oh, my God!' She sat down amid the tins of flowers in the garden and put her head in her hands. It was Kitty's ability to get so far away from her, her independence more than the possible hazard of flight, that distressed her. 'How did she get there? The boat doesn't arrive here until noon and it doesn't go back till the afternoon.'

'She went with the fishing boats. The fishermen told us,' Lulu said.

'But she's only a child. Why did they take her?'

'Oh, you know Kitty. She told them some dire story that touched the core of their simple hearts.'

'Well, I'm off to look for her,' Harriet said.

'You can't, Ma,' Tim said. 'Not yet. You just said – the boat doesn't go until three.'

Harriet shook her head. 'I can't wait that long. I want to go now.'

'But, Ma!' Tim's voice grated with impatience. 'The boats go out at dawn anyway. It was no trouble for them to take an extra passenger. You don't expect them to make a special trip just for you.'

'You never can tell,' Harriet said mysteriously.

She found Apollo at the little bar on the beach, meditating upon a cup of black coffee. A day ago she would have sworn that she would never have the nerve to speak to him again. Now she did not care. She went to the bar and stared at him until he was forced to give her his attention. 'Let me buy you a drink,' she said.

'Ha! You buy me a drink?' He laughed in outrage, feeling it an offence to his pride.

'It would please me,' she said solemnly and after a brief hesitation Apollo conceded.

She ordered coffee for herself and two Metaxas and paid for them. 'I want us to be friends again,' she said, not looking at him. 'I want you to do something for me.'

She could feel his confusion burning through her. She did not dare to meet his eye. After a very long pause he spoke hesitantly, 'Yes. I will. I look after everything.'

She thanked him with a smile. 'Oh, you understand. I'm very grateful. Can we go now?'

'Of course,' he said and then he gave a little smile; a leer. 'Very difficult,' he said. 'Very expensive.'

'Oh, of course! How stupid of me,' Harriet apologized. 'Let me pay you.' She opened her bag and began to remove some money.

'Ha! You pay me?' His furious laugh told her that she had gravely compounded her earlier offence. He made no move to take the money. Instead he was removing something from his own trouser pocket, a little package which he handed her. It was written on in Greek and she couldn't understand it. She thought it must be a present and opened it.

'Oh,' she said.

It was a packet of contraceptives – condoms. The thin foil envelope caught the sunlight and the eye of the barman and she pushed it back into its box.

'Ah,' she said.

Apollo was grinning proudly. 'You have problem – I fix.'

'You misunderstand.' Dismay lit up her face with a smile. 'This is not at all what I require.'

'You are shy.' Apollo looked pleased. 'Not to worry. I look after you. You write to me. You say you are afraid to make love because of the children. Now you are no longer afraid because these' – he pointed to the box – 'are anti-babies.'

'No!' Harriet cried. 'It's a mistake.'

'But you write ...!' He took from another pocket a crumpled note and there she was, in her own hand, damned by manners – concerned for the children.

'Oh golly,' Harriet said.

'You come.' He gave her a meaningful look and took her hand, running circles in her palm with his thumb.

She was irresistibly drawn by him a little part of the way. 'Look, wait a minute!' She stopped like a donkey.

'No,' he said petulantly.

'No!' she said, firmly but gently. 'Not now. I'm in terrible trouble. I need your help.'

'I don't understand.' His eyes were puzzled and hurt.

'I know. It's my fault. I feel awful, but just for now will you be my friend? My brother?' Quite unexpected tears came to her eyes as the beautiful youth considered her with a frown. He slipped his precious package into his pocket. 'Yes,' he said. 'I will.'

'My little girl has run away,' she told him. 'I have to find her. She went to Psiros with the boats.'

'Big girl!' The boy's face brightened. 'Very pretty.'

'Yes,' Harriet admitted. 'She's only little really.'

'She not run away. She go to Psiros to fetch her father. She say she need to get her Daddy.' Apollo laughed. 'Maybe he go there and drink too much.'

'Apollo!' Harriet seized his hand. 'Her Daddy left us when she was just a baby. That was only her excuse. She was upset by something else and she ran away. Please, please take me to Psiros. I must find her.'

'Okay.' He covered her grasping hands with his. 'We go. No problem.'

'I'm very grateful.'

'Sure.'

When they got to the harbour the boat from Psiros was just coming in. Harriet touched Apollo lightly. 'Wait a minute. I just want to check the passengers in case Kitty's with them.'

She was reminded of the day when she had first had intimation of Joe's arrival from Melina and had searched the arriving passengers so eagerly for his face. Watching the new arrivals jumping from the ferry on to the quay – the happy holidaymakers and homecoming workers, the few nervous animals, their behinds prodded by twigs – she could see immediately that Kitty was not among them and her first bitter thought was not alarm but disappointment. 'She doesn't even miss me. She doesn't want to come home.' She felt foolish and angry with herself for having given so much attention to Joe Fisher. Already, on that occasion of her earlier disillusion, she had deduced from his letters that he did not love her. She opened her handbag and, from the debris within, fished out that little bundle of powdered correspondence. Very slowly (and with set jaw) she tore the bundle across and then launched the scraps on the hot breeze towards the sea. Some of them drifted on to the water and were agitated by little waves so that they lapped like tongues. Others drifted on to the grey heap of a man who sat desolately on a bollard close by the boat. He turned, very slowly, to examine the fall of litter which clung to his tweedy clothes.

His face had a boiled quality, it was the weight of his winter clothing.

'Joe!' Harriet said. 'Silly sod,' she thought first and then; 'Oh, love!'

'I'm waiting for the boat,' he said.

She walked over to him and plucked paper from his suit. 'You're a fool, Joe,' she said softly. 'You even look a fool. Why didn't you come back into the house and take off your coat? The boat doesn't go until three.'

'I was hoping it might leave earlier. If I could get back to the mainland I might get a flight this evening. I'm afraid of missing the boat.'

'Poor boy,' she said softly. 'You've missed the boat. We both have. It's our age. It's the age we were born in.'

'Please, Harriet. None of your profound confusions. I just want to go home.'

Sweat poured down his face. He looked like a soul in hell. He needed rescue. He needed Georgy.

'I'm going to Psiros now,' she said. 'One of the fishermen is taking me. You can come if you like.'

His whole aspect brightened. He looked at her with love. 'Oh, darling, that's kind,' he said.

She walked away from him and went back to Apollo. When she returned she had the youth held firmly by the hand.

The physical contrast between the two men was so great that Harriet experienced a small unwholesome pleasure. 'This is my friend, Apollo,' she said to Joe. To Apollo she said: 'It's Joe, my brother – he wants to come with me to Psiros.'

The two men glared at each other. 'Why he no help you?' Apollo wanted to know. 'Why you have to come to me?'

'Because he's no bloody good,' Harriet sighed.

It was an uncomfortable journey. She was glad that the smaller island was less than a mile away and that they would reach it in twenty minutes. At first she stayed on her own and leaned over the edge of the boat, peering into the water, looking for traces of ancient palaces and monuments grinning up out of the green, like the skulls of drowned sailors. It was rumoured that Psiros had once been linked to Keptos by a thriving city but it fell beneath the sea and severed the island in two. She could see nothing except an empty mineral can and a dead fish which rocked about, fixing her with its morbid eye.

'Harriet . . .'

Joe came up behind her. He still wore all his tweed and he looked like people she had seen in a space film, who were in a craft that passed too close to Mars, and their faces melted.

'Oh, love,' she thought.

'I'll get in touch as soon as I can.'

'Take your time,' she said in a little flat voice.

146

'I'm sorry.'

'Just tell me –' her head jerked round to face him – 'were you happy?'

'Yes, yes. I've never been so happy in my life.'

She wanted to question him in the closest detail, to know if it was the sun that made him happy, the island, the brief freedom from his wife and business, or was it in some measure because of her. Instead she said carefully. 'Tell me, was there ever a time – even a moment – when you thought you might throw it all up, your family, your friends, to be with me?'

Joe sighed. He circled around her in distress, wanting to touch her, but he did not dare. 'I am just an ordinary man,' he said. 'I do what I can. I do my best. I go ninety-five per cent of the way with people.'

'It's the other five per cent that counts,' she thought and she walked away from him and perched on a coil of rope close to Apollo.

'Poor lady.' Apollo patted her despondent shoulder. 'Many brothers, no lover.' A mild, possessive condescension had crept into his voice and it irritated her but she merely laughed agreement: 'No lover.'

'When we find your daughter . . . !' He winked at her and patted the pocket of his jeans.

She winked back. What else could she do? It was a small thing to do for a friend.

TWELVE

As they neared the island, they were greeted by a flotsam of pedaloes. Blue and red and iced-lolly orange, they ploughed a solid course around the glittering bay, motivated by the flailing knees of their pilots. Behind, the sombre massif of the new hotel towered over the hills. A patchwork of blues and greens – the two swimming pools for adults and children, the golf course, the instant garden – spread out beneath it like a child's apron and Harriet noticed a tide of brilliant pink rising from the base of the building. They had completed the painting of the ground-floor buildings and staked up trellises which had been threaded with plants already drooping with heavy blossom.

She gripped the edge of the boat and peered hard at the bright, mobile plastic cartons and their human content. She was mad with curiosity. She knew now she had been fated to come to Psiros. Even though her earlier planned missionary trip had been thwarted by the arrival of Joe Fisher and although he himself had broken his promise to bring her to lunch in the new hotel, still she was compelled to come. She felt that the temporary islanders had some clue to offer her, some key to the puzzle of unresolved lives. All her years she had been living up to the standards of an invisible god, her husband, and had been searching for positive evidence to support the quality of her existence. She now believed she had been mistaken. It was negative evidence one needed to buoy up the case for a life. She sought for agitation in the gaiety of the holiday revellers, for jealousy in their romances and behind the dyed hair and painted eyes, a fear of old age – a terror of death.

It was clear the holidaymakers were as curious about her as she was about them. The knees in the pedaloes pivoted with vigour. The little boats converged like ornamental fishes. Harriet found herself engaged in a lopsided gaze with a middle-aged woman with a wall eye and stiff golden hair. Rings of gold tin were looped through her ears and her bosoms lounged like white rabbits in a low-cut swimsuit. The woman latched her crooked eye on to

Harriet. Harriet stared back. So intent were they on one another that the passenger in the pedalo, a man, became bored and his fat fingers delved in his glass for an ice cube which he thrust at the cleavage of the woman. 'Heh, heh!' he cackled. The woman squealed and wriggled with joy like a toddler. Her wild happy eye rejected Harriet's morbid look and roved on to Apollo who whooped with youthful approval.

When she got on to the island Harriet wanted to be alone. Joe had to wait for the hydrofoil. He had decided to remain at the harbour and she did not try to dissuade him. They said goodbye.

'Thank you,' he said. 'It's been lovely.'

'Thank you for coming,' Harriet said.

They had both modestly assumed formality. It was a gloved farewell. They stood stiffly until he realized with dismay that she was waiting for her hug. He leaned over and put a dry kiss on her cheek. He patted her shoulder. 'There.'

Huge tears spilled down her face and down the back of her throat, choking her. She went on, helplessly shaking and choking, blaming him with her ugly crumpled face, while he watched in misery. She shook her head to show that she was ashamed of herself, that he must take no notice.

'I'll be there, you know, if you need me,' he said, but it only made her uglier and angrier and eventually there was nothing to do but turn her back on him and walk away.

'No bloody good,' Apollo grumbled, giving Joe a dark look. He led her away. 'I am your brother. I look after you.'

'Leave me alone,' she said bleakly.

'I wait,' he said.

'Yes please. You wait.'

The hotel was built on the beach and it had claimed the bay, criss-crossing the sand with bright deckchairs and umbrellas. As she picked her desolate path through the sunbathers she found that she had to pause every now and then to examine them. It was partly to keep an eye out for Kitty but she was curious too. She had to find out what they looked like. They all looked alike, she thought; men and women, pink and glistening, resembled awful North Country specialities in a butcher's window.

A verandah had been stitched on to the front of the hotel over the beach. French windows opened out from the restaurant and tables with white cloths and pink flowers had been introduced on to the balcony so that some of the diners could eat out of doors. She experienced a desire to go into the restaurant, as Joe had promised and she had imagined, to eat some large expensive meal with cold wine, unimpeded by the bad manners of the children or the poor meat on Keptos. She would like a steak or a lobster or a nice piece of duck. It was almost lunchtime and inside, white-coated waiters were administering little baskets of bread and jugs of iced water to tables, propping up crisp menus. She could imagine bowls of salad and trays of chips, some meat or fish in its own juice with a grilled tomato and a spray of watercress.

The restaurant was plain and nice. It reminded her of home and the dignified fish restaurants where you could have buttered asparagus and sole and raspberries and not feel greedy because there was nothing minced or cheap on the menu. She was ravenously hungry. She stared in the window like a savage. A startled waiter peered back out at her and she realized she looked a savage, with her wild, dirty face and her old clothes. She had to have a drink. She really couldn't even face dear little Kitty without a drink.

She moved around to the side of the hotel along the alarming blue swimming pool and the frilled awning of the poolside bar. Dripping bathers blotched the dull concrete patio and around its edges white tables sprang up like daisies. There was a small platform where musicians played in the evening (and where, no doubt, Miss Psiros was elected at the end of each happy fortnight). The pool rang with the muffled crunch of descending divers. Their excited shrieks were underlaid with the pleasant sounds of drinks being served and sipped. Most of the tables were occupied but Harriet found an empty one in a shady corner and she sank wearily on to a metal chair. She felt incomparably gloomy and dowdy. Coming to Psiros had been a mistake. She knew perfectly well that Kitty would come home sooner or later in one piece (or two – she might be pregnant). The people at the Paradise were a different species to her. She could not compare their lives with hers. In any case they seemed happy. It was a hollow happiness, of course, the brittle cheer of superficial types, but their laughter was getting on her nerves.

The waiter came. She ordered, without looking up, a gin martini. Infected by the meaningless gaiety of the holidaymakers, he laughed at her.

She directed a bitter glance at him and was perturbed to see that it wasn't a waiter, he wasn't wearing the regulation white jacket. He was wearing hardly anything at all, except a scrap of yellow swimwear. Good Lord, it was the lecherous lifeguard whom she had earlier spotted through her telescope. 'What do you want?' she said.

'You really want to know?' He gave a winning, wicked smile. 'It is you.' He sat down. He really was quite astonishingly handsome. He was older than Apollo and had the bad, mirthful eye of the habitual seducer. It made her unsure of herself. She clawed her hair out of her eyes, then, remembering the state of her face, clawed it back again. 'Well, I don't want you,' she said.

'Why not?' His tone was gentle but astonished. His body and the features of his face had been flawlessly structured. Only the shortness of brow and the tightness of his wavy hair bespoke peasant origins.

'Because I'm married. Because I'm hundreds of years older than you.' She was annoyed to find that her tone had taken on something of his light, bantering one.

'How old?'

'Forty.'

'Oh, my God!'

Harriet felt oddly let down.

The boy rallied. 'I don't care.' He shrugged. 'It is not, after all, catching. You have nothing catching?'

'Despair,' she said, but she could see that he did not understand the word.

'Is that all?' he laughed fearlessly. 'No problem. We will make love.'

'Certainly not,' Harriet said.

'Why not?'

'Because I don't believe in casual relationships. I think sex should be beautiful and meaningful.'

'I think that's a load of sheet.'

'Well then, sheet is all you're going to hear.' She giggled. She felt as if she had already had a drink. And she was learning to use swearwords. Only this morning she had said 'bloody'.

The lifeguard grinned at her. 'Okay, but I think you should wear dark glasses when you talk sheet.'

'Why? Don't you like the way I look?'

'I like the way you look, but your eyes they say different to your mouth.'

For some reason she felt cheered. The lifeguard was very good company. He was intelligent in a way. He had sexual intelligence.

Her body tingled pleasantly with all the talk of sin. She had the feeling that the love he offered really was free. One wouldn't have to pay with grief or guilt.

'You are a very handsome man,' she said

'Sure,' he said modestly.

'Are you ambitious? You speak very good English. What are you going to do with your life?'

'Yes, I am ambitious,' his brow lowered and for once he looked entirely earnest. 'I want to get a big flashy car.'

'But your life here, this job! It's a dead end,' she protested. 'You should be thinking of something better.'

He smiled. 'What is better? I have the sun, good food, some money, a lot of girlfriends. What more has the world to offer?'

'I don't know,' she said. 'Marriage? A family?'

'Ah, yes,' he said. 'These things I will have, but later, when I am not so young – a good woman, perhaps also not so young.'

She saw it then, some older woman alone at the island resort. A widow? A divorcee? He would look for an insecure woman and one with plenty of money. She tried to feel harshly towards him but why bother? The widow would be delighted. Why should she not spend her money on him? She would probably have put in years of misery with some dour and responsible fellow who worked himself into the grave wherein one foot had already been securely lodged.

A tall, striking young woman, with abundant red hair and prominent teeth, strode past in a green swimsuit. She reminded Harriet of Hawna Maroyle. As she passed, she gently grazed the lifeguard's hair with her long nails. His gaze followed her and he sprang to his feet.

'Excuse me,' he said courteously to Harriet.

'Yes, of course,' she said.

'My name, it is Costas,' he said. 'I will see you again?'

'Of course,' she said.

As he unwound, she could not help giving the quickest of glances to his boastful crotch in the brief scrap of swimwear. He noticed this, although his glance was torn away to the younger, bolder redhead, and for an instant he posed and he looked absurdly magnificent.

'Costas,' she called after him.

'Yes.' He turned back, a tiny bit impatient.

'Are there other jobs here for good-looking young men?' She had an idea.

He shrugged. 'Yes. Waiters, barmen. The management, they like the handsome ones. God knows why.' He laughed and sprinted off after his prey.

A moment later the barman came – another gleaming, grinning young man though not nearly so well structured as Costas. 'I'd like a gin and vermouth,' she said. The barman nodded.

'I should have the Paradise cocktail, dear,' said a gruff, cheerful voice.

It was a woman in her forties, firmly corseted into a blue dress. Blue eye shadow had been generously applied to match the dress but it had suffered from the woman's habit of squinting around her well-clenched cigarette.

'Why should I?' Harriet said.

'It's got joie de vivre,' the woman said.

'Then I don't think I shall,' Harriet said stubbornly. 'I've got no room for joy. My daughter's run away.'

The woman in blue sat down. 'Yours too? Energetic little sods, aren't they? It's all the vitamins nowadays. Sti-i-ill,' she threw back her head and stretched her arms, 'it does them good.'

'I don't see how you can say that,' Harriet was reproving. 'She's only fourteen. She looks more, she's a big girl, and very pretty. She could be anywhere. She could be with a man.'

The woman looked alert. 'Big girl? Very dark, very pretty? You mean, here on Psiros? Oh she is dear, she is.'

'She is what?'

153

'She is with a man. I'm sure I saw her go off with one of the waiters. Oh, you don't want to worry, dear, he's a nice boy.'

Harriet stood up. Her face went white underneath the sunburn. She had never really believed that little Kitty would go off with a man.

'Excuse me,' she said. 'I've got to find her.'

'Let her have her fun.' The woman waved a plump pink arm. 'Here, have a ciggie, have a drink.'

'Fun?' Harriet's voice rose and her chin trembled. 'You call it fun for a fourteen-year-old girl to have sex with a waiter? No wonder the world has gone the way it has. It's people like you with no standards that set the example.'

The woman's broad hand, hazardous with rings, trapped Harriet's. Her free arm retrieved the departing waiter. 'Two Paradisos, dear,' she said to the boy and then she turned back to Harriet, who was struggling to escape.

'You really are in a state, aren't you, dear?' She shook her head. 'Who said anything about sex? It's not that you want to look out for these days, it's the judgement.'

'The judgement?' Harriet felt too shaken and too weak to move. She sat down again, her hand still in the grasp of the woman in blue.

'Yes, dear. They sit in judgement on us. They think we're disgusting. They're very fastidious. Don't be fooled by their noise and their mess. What about all those vegetarians and anorexics? They aren't at all keen on flesh.'

She wanted to tell the woman she was mad, to laugh in her face and tell her for her information there was no connection between vegetarianism and anorexia. At the same time there were grains, which stuck like sugar, of truth. She had never had an opportunity to exchange truths with another woman. The cocktails came. The waiter grinned as he placed them before the ladies. They were the large drinks in pottery vases, garlanded, from which Harriet had once vowed to save the solitary ladies of Psiros. She removed a paper parasol and some flowers and then she ate, one by one, the pieces of fruit which were piled up on top – a cherry, a piece of pineapple, a strawberry. She sipped the drink. It was cool and very strong. She sensed rum and gin and some orange-flavoured liqueur sharply blended with pineapple juice. She bent her face to the stone mug and gulped. 'What should one do?' She dropped her words into the hollow top of the vessel, where they echoed.

'You've got to stop protecting them,' the woman said. 'They have to learn to survive on their own.'

'They'd get hurt,' Harriet said. 'I couldn't bear it.'

'No, I know – but they can. They adapt. They get hurt, yes, but they find a crutch.'

'What crutch?'

'A person, a drink, a cigarette. They find out that they're just like you after all. Occasionally, they become your friends.'

Harriet looked up. The woman in blue was no longer laughing and Harriet saw that behind the bright smile and reckless, gravel-pit voice was an ordinary woman. Beneath the exotic blue drapes of shadow were plain dull blue eyes, tolerant. 'I'm Janice,' the woman said.

'Janice, why did you come here?'

'Get away, it's very good value. It was a bargain because the hotel's only new. All mod cons, luxury up to the gunnels, waited on hand and foot. My old man's here too but he's a quiet type and I like a bit of company in the evenings.'

'But it's artificial!' Harriet protested. 'This is not the real Greece. It's destroying the natural beauty.'

'Well, I'll let you in on a secret, dear,' Janice smiled. 'This is not the real me either. The real me is a twenty-seven-year-old raver with legs that would knock the sight out of a fella's head. Then life came along and destroyed my natural beauty. Well, I like it here. It looks beautiful after a drink and so do I, dear, and I'm out for a good time.' Janice looked sadly at Harriet for a moment but then she broke into a gusty laugh.

Harriet felt she was being teased. 'I have to go,' she said. 'I must look for my daughter.'

'My guess is she's with her little foreign friend in his bedroom.' Janice indicated a spartan prefab unit partly concealed by palms and clearly designated for the lesser comforts of staff. 'Now don't look like that, dear!' Janice's finger withdrew to waggle a reproach at Harriet. 'The picture isn't at all as clear as it's painted. That's

155

right. You go and sort out the juveniles and maybe we'll meet up later for a spot of lunch.'

'Oh, I don't think so. I don't feel very tidy.'

'Tell you what,' Janice said. 'Use my bathroom. You'll get the key at the desk – room 2254.'

The thought of a hot bath, a proper lunch, made Harriet feel tearful with gratitude. 'Oh, I couldn't,' she said. 'You're very kind. What would your husband think?'

'Never mind about that, dear. Just you enjoy yourself.'

When she stood to leave Harriet found that her feet had turned to rubber. It was the effect of the cocktail. She clung on to the metal ladder which led to the diving board and watched a downpour of bodies fall with distorted thumps and cries into the water. Janice nodded encouragement and Harriet waded on determinedly, past the palms and a further strip of neglected geological stubble where crates of bottles were stored out of sight, until she reached the workers' quarters.

She found Kitty in one of the small utility rooms of this block. She was on a bed with a young man.

'Kitty!'

'Oh-oh!' the child said, with a glance at the boy, acknowledging her mother with a faint curl of the lip.

'I've been looking everywhere.' She felt crushed by the child's contempt. 'How could you do such a thing?'

'You know.'

'What are you doing in bed with this boy?'

'What do you think?' Kitty gave her a look of exasperation. 'I'm eating Rice Krispies.'

'Rice ...'

'I was bloody starving. I got nothing to eat after that sod locked me up. I might have starved to death if it hadn't been for Christos here. Mum, it's really not so bad here. They've got Rice Krispies and ice-cream cones and doughnuts. See!' She held up the bowl that had been buried in her lap and showed off a silt of sodden cereal at its bottom.

'Rice Krispies,' Harriet moaned faintly. 'Come *home*, Kitty!'

Kitty spooned the last of the tinned milk and sugared cereal into her mouth and shook her head. 'No, Mummy. I'm staying here until . . . I'll stay here with Christos for the moment. He said he'll get me anything I want. I don't fancy getting the wrong side of your lover, the lock freak, again. It's disgusting anyway, you think of nothing but sex.'

'And what do you suppose this young man's got on his mind?' Harriet's voice shook in sympathy with the vibrating finger she jabbed towards the young animal who was crouched on the bed, poised but languid, a handsome hound. 'Or is sex just disgusting if you're not young and beautiful?'

'Mummy, don't be *gross*.'

'Now, don't try and put me off.' Harriet knew she looked and sounded crazed. She remembered Betsy throwing chairs into the water after her refreshment by the hotel cocktail. 'If you're so superior, how come you keep disappearing with men the moment I take my eye off you? How come I find you in bed with a strange young man?'

'Well, not for *that*.' Kitty glared back. 'If you want to know how come it's because nobody takes a speck of notice of me at home.'

'You mean you haven't . . . ?' She felt quite giddy with relief.

'Fucked? Oh, Mummy, you're so crude. You're so old-fashioned – so *primitive*! Of course I haven't. Don't you even know it isn't cool to abuse your emotional capacities with superficial sexual stimulus? And it's not hygienic. Yee-uch!'

'But Lulu does. Is she old-fashioned too?'

'She does *not*!'

'But . . . ' She felt like Dorothy in *The Wizard of Oz*, as if she had stepped out her own back door and found an entirely altered world there. For a wild moment she wondered if the young generation was a wholly new species – not human at all; they might even have a different method of reproducing. They were different. Of course they were. They were modern and she was old-fashioned. How did other people know about these things? How did Janice know? Did her children talk to her? (Harriet suffered a sharp pang of jealousy at this notion and dismissed it out of hand.) Were there notes about them in the popular magazines? 'But Lulu sleeps with Roger!' Even as she said it she knew she was betraying some hopeless naivety, some *grossness*. It didn't mean the same thing it had in her youth.

'Yeah. *Sleeps!*' Kitty emphasized scornfully.

'But you said it yourself!' Harriet remembered with a certain hysterical triumph. 'The day Roger arrived you came running out on the road to me. "I'm not going back there," you said. "They're at it – fatty and the beanstalk." You said it, Kitty! "They're at it!"'

'Mummy!' Kitty's voice was a growl of shame and rage. 'You thought I meant *that*? I meant they were kissing – on the mouth. Yeuch!'

'You mean . . . nobody makes love any more?'

'Yeah, well – maybe wallies and posers. Maybe older people who are really involved – and married people.'

'Timmy?' Harriet's voice was a tiny quiver of hope.

Kitty hesitated and then wriggled uncomfortably. 'Well . . . he's a bit of a wally.'

'Kitty – you must tell me; if Roger isn't doing it with Lulu then . . . are he and Tim . . . ?'

'*Mummy!*' Kitty jumped with annoyance so that milk and sugar sprayed from their respective containers on to the blankets. 'You're hopeless, you're *perverted*. Tim and Roger are certainly, bloody well not. Tim and Roger are anything but lovers. If you want to know the truth, Tim and Roger are . . .' But here she stopped.

'I do. I want the truth,' she begged.

Kitty turned a round, impassive face, as unpleasant as a cold pudding. 'If you want to know the truth I think that you and Joe Fisher are a pair of ridiculous old farts trying to be sexy and succeeding about as much as . . . David Niven and Deborah Kerr!'

How horribly true, Harriet thought with interest.

'If you want to know the truth this room belongs to Christos and he hasn't invited you here so I really think you should go.'

'What about Christos, then?' Harriet was fired with inspiration. 'Is he a . . . a wally? Did he really just bring you to his room for Rice Krispies or might he be hoping for something else?'

'You have a filthy mind, Mother,' Kitty said on a thin, dangerous note. She turned to Christos. 'Did you bring me here to fuck me?'

The boy looked delighted. He bestowed an amused glance on Harriet and returned to Kitty, touching points of her face as if she was a little dimpled doll instead of a huge, threatening woman, 'I bring you here because you are helpless and hungry. I bring you here because you are very pretty. I bring you here because I love you and I want to ...' he darted another look at Harriet and then leaned over to whisper into Kitty's ear. Kitty's face boiled with fury. 'You dirty creep,' she said. She jumped off the bed and upturned her cereal bowl, still with dribbles of milk and a few wet warts of cereal, on top of the boy's head.

'Let's go, Mummy,' she said with dignity.

Out in the sunshine people were finishing their apéritifs and moving, in chatty, tipsy groups, towards the restaurant or to shady outdoor tables, for lunch. She saw a small woman, with nice wavy brown hair, doing a slow pirouette between the tables. Her pretty face was in a transport and, as she executed some complicated little twirl and plié, she missed her footing and fell into the pool. 'Betsy!' cried a male American voice with desperate tolerance.

'Delbert!' Harriet cried.

'What?' Delbert J. Mallard rolled up his sleeves and his trousers as he looked around. 'Oh, hi there, miss! Good to see ya!' he waved and smiled before lunging into the water after his wife.

She saw a group of office girls in cotton tops and wrinkled jeans, arm in arm, their bosoms bronzed for the dress dance season. A very thin young man and woman, unnaturally bleached and dressed in new clothes of which hers were frilled and colour-matched in every particular, walked sideways for their eyes were so closely locked that it was impossible to avert the parallel. The honeymooners, Harriet guessed with excitement. She noticed other groups and figures she thought she recognized and she felt a thrill of achievement, like a teenage autograph-hunter.

'Kitty!' she gripped her daughter. 'Let's stay and have lunch.'

'Great! Fantastic!' Kitty, said, but then, sensing better advantage in resistance, she whined. 'Oh, I can't, Mummy, I'm filthy. I have nothing to wear.'

'Never mind,' said Harriet recklessly (and satisfactorily). 'I'll get you something.'

'Okay.'

She had to find Apollo first. He was at the bar, drinking fruit juice and talking to a blonde Scandinavian girl who wore a brief outfit of tie-dyed rags.

'Apollo!' She tapped his shoulder. When he saw who it was his expression altered to that which the very young reserve for Totally

Uninteresting People. She was taken aback until it occurred to her that the boy had never been to a tourist resort before, had never had a choice of young women (for whatever Kitty said, Harriet was convinced that sex still survived at the Paradise Hotel). She realized with relief that the boy would no longer be determined to reserve the precious package in his pocket for her.

'I've found my daughter. We're going to have some lunch.'

'I am happy for you,' he said politely. 'It seems that we have each of us found what we require.'

'If you and your friend would like lunch,' she said, 'I will tell the restaurant to put it on my bill.'

'Thank you, no.' He was eager to be rid of her. 'Younger people do not eat lunch.'

'Well then,' she shrugged humbly. 'Whatever you want, I will pay.'

The boy glanced at his eager young companion, then back at Harriet and he laughed good-humouredly.

'He's thinking of me as a sin-eater,' Harriet thought. 'He thinks his luck is too good to be true but that I will take the retrubution.' She hurried off, feeling haunted.

She went into the hotel with Kitty and asked at the reception desk for the key to Janice's room. There was a boutique in the foyer and while they waited they examined its display. There was a predominance of bright yellow and glitter but Harriet noticed a range of coarse linen separates in black and white. 'I promised I'd buy you something,' she told Kitty. 'Would you like one of those?'

'Cosmic!' Kitty said.

They bought the tops and took the lift to the twentieth floor. Janice's room was bright and neat – a hotel room from anywhere in the world. It had a huge bathroom with a pile of stiff white towels. While her bath was filling, Harriet stood on the balcony and looked out over the sea to Keptos. With its poor vegetation and the long hump of its back, it looked like a balding badger.

She had a wonderful bath. She found shampoo and washed her hair. She rinsed her face clean of the tears shed for Joe Fisher.

Kitty bathed too. After Harriet had scrubbed the bath, which retained a substantial grey ring, and replaced the towels and scents and dried her hair and Kitty's, they dressed in their white tops and their jeans and looked as new as First Communion girls.

They returned Janice's key and went in to lunch. They drank cold wine and ate shrimp cocktail and ham salad and chips and strawberries. It wasn't good food. There was no lobster on the menu, the Greek dishes were framed in a separate little section, as if they were a joke and the shrimp cocktail was a shrill and viscous preparation. Kitty thought it was wonderful (apart from the ham) and Harriet ate as though she had never tasted food before. As she chewed and sipped consideringly she looked all around her, absorbed the bright, intricate pattern of people who moved in a body across the world and fortified themselves against its foreignness in every respect except their distance from the sun.

There were girls who had come for Romance. She noted the bold gaze of a waiter at one table and the fluttering, blushful response from its recipient and all the table a-twitter with conspiracy and jealousy. There were married couples – a boiled assortment of reckless extremes (mini-skirts and varicose veins, carmine lipstick and incipient moustache, plunging neckline and plummeting bosom). The husbands, in their holiday clothing, looked like wistful children whom wicked time had punished by pulling out their hair and teeth and puckering their chins and blowing out their bellies. They made jokes about sex and the wives' scornful laughter was full and rippling as sails in the wind.

There were the older solitary women. Some smoked through the meal and read a paperback. Others compounded the cocktail they had drunk before lunch with wine and brandy. They all exhibited some vivid feature – bright beads or a transparent top or some strange shade of dye in the hair – and she assumed that this was a signal for men, so that it would be known they were available and they wouldn't have to interrupt their reading or their smoking to inform anyone of the fact.

There were some men on their own too. They did not read but kept predatory watch. They were blond foreigners who wore shorts without looking absurd or vulnerable.

They were all familiar to Harriet, not just because she had seen them or imagined them through her telescope on Keptos but because they were the logical successors to the people her parents

161

had been, to the company they kept on their holidays at the seaside. They no longer made her feel superior or caused her lip to curl in scorn. They made her feel bewildered. She had liked Janice. She found her kind and very interesting but although she spotted her lunching at the opposite side of the restaurant and waved to her, she couldn't bring herself to invite the woman in blue to her table. She had been entertained by the lifeguard and cheered by him yet if anyone of her own acquaintance had arrived while they were flirting, she would have cut the boy dead and pretended she did not know him. She could not relate to such people. She had to relegate them to a pack or a point of view. It disturbed her slightly that they did not recognize this fact. They accepted her as one of them. They did not seem to know she was different, that she had struggled against the tide and been washed up on more exclusive shores.

This was not her only confusion. She had opted, at considerable expense and with difficulty, for the simple life on the remote and uncluttered island of Keptos. In truth, it had never been simple. It was inconvenient and laborious; the simplest acts of washing or cooking were a torment and, because of the travel complexities and the limited accommodation, even friendships and relationships were complicated.

Here life was simple. The drinks were strong and cool, the baths warm, the towels copious, the food was cafeteria food which appealed to children and did not disturb adults; if one wanted ciggies one merely waved at a waiter – the same, presumably, if one craved the act of love and, because of the abundance of opportunity, the wave could be turned into one of dismissal should the desire have passed by the time the service was on hand.

She felt elated. She felt bewildered. She had the unpleasant suspicion that the people who languished in the giant pool all day and in warm scented baths each evening paid less for their trip than she who patted her armpits from a tin basin of warm water. How should she prove that she had been right all along – and to whom? The answer, or part of it, came to her as she finished the wine and waved to the waiter for two coffees and a brandy. She must simplify her life. She would get rid of Roger and allot domestic chores to the children. She would put meal-making and shopping on a rota so that she was not permanently shackled to the stove or anchored to bags of messages. Every so often they would take their meals at the restaurant on the beach. She would swim. She recalled how much she had enjoyed her swim with Joe Fisher. She would swim from the beach to the same rock and then dry off in the sun. For the moment it would serve almost as well as a bath and next year she would seek Melina's permission to have a proper bathroom installed at the cottage. There was nothing, now that she came to think of it, to stop her importing a suitcase full of fluffy towels to the island and leaving them there for her use year after year.

Year after year after year after year. She saw those years, continuous as the stars that shine, stretched in never-ending line. It was a moment of real fear. The years ahead were like figures in a nightmare; they had no features. She was a young woman. It was only living with teenagers that made her feel a hundred. She had forty years or more – as many years as she had lived – before she could properly call herself old and languish upon the whim and charity of others. In the meantime she must draw in the faces of the more immediate years and accept whatever disfigurements the unpredictable will of the children imposed on them. She might be all alone. She might be invaded by hordes. She might be turned into a grandmother – or a jail visitor. She must not seek for personal change or gratification for that would make her a bad mother and justify the failure of her children, but she must accept, unquestioning, uncritical, whatever changes the children engineered on their own behalf and admit readily that the creditable changes were their own achievements and the disgraceful ones entirely her fault. She must not fall apart. She might loosen a little but then she must pull herself together.

The diners in the restaurant were finishing their meal. One by one, two by two, in little mirthful knots or happy laughing bands, they strolled out to bronze contented stomachs in the sun or to bear their wine-soaked passions up to a pleasurable siesta. She could see now the sense of the hotel. It was a defence against the unforeseen. Even if lovers or children let one down, the routine of the hotel would not falter. There would still be people to lie down with or talk to and meals at set times and the beds would always be made.

When she had first looked on the visitors to Psiros she thought that they were stupid, second-rate people with nothing in their heads. After talking to Janice she realized she had been mistaken. It was merely that they had nothing on their minds.

But it wasn't as simple as that. Beauty fed the spirit. Beauty was faith and hope. To raise children without it would be like giving them no liver or oranges, no love. She had often felt a soaring of the spirit, a feeling close to joy, when she looked down from the high field and saw the great spangled sweep of the sea; or at night with animal noises faint and contented as the grunts of sleeping children and the cottage roses, damp and blue in the dusk; or in the very early morning, with the sun's first seepage into the sky. Nothing worthwhile was easy and facility of access seemed itself to lend a devaluing quality.

'Come on, kiddie,' she said quietly to Kitty who was tenderly feeding herself with strawberries. She wanted to go home now, quickly, before her argument developed some fatal flaw. She would start again; shop in the village for nice food and wine and when the evening came she would be back in her own pretty garden, the storms of recrimination and exclamation abated, a drink in her hand and the smell of roses in her head.

As they got up to leave, she noticed the restaurant's one remaining occupant, a woman sitting by the window with a drink before her, very composed, neither reading nor smoking but watching a sea view out of the window.

'Just a moment,' she said to Kitty.

'Oh, Mum, don't start,' the child begged.

The woman was about her own age with handsome loops of grey in her strong waving black hair and a remarkable face, weathered but beautifully featured, like an expensive handbag. She wore a long black vest for a dress and had silver sandals. When Harriet reached her table the woman looked around slowly. 'You're the painter,' she said. It was as if she had been waiting for her.

'Yes, I'm Harriet Bell. How did you know? Who are you?'

'My name's Anne. I know your work. As a matter of fact I was at your London show and I bought a painting. I took the boat to Keptos the other day and I saw you. I would have said hello but you were with a rather dishy man. Lucky you!'

'Not very.' Harriet liked Anne. The nails on her broad hands were neglected and her feet were quite dirty but she had a valuable look. 'What are you doing here?' The rude question was out before she could stop it. 'Mummy!' Kitty protested in agony.

Anne was not put out. 'I'm thinking.' She pulled out a chair for Harriet with her dusty foot.

Harriet was tempted to settle but Kitty had commenced a dangerous growl, salty with threats.

'I'm sorry,' Harriet said. 'I have to go. I hope we'll meet again.'

Anne smiled warmly and put her feet up on the chair she had withdrawn for Harriet.

On their way out they were accosted by Delbert and Betsy. Betsy looked perfectly composed now. She had a white bag with matching sandals and a cotton dress with a print of pale grey to match her eyes. 'D.J.'s been telling me about you,' she said to Harriet. 'Come and have a drink and a game of cards with us. You know what they say – unlucky in love, lucky in something-or-other.'

'I told Betsy how your daughter ran off with your boyfriend,' Delbert said. 'Gee! Kids! Our Betsy hasn't been herself since little Libby got in trouble a few years back.'

'Your little girl got pregnant?' Harriet was sympathetic.

'Naw. She was one of a motorcycle gang that held up a bank. A motorbike! Betsy gets mad as hell when she thinks of all the money we spent on pony lessons. She gets so mad she has to let off steam sometimes. Still, nobody minds out here. I guess everyone acts a little wild on their holidays.'

'Yes,' Harriet said sadly. 'They do.' The Mallards were happy together, one could tell that they were. She wondered if their conspiracy of mutual satisfaction had driven Libby to crime or if disappointment over the wasted pony lessons had been their unifying factor. She would be interested to find out. 'I must go now,' she said. 'I'll come back sometime. I'll look forward to the cards.'

'Sure thing.' The couple waved.

Now that her immediate aim of Kitty's safe retrieval had been achieved she did not want to leave. She imagined how pleasant it would be to pass the day with cocktails and bouts of unconsciousness and in the evening to float about in a pleasant haze with familiar music in the background and a stranger's body in the arms.

She was not the only one. Apollo was in love. His beautiful face clouded with pain when she told him it was time to go. The young woman looked unhappy too and Harriet felt ashamed for having treated the boy with such carelessness. 'I'll make it up to you,' she promised. 'I have a plan.'

Her plan was to help him get a job on the island. With his good looks and passable English she was sure he would find employment in the hotel. In due course he would forget about his many fatherless nieces and nephews, he would become as happy and feckless as Costas the lifeguard, with an endless stream of girlfriends and dreams of rich widows and flashy cars.

Kitty too, was reluctant to return to Keptos. At the last minute, waiting on the now-deserted harbour for Apollo to help her into his boat, she had turned into a solid column of recalcitrance.

'What is it, kitten? What's the matter?' Harriet said.

'It's him.' Kitty looked genuinely fearful. 'Fuckface Fisher. Mummy, promise you won't let him lock me up again.'

'Oh, poor baby, I forgot to tell you. Joe Fisher's gone.'

'Oh shit,' Kitty said confusingly.

THIRTEEN

She told Roger he had to go.

'I am in your hands.' He grinned and gave his little, mocking bow.

'I want you off my hands.'

For a moment his eye narrowed but then he smiled again, showing fishes' teeth, and his head jerked about as if in rhythm to some violent tune, as he sought the attention of the other children, and their alliance.

'Perhaps.' he said, 'we should put it to a vote.'

Everyone except Roger looked uneasy. 'Do you want me off your hands?' He spoke pleasantly but Lulu grew alarmed under his hooded look and had to concentrate on her hands, as if hands were the matter for consideration. She bunched them suddenly into fists and banged them on the table and rounded on Harriet. 'Just because your lover walked out on you . . . !'

'Are we talking about lovers?' Harriet said quickly. Her own hands clenched with nerves beneath the table. 'Is Roger your lover?'

'No.' It was a miserable confession.

'It's all right, dear.' She was dismayed at having drawn such pain. 'Just one thing more – do you love him?'

'No!' This time, an angry, demented shout.

'I see.'

She turned to Tim. 'Do you love him?'

Tim looked ill and frightened. 'No.'

'I'm sorry.' She looked away. She hated all this. She recoiled as did the young mother from a toddler with worms, but one could not run away. She produced the ghost of a smile. 'No, I'm not sorry. I'm glad. Now we'll have dinner and in the morning, Roger, you must go.'

He was still smiling, still insolent. 'You're afraid of me, aren't you?'

'No,' she said hurriedly.

'You're afraid for your precious darlings. You think I'll corrupt them.'

'Yes.'

He leaned across the table, his sharp head looming. 'Let me tell you, ma'am, they have nothing to fear from me. There are no innocents here, dear lady, except yourself.'

'What are you talking about?' For some reason she knew he was telling the truth, as when Kitty had spoken of the new celibacy.

'Shut up, Rog,' Tim protested angrily. 'Take no notice of Mum. You can stay if you want.'

'No,' Harriet said.

'You think your little girl's going to be a teacher, don't you?' Roger went on. 'She's a little fibber. She got nabbed for smoking funny-smelling cigarettes – and selling them to her friends. She doesn't go to school any more.'

'Oh!' Harriet said.

'And what about Tiny Tim here – mother's pride, the accountant. Don't you want to know what he's been up to?'

She shook her head and then her distant voice said, 'Yes.'

'He's a thief. He borrowed a car to take some little bird for a drive and left it neatly folded in a wall. He got done over by the pigs.'

'Tim!'

'I had to.' He was embarrassed, defensive but not, she thought, ashamed. 'Everybody's got a car.'

'Why wasn't I told?'

'I didn't give my real name or address.'

'It's stupid, Tim. They'll catch up. It's all so stupid. Why didn't you come to me if you needed a wretched car so badly?'

'You'd done such a lot. We didn't want to let you down,' Lulu said miserably.

She put her head in her hands and squeezed her forehead. She must pull herself together. 'Okay,' she said gently. 'I understand.' She used up her anger on Roger. 'It's you I don't understand. You're not a friend. What are you? What do you want from them?'

'Whatever I can get.'

'You can get out!' She made a cat's swipe at him. Her nails left a little sliver of blood on his cheek, which pleased and horrified her. She brought her arm back to pat her daughter. 'Oh, Lulu. Are you all right?'

'For God's sake, Mum, it was only grass.' Lulu shrugged free. 'And a little coke. I can handle it.'

'I should have guessed something was wrong,' Harriet said. 'It's just . . . you seemed so pleased when Roger arrived.'

'I was. I thought he was my pal. We never even guessed until he started to put the bite on us.'

'What do you mean?'

'He likes Keptos. He wanted us to keep him here. He wanted money.'

'Why didn't you tell me then?'

'That's the whole point, Mummy – he was threatening to tell you.'

'He was blackmailing you?'

'I guess. He wanted Tim to sell his telescope but that wasn't on – it was all you had. That was why we decided Joe Fisher should stay. We thought if anyone could deal with Rog, he could.'

'I can deal with Roger,' Harriet said. 'I've changed my mind about sending him away. I'm willing to bet he's got something incriminating hanging about here. I'm handing him over to the *astinomikos*.'

'The pigs?' For a moment Roger looked afraid but then he sized her up and he sneered. 'Okay, I'm a handler but she's a user. They might not know the difference around here.'

She wished she could be resolute but he might be right. 'Well then, you will leave first thing in the morning,' she said in a remarkably ordinary voice. 'In the meantime perhaps we should have something to eat?'

When she rose from the table her dress stuck to her in clammy patches. In a sickly daze she put chops beneath the grill and made salad. She brought wine to the table. As she poured the wine she noticed that her hands were colder than the wine, although the day sweltered. She felt chilled right through, even her head. A kindly thump on the back from Kitty thawed her slightly. 'Oh, Joe,' she thought.

She had summoned the children together immediately on her

169

return from Psiros. Full of lunch and mixed drinks it had seemed perfectly reasonable to proceed with her plan for the simplification of her life, but now she realized she had known all along that the disturbance of Roger would uncover some appalling unpleasantness. In an odd way she was relieved to know the worst. She did not feel personally affronted about the waste of money on education as Delbert's Betsy had been. Perhaps that would come later. There was even relief in the fact that she was no longer excluded. If Lulu had been telling the truth about her drug problem then none of the difficulties was hopeless. The children were, after all, only ordinary people, already beset by secrets and lugging life sentences. She was grateful to them for having tried to protect her. She even derived a kind of satisfaction from loving them all the more fiercely now that they were less admirable.

They ate a subdued dinner and went early to bed and Harriet surprised herself by sinking into a swift and bottomless sleep. Early in the morning she was wakened by a small noise which she could not identify, like the saw blade of a knife drawn across a crust of loaf.

It must be Kitty. No one else would bother her in the middle of the night. She was too tired to argue so she resigned herself, grunting invitingly, reaching out an arm to greet the hovering presence. It took a moment for her sleepy mind to register that the arm she touched was thin and bony and had hairs on it, another for her to unlock her eyes to define the curious greenish-white form – a sea cucumber – which suddenly became human and moved into the bed on top of her.

'Roger!'

'Ssh! Take it easy.'

Surprise made her struggle ineffectual. It was the shock of touching a snake. Roger did not feel cold or slimy. His body was warm and slight and weightless. Curiosity made her hazard a touch at his skin and hair and both were smooth and fine.

He burrowed against her, holding her very tight. He felt boneless. She thought that perhaps he had held Lulu like this in their early sexless nights. Perhaps he was some kind of eunuch. But then she knew he wasn't a eunuch.

'You *child*!' She braced herself and struggled up.

'I'm not a child,' Roger said. 'I'm the only grown-up you know. I want you and you want me and that's a fact whatever your prissy lips might say.'

It was her eyes, her bold eyes. Everyone could read her face like a book, although she thought the only thing she had registered was an instant's relief on realizing that Roger was not gay, that Tim would not be found on the beach, kicked to death by Manolis and his friends.

'You revolt me!' she said.

'No,' he said. 'You revolt yourself because you want me to love you. You see! I know you. You don't just want to be loved. You want to be known and loved. You want to know the worst, to sweep away all the surprises and still have love.'

She could see his smile through the dark and his unflattering knowledge of her was a kind of comfort. She wanted to be loved. She wanted to ease the hunger she had let build up for Joe and avenge the love.

'You hurt my children!' she accused.

'Your kids are off the rails,' Roger said. 'You've brought them up too soft. Someone was going to take advantage of them. Be glad it was just a plain grown-up grafter and not a spacer. I've done them no real harm. I've taught them a lesson. They're going to find it useful. I was never really serious about wanting money. That was just to sharpen their wits. All I really wanted was you.'

He stroked her face and calmed her down and bent to kissing her again. She was excited by his pure baldness, the fact that someone like him could be moved by her. She was about to open to him when she felt in his body a little shudder, not of tension or excitement, but of triumph.

'You bloody little rat!' She scrambled from under him. 'You're trying to do to me what you did to Lulu – breaking me down so you can do whatever you want afterwards. Would you have come looking for money tomorrow? Or is it just that you like it here? You don't want to go in the morning. Well, you're not going in the morning. You're going now!' She got out of bed and picked his jeans up from the floor, recognizing as she did so the zip as the source of the sawing sound that had woken her. She flung them at him. 'Out!' she ordered.

171

'It's the middle of the sodding night,' Roger whined. 'I'm not going now. For God's sake, I'll go in the morning.'

'You won't live that long,' Harriet said. 'Lulu! Tim! Kitty! Come quickly. Roger's in my room!'

'Shit!' Roger said in terror, dragging on his jeans, hearing the thud of amazon feet in the hall. 'What about my things?'

'Your bag will be left on the beach at noon tomorrow.' Harriet opened the window.

He scrambled out and she watched his wan form on the track, spiritual in moonlight. She shivered and pulled on her dressing gown. What wretched madness had possessed her to let him put his arms around her? She scrubbed at her mouth with her hand and then slammed the window.

The children burst in.

'It's all right, it's nothing,' she said. 'I got a fright but it was only Roger. He just came to say goodbye.'

'What about his things?' They looked disappointed.

'He didn't try anything funny?' Tim said.

'No. Nothing funny.'

'Can I get into bed with you?' Kitty said hopefully.

'Yes, baby,' Harriet reached for the succulent arm.

FOURTEEN

She was glad to have the children to herself again although she did not really know these stained new adults who sat about in the sun in their nightwear, heaping brooding looks on the innocent flowers. Occasional drab scraps of conversation were tossed out and she leaped to catch them.

She did not try to lead them but ran behind in the manner of a sheepdog, hoping to direct them. She dared not interrogate in case it would lead to bitterness – theirs or worse, hers. She intruded only on paths of inconsequence as if they were someone else's children. What kind of car had Tim taken? Where had they met Roger? Where did Lulu go in the day when she was supposed to be at school? Why had they lied so pretentiously about their futures to Joe Fisher?

'Don't you understand *anything*, Mum?' Lulu pleaded.

She understood none of it. She felt obliged to compensate for this failure. She made a lovely picnic lunch, spreading out the pink tablecloth as she had done for Joe Fisher, putting strawberries in a bowl and wine in a bucket and bread and cheese and apples in a basket lined with its own chequered cloth. They fell on the food with their unwashed faces and straggling hair and stuffed their mouths like refugees. Harriet turned away to hide her revulsion and pretended to admire some scenery.

The forgotten bell of Lulu's laughter rang out; 'Mum, remember the day Joe Fisher threatened Rog with the police?' She turned to her daughter with a delighted smile, but Lulu was talking with her mouth full and a little worm of hysteria writhed in her when she saw her pretty cloth, now daubed like an ambulance blanket with squashed strawberries and spilt wine. 'He ran about like a fool trying to catch a fart,' Tim snorted and her tatty little band rocked and squawked. Oh, she was superficial. How could she care so much about appearances when her own had suffered such wear over the years? Chilled by her critical smile the children ambled off in their frowsty nightclothes to sit in the sun and resume their geriatric study of space.

After she had tidied up the lunch things (in a day or two, when the children were better, she would broach the subject of shared domestic duties), she instructed herself to go for a swim. She forced herself to enter Kitty's room and remove from a drawer the beautiful blue swimsuit. 'Thief! Thief!' Kitty would cry if she caught her but the knowledge of Tim's pilferage had taken the claws out of her scruples. She did not even attempt to hide her crime but dropped her dress on Kitty's floor and smoothed the blue costume over her limbs. It was lovely. The blue made her eyes remarkable and showed her hair the colour of a Florentine angel's. She had a tolerable figure, although mostly bones and bust, and now that she had gone brown all over she looked (perhaps) more textured than ravaged.

Why had she never bothered to steal back her swimsuit when she had Joe? He might have carried off the kind of enhanced picture of her that would have made his parting from her more a loss and less a lucky escape. She knew the answer. It was as Roger said. She did not just want to be loved. She wanted to be known and loved.

Thoughts of Roger reminded her that she had not brought his bag to the beach as she had promised. She slipped on her dress over her swimwear and quickly and distastefully crammed his few things into his mouldy-looking zipper bag.

He was waiting for her on the beach. Dressed only in jeans he looked skinny and vulnerable. His nose and the bones of his shoulders were rasher-coloured. He looked anxious. 'Hard-hearted Harriet.' He attempted a smirk. 'I've been waiting for you. I've been here all night.'

She thrust out his bag of clothing on a rigid arm.

'Okay, I'm going.' He rooted in the bag and withdrew his black tee shirt. When he pulled it over his head his hair sprang through like the feathers of a startled bird. His face emerged and his eye was on her as if he had been able to spy on her through the fabric. 'Come with me.'

She did not trust herself to speak in case she would begin to feel sorry for him. She jerked her head dismissively in the direction of the fathomless ocean.

He swung his bag on to his shoulder. 'You should, you know –

come with me. You'll be lost without me. You've invested everything in your family but the bottom has fallen out of that market. You know what they'd do if you never came back?'

She shook her head.

'They'd sell your clothes.'

'Get out,' she cried. 'Leave us alone.'

'You're good out of bed,' he said, 'and I think you're good in bed. We'd make a lovely couple. You're not going to make me beg, are you?'

'I'm not going to make you do anything,' she said stiffly.

He came over and touched the side of her face. 'Never mind. I've a nerve to even ask. I would like to ask a small favour, though. Just a teeny one.'

The kind touch disarmed her. 'All right,' she said.

'Give us some bread,' he grinned. 'Blow me, I'm broke as a biscuit. Unless you see fit to sponsor my voyage, dear lady, it looks as if you're going to be stuck with me.'

For a long time she was busy trembling. 'I haven't got that kind of money,' she said.

'Sod it, any kind of money will do. Give me enough to get to Psiros. I'll work something out when I get there.'

She counted the money from her bag. He kept his hand out after he had taken it from her.

'What do you want from me now?'

'Don't try to bullshit me,' he said. 'I'll have to stay in one of the houses until the boat comes in. I'll need some money for food.'

She pushed more notes at him. He put it away. 'Sorry about that.' For a moment he managed, almost, to look embarrassed. It helped Harriet to recover. 'Not at all. If it gets rid of you it's a bargain.'

'And you like to pay for your pleasures.' He tapped the side of his cold little eye. 'God sees all things. Perhaps I should have made you pay last night. You'd have liked that. Maybe we still have a future. I might wait for you.'

She ran away behind a rock to take off her dress. When she had changed she remained crouched there, fussily folding her handbag up in the dress and tucking both into a damp crevice. When she peeked Roger had gone.

She struck out stoically to fulfil her swim. The moment she felt the water slurping warmly at her ankles she experienced the same terror as when she had gone swimming with Joe, but she kept her eyes closed and put her head down and beat at the water as if it was entirely to blame. She did not look again until the floor of the earth had receded from reach and the beach had been shrunk to a harmless miniature. She opened her eyes then to see the peppery sprinkling of beach, the toy taverna and a pocket-sized voodoo doll – Roger – watching.

Experimentally she flapped her arms about as if she was drowning. Roger watched. She lowered her head beneath the waves and remained submerged while her breath held. When she broke the surface and looked again, Roger was walking slowly away.

She came to the place where she had made love with Joe Fisher and pulled herself up on the baking rock. She lay back to receive the satisfaction of the sun. Ah, bliss.

But it was not. The hot rock had the quality of a torture implement. She was scalded and scathed from beneath and impaled from above by probing, cancerous bolts of sun. How could anyone be expected to sunbathe in such a place? How could anyone make love in such a place? She forgot now how lovely it had been, was filled only with irritation at his thoughtlessness. Having found a chink in her relentless worship her mind dragged her down other tunnels of treachery. Why could he not have simply gone to Psiros and phoned his wife from the new hotel and told her he had to make an urgent call on a client in, say, Petrograd, and he had no idea where the fellow had booked him in? He could have then come home quite plausibly with a brown and guiltless skin. In any case, if his wife was as sharp as he suggested, she would have long ago spotted that his passport was missing? No, it was not Georgy he feared. It was himself, her effect on him, the way she disarmed him and left him naked like herself.

She sat up angrily and miserably and clenched her arms around her boiled, bare knees. She felt wretched. It was the rock, the damn bloody rock. He had haunted it. He had made it his territory, like a tomcat. She would have to go back. In any case, she had never liked swimming.

She swam back. She shopped, she cooked; she put a cloth on the table and a smile on her face.

The children looked so awful when they came in to dinner that she thought she ought to ring a bell and cry out, 'Unclean!' But she had to show them that she did not mind, that her finding out their small failures lost neither their face nor her trust. 'I've been for a swim,' she confided heartily. She poured out wine and cut bread and she smiled and smiled.

There was silence.

'I want you to know you have nothing to worry about as far as I'm concerned. Everything that was discussed yesterday is forgotten. From now on all we have to think about is the future. Even that doesn't look so bad.' She smiled primly. 'I'm sure if I talk to the proper people, I can get you both back into college.'

'Oh, lay off, will ya,' cried the jaded children.

It transpired that they did not wish to return to college. 'If you've got bread to burn, I can think of things I'd really rather spend it on,' Tim said.

'You have to think about your future.' Harriet was at bay.

'That's what I'm talking about. I'd like to set up a little business.' He explained enthusiastically some illegal-sounding plan involving violent movies on video tapes. She interrupted to avoid the details. 'I haven't got that kind of money, dear. It would cost a fortune to rent a warehouse.'

'Not if I lived in it too,' Tim said. 'I've got it all worked out. If you let me use the house as security I can borrow enough bread. All I'll need from you is a bit of extra for rent and furniture. And if Lulu shares with me, once she gets a job she can help with expenses.'

'Why would Lulu want to live in a warehouse?' Harriet said contemptuously.

'I don't mind, Mum,' Lulu said. 'Anywhere'll do for a start. One of my pals works as a cigarette girl in a night club and I'm sure she can get me a job.'

'A glorified waitress? No!' Harriet cried.

'Don't be such a snob, Mum. The money's good.'

'But why leave home?' Harriet said. 'I won't interfere with your plans but don't go just yet. You're much too young, both of you.'

'Mum, don't lay a guilt trip on us – please.'

'I'm not blaming you,' Harriet said quickly. 'If it hadn't been for Roger . . .'

'If it hadn't been for Joe Fisher and his duty fucking free,' cried Lulu with alarming passion.

'Now that's simply ridiculous!' Harriet said. 'How could it possibly be his fault?'

The children exchanged strange twinnish glances. 'You're right, Mum,' Tim said, with the same curious look. 'It's got nothing to do with Joe Fisher. If you want to know it's your fault.'

'What's my fault?' She blinked at them, through the pink dimples of offence.

'Everything.'

'You've made our lives impossible.'

'Right from the time we were little – always asking were we happy.'

'I cared,' Harriet said.

'When we were kids at school it didn't matter all that much because there wasn't a measure by which we could judge. One kid's life seemed much the same as the other. But university students are a different matter – some are swots, some are ravers, and some are stinking, filthy rich. And happy.'

'You do see, don't you, Mummy, that you've landed us in a mess?'

'And the best way you can help us now is to give us the money and let us go.'

Harriet sat perfectly still. She examined her hands, her fingernails, her wedding ring. She tried to keep her feelings under control but she feared her restraint showed as a small, cruel smile. 'I think,' she said quite brightly, 'I'll go for a little walk.'

She walked down to the beach and sat at the deserted bar. She stayed there a considerable time, drinking Metaxas, longing for love. It was love she wanted, she was stubborn about that. In spite of her pain she would not have settled for a sympathetic ear. Never mind her body's response to Apollo or Costas or even, in an unguarded moment, Roger, she was prepared to sit it out in unnatural discomfort, like an Eskimo on an ice floe, until tempted by the proper package of true devotion, tender and comforting pats, an eager mating of the brain – as well as the other thing which shook or peopled the earth.

178

It was Joe she blamed, for giving her ideas above her station. She blamed her mother for never telling her anything. She saw then, quite clearly, that the fault was all her father's. Where had he been, all the years of her growing up? Why did he leave her to the mercy of her mother, and the young men who bullied her and the one who carried her off? He had never actually packed his bags. He simply grew invisible. It was his fault that she was still compelled to seek a father under the romantic layers of every man she met, his fault that she still sought approval for everything she did. He had forbidden her to roller skate or ride a bicycle, to play in the park or join the guides. 'You'd knock your front teeth out,' he reasoned mysteriously. It was why she was so useless, why her hands dangled in a crisis.

He had carried her on his own bike, though; not on the crossbar but in the basket, her legs dangling over the front, his free arm restraining her. They went out together on secret errands that ended in sweets. They sang: *The Yellow Rose of Texas, Rosemaree, The Teddybears' Picnic*. Sometimes he brought her home presents, a cream meringue in a paper bag, a set of foreign stamps. 'I paid for those,' he would point out.

He collected comic records and called her in to hear them. They listened together solemnly, exchanging faint smiles of relief when the jokes were successfully achieved.

He bought her a doll. It did not resemble anything in their lives. She was a fabulous creature, rosy and thick-lashed with golden curls and dazzling blue eyes, a glistening, dimpled mouth and a charming, avaricious little row of teeth. Her dress was made of taffeta and she had mountains of lace and net underwear including a perfectly made pair of knickers. She even had socks and white buttoned shoes that fastened and unfastened. Her price was still pencilled on her tummy where it was left to impress as it was meant to – and did; forty-nine and eleven.

He was bitterly disappointed when she put it on a shelf in her bedroom and left it there until its look of delighted surprise grew macabre under a veil of webs and dust. 'You don't like it,' he complained. 'You never play with it.' She shook her head in protest, unable to explain her fear of knocking its teeth out.

Up to a certain stage he had, in a timid way, been her ally. How had she lost him? When had he deserted her?

Even when she was a young girl he had been meekly on her side, telling her she was a bobby dazzler, giving her the money for a stiff slip. It was only when Martin came to claim her that he turned against her. He told her she was throwing herself away, that she had as much taste as a boiled boot.

'You don't know him, Daddy,' she had pleaded. She did not know him either but she was drawn to him and his hostile sexuality made her father seem old and moth-eaten by comparison. 'He's wonderful.'

He had turned to her mother, their common enemy. 'She thinks he pisses Eau de Cologne,' he sneered in a unique display of vulgarity.

That was unforgivable. She did not speak to him after that – not until after the twins were born and she was sick with her first taste of the terror of loneliness. She needed some comfort then, some link with the security of her own childhood. She went to see him. 'What do you want?' he said in a sour, hopeful voice.

'I want my toys,' she said. 'My doll. I want my teddies and all that. For the children.'

'Is that all?' he said. 'I burnt the bloody things.'

It was a staggering blow. The memory of her, the souvenirs of her childhood, had been just so much rubbish cluttering up a room that he had burnt them. She never had anything to do with him after that, never asked her mother how he was. She had forgotten all about him. Good enough for him. She had banished him as effectively as he had banished her.

Still the memory, now that she had found it, cut into her, but it was only a scratch compared to the loss of Joe. He would get in touch with her in due course, but if she took him back (and she probably would) she would have to face the fact that nothing he might say to her was of any consequence. It was a life of deprivation, interspersed with tantalizing bouts of furtive celebration; Hell's bells.

Everything she did seemed to aggravate the pain. She took the children to the restaurant where they had laughed together at the dancing lobsters. Kitty grizzled about eating in the dark and the non-availability of Coke or Pepsi. She blinked back tears as she chewed on the greasy dolmades without the touch of his leg on her

180

leg. She went up the field with her telescope to take a look at Psiros but all she could see was the tree beneath which they had made love and the ledge where, looking out afterwards, they felt as if they had conquered the world. She pulled herself together and went to fetch her paints. When she opened the wardrobe, she caught sight of his silly, artless summer clothes, in which he had climbed up to meet her and had brought the gift of his flowers and the boundless, dizzying relief of his presence.

The clothes completely unhinged her. She cried like a baby. She wailed and chattered. She fell on her knees and buried her face in them, choking on his name. But then she got a grip on herself and gathered up the foolish holiday garments in a little bundle and ran outside and threw them down in the yard. She poured oil on them and brandy and flung on a pile of sticks and set them all on fire and then she felt much better.

FIFTEEN

The boat that took Roger away brought new visitors to Keptos.

A scrap of black on the track (like a blackened fragment blown from Harriet's bonfire) broke a membrane of haze on the horizon. It was Melina, bringing intimation of fresh disturbance to their lives. She chanted as she clambered: 'He is coming!'

Harriet came to the door. She stood with her hand to her eyes until Melina had arrived and stillness reassembled in her wake. 'Who is coming?' she said patiently.

'Stefan. He has come.'

'Then let him come.'

She no longer believed in Stefan. The widow was mad. It was habit and not faith that roused her to tidy her hair after the woman had departed and enliven her face with a daub of lipstick. To conserve movement she used a sunless window for reflection and was shocked when this presented her (behind the watery shadow of her face) with a more substantial image. A man was staring in the window at her. Stefan! She saw her own birdlike dismay flung back at her in the funereal panes of his glasses. The huge stranger was scowling at her and Harriet shrank back from view, guiltily concealing the artefacts of adornment, forgetting her unfinished upper lip.

The man burst into the cottage. 'Yes, it's me,' he said, seeing her shocked face. 'I have come back.'

For some reason he looked familiar although she had never known a man of such dimension. He was enormously fat. She was glad the children were in the garden for he seemed to use up every inch of space in the house and even its air.

'All those years! We thought you were dead.' She averted her eyes and busied her hands with the breakfast dishes. She could not look on his blazing lenses. A speech about tenants' rights, prepared in the days before she lost faith in Stefan's existence, drained from her brain. 'You might have written!' She kept her hands diligent, her eyes anywhere. She knew, all the same, that he was staring at her.

'Shut up, Harriet,' he said.

Her hands froze on a clutch of cups and a saucer of butts crumpled into ashes. He knew her name. Had he not been so rude they might have sorted out their difficulties for it appeared that he also knew some English.

'Where is the man? Where is your lover?' Stefan demanded.

'He's gone,' Harriet said and little pink spots appeared in her cheeks.

She turned irresistibly and was shaken afresh by his familiarity – not just a vague provocation of memory but recognition. She *knew* him. Of course! He was Melina's nephew. There were no obvious resemblances but blood must show. 'Look here,' she said uneasily. 'My friends are none of your business. I am perfectly prepared to discuss whatever problems you might have.'

'The children,' he said. 'They are my business.'

'She told you!' Melina must have complained of her behaviour, bringing the children in as additional evidence of her irresponsibility. 'She's just a trouble-maker.'

'Relax. She comes with me.'

'But . . . you came for the cottage!'

'What would I do with this heap of junk?'

'It's your home!' She had rarely been so confounded by an adult. Until now, only the children had this capacity for knocking her off guard and jumping on her where she lay. 'For heaven's sake, Stefan!'

'Who the hell is Stefan?'

Her mouth gaped. 'Who are you?' His voice, she realized, was without a trace of an accent.

'Close your mouth, old pal,' he laughed, removing his sunglasses and folding them into a pocket. 'You look like a trout.'

'Daddy!' The door was flung open and Kitty made an elaborate entrance.

'Martin?' Harriet moaned and she self-consciously snapped shut her jaw.

Kitty embraced the fat man and danced about delightedly. 'Oh, Daddy! You came, you came.'

'Of course I came, precious. I took the first plane I could. You don't think I'd leave you here after what you told me.'

183

They were so large, so loud, so *irrefutable*, that Harriet felt herself fade away and almost vanish. 'Told him what? What did you tell him? You don't even know him – he left when you were a baby,' she argued weakly with herself.

'Gosh, Mummy!' Kitty remembered her. 'It's why I went to Psiros – to telephone Daddy. I was afraid of Joe Fisher and I didn't know what else to do.'

'How did you find him? How could you have recognized him?'

'Don't be cross, Mum. I needed a Dad. I found him. We've been writing to each other for years. He sends my letters to the post office. We send each other photos too.'

She felt the cut of this infidelity. 'It's all right. I'm not angry – nor at you, Martin. It's just . . .' – she sagged on to a chair – 'a bit of a shock to see you after all these years.'

'You too,' he grinned. 'You look well. I'm sorry to have jumped on you, Harriet. It sounded so damn rotten, what the kid told me.'

'Yes, I expect it did. You look . . . prosperous. How is . . .?' She could not remember the name of his new or not-so-new wife.

He did not supply it. 'I'm on my own again. I mean, I was on my own.' His attention wandered away from Harriet and alighted on Kitty, moonstruck. His look was still foolish when it found its way back to her. 'This is all so strange. I don't know what to say. Look, I'm sorry, Harriet. You've done a great job bringing her up and I'm grateful.'

'You don't have to be.'

'No, but it looks as if I'm taking over at the easy stage.'

'Taking over what?' she smiled.

'No, not taking over – no, of course not. I know she'll still want to spend a lot of time with you. But you'll miss her.'

'Miss . . . what?' She looked at Kitty. Kitty's face was laden with guilt, a comic parody of grown-up gloom. 'He's going to buy me a pony, Mummy.'

'We have nowhere to put a pony.' She laughed harshly.

'Don't be silly, Harriet,' Martin said. 'Kitty's coming to live with me. Stop pretending you don't know.'

'She doesn't know.' Kitty kept her eyes lowered. 'I meant to tell you, Mummy.'

184

She looked at them; first one, then the other, her mouth working to assist the agonizing sloth of her brain. When she finally found words they were flung out on a little mocking laugh: 'You can't!'

'Not right away,' Martin said. 'I'll wait for a day or two. I'd like to see the twins. When the boat comes back . . .'

'No!' She left her chair and ran to Kitty, putting cold hands on her face. 'Kitty!' Kitty tried to turn her face away. Harriet thumped her and spun on Martin with her clenched fist. 'No! I'll fight, I'll stop you! The courts . . . !' A burning in her chest and throat made it hard to form proper sentences.

'Not when they hear how your boyfriend's been behaving. Look, Harriet, you can do this your way or mine. My way, Kitty is free to come and go as she pleases. Your way, the courts decide and you may only get limited access besides putting the child through the unpleasantness. I doubt if you really want that.'

'She's mine!' Harriet wailed. She shook her head. She shook all over. Her eyes and nose began to drip.

'Mummy, don't cry,' Kitty begged and she put her arms around her.

She let herself sob into the comfort of Kitty's bosom. For a moment she was tempted to abandon herself to grief. She had never allowed the children to see her tears. She knew the binding quality of pity. 'I'll put the kettle on.' She wiped her eyes and swam towards the sink, all sense of weight and substance departed. Her hands groped for the kettle and clung to its reliable squatness. Faithful companion to crisis, it knew its routine by heart. Waiting for it to fill, she remembered with hallucinatory vividness a day many years ago when the twins had gone missing. 'Put the kettle on,' she had said distractedly to Kitty, when a policeman called and she thought he was bringing news of death. Long after, she remembered the child and hurried to the kitchen to find four-year-old Kitty patiently standing on a chair at the sink, the spout of the kettle held to a dripping tap. 'Kitty! Kitty!' she whispered. 'Oh, God!' For once she assigned a presence to the formula, an omnipotence with whom she might recklessly bargain. 'Let me have Kitty and I won't mind anything else.' 'All birds must fly,' came the stern reply in her head. Had her own mother known such grief? 'Mother?' she whimpered.

She became aware that some sort of commotion was going on outside.

'Mother!' cried out the new generation, in voices lightened by alarm.

There was a banging at the cottage door and a confusion of voices. The twins had come in and some others whose tones she did not recognize.

She emerged from the kitchen as one walking a plank across a gorge. Lulu and Tim guarded the hall and a family was coming into the cottage – a tall, swarthy man with a moustache, a shy, well-dressed woman and five or six children in adolescence and teens.

'It is I, Stefan!' the man announced.

'*Stefan?*'

'This is my wife, Eleni, and my children.'

'Your wife? Your wife is dead.'

'My second wife. Did Melina not tell you I am married?'

'Perhaps she did.' Harriet recalled one of many earlier confusions.

'And now we have come home.'

'I'm not leaving!' Harriet blurted.

'Of course not!' The dark man made expansive movements with his arms. When he smiled his moustaches pincered his nose.

'Sorry if we've caused you any inconvenience,' Lulu said with insolent sweetness.

'No, no! It is I who must apologize,' Stefan insisted.

'What for?' Harriet said.

'The noise.'

'Noise?' Tim snorted. 'On this cataleptic bloody kip?'

Harriet glanced at Stefan's children to see if they threatened rowdiness but his brood emanated a well-bred moroseness.

'I am sorry in advance for the noise of the building,' said the Greek. His handlebars tweaked his nose as he struggled to make himself understood.

'Building?' she echoed stupidly.

'My little project.' He put his hand on his chest and grinned modestly. 'I leave here a poor builder's labourer. I work hard and now – a wealthy man with my own company – I come back to build on the best site in Keptos, my beautiful new hotel.'

'Oh, golly!' Harriet said and with a hand to her mouth as if she had to be sick, she beat a path through the density of giants.

She ran, she ran.

When she got to the beach she stopped, feeling that some warning was due. Timeless, blameless, it mocked her woe. Mineral particles glittered in pebbles on the strand and the sea teased her with its lights. Stones shuffled at the water's edge and the hulks of boats groaned as their bottoms were shifted by the tide's pull. Harriet stood on the shingle panting, her face desolate, her hands gathered into fists. She drew in breath until she had accumulated strength and then in a great vituperative stream she shouted out every swearword, each coarseness and profanity that had ever emerged from the children's mouths. She could sense the shock on the air. All the innocent sounds had ceased. The hideous verbal mutations of anatomy and biology spewed out so fluently that she thought she could see them depart and roll away over the ocean, a sulphurous plume like dragon's breath. 'Cosmic,' she murmured.

When she looked again she was embarrassed to see that there was a woman watching her. She noted two brown and slightly soiled feet in silver sandals, the dusty hem of a black vest dress and a weathered, smiling face. It took some time to assemble the parts to a whole. Dimly she recalled a similar foot or the same one, hospitably drawing out a chair for her to sit on in Psiros, in the hotel. It was the woman in the restaurant. 'Anne?' she remembered vaguely.

'Hello, Harriet.'

'What are you doing here?'

'I came on the boat this morning. I was hoping I'd find you.'

'What do you want?'

'Buy you a drink,' Anne said, getting the answer right at once.

She went away and returned from the bar with two well-filled glasses. 'I came at a bad time,' she said, looking into Harriet's blotched face as she handed her her drink. 'Talk?'

Harriet shook her head. How could she tell a total stranger that the very smallest and nicest of her dreams had died along with the grand ones. If Anne had been less of a stranger she would have simply told her to go away – or if she herself were less polite. It was good manners that goaded her grudgingly back to her companion.

'You talk to me,' she said to Anne. 'Tell me what brought you here.'

'To Greece?'

'No. Here, to Keptos, today.'

'I wanted to see if I could convince you to let me sell some of your paintings in the hotel. There are people there with lots of money and nothing to spend it on.'

'Oh, no,' Harriet protested. 'I couldn't do that. Those paintings are not for sale.'

Later they returned to the question of why Anne had first come to Greece and she told her story. It took a long time and required a number of pauses for refreshment. By the time the two women parted and Harriet returned to her family, the sun was easing into the sea and she had a new lesson in her head: in Pandora's box, there are many mansions.

SIXTEEN

Next day the boat came in – not the familiar little fruit- and sheep-smelling vessel that was the island's regular water traffic but a big, oily tug swaying and grumbling with the burden of the earthmovers from Psiros.

Like dinosaurs they lumbered on to land and heaved themselves up the hill, screaming and sliding and clawing stones and clumps of flowering weed from the track as they made their ungainly ascent.

Harriet watched from her window. They conquered the hill and began to tear apart the earth. Whole fields were dismembered. Brown lumps of land were held aloft, crumbling, and then dashed back to earth. Goats and sheep, demented with fear, made low shuddering cries.

She was annoyed about the noise. If it had not been for the noise she might have been unconscious of these small events. She had withdrawn into a sealed world. Like Anne, she was thinking.

No one had had to break her fingers to prise free her possessions. In the end they had gone numb and let them drop of their own accord. Each of the losses caused her pain but the cumulative effect was a feverish lightness. She was happy to devote her life to the children in whatever manner might be most useful, but the fact that the larger part of her drifted free was a cause of nervous excitement; it was the way all the blows had fallen at once, cutting her loose (or almost) at a fell swoop. She was not left clinging and hanging as other women are. She had fallen through the chasm of adult expectation and was like a child of six or seven, secure in the present and indifferent to the complicated seethings of humanity.

She used to pursue an ideal life which was a sort of still-life-in-locked-embrace, with a broad shoulder to block out the terrors of the world. Now a different ideal was emerging. She conceived of life as a dance in which only the exceptionally gifted or stupid stayed together, the more naturally suited partners lingering a little longer than the music and then moving on. But each of the dancers left a layer of themselves behind and this shadowy garment became the substance of oneself.

The life she had sought for herself was like the one she prescribed for her beautiful doll – shelter and decay. One ought to be like a tree, out in all weathers and showing off the layers of the years. She began to believe that there had been nothing the matter with her life all along except her habit of depositing it wholesale in the arms of every man she met, and then running away.

She was not, after all, she thought, a failure.

It was an exclusively held view not, alas, shared by those with whom her life was.

Martin berated her because of the way the children buzzed around him, trying to extract money. 'You've brought them up like bloody little leeches, Hat,' he said, retrieving from an attic of memory his unpleasant pet name for her.

Repulsed, the leeches sought fresh blood. 'You know what you are, Mummy?' Lulu came to join her at the window and clawed irritably at the glass. 'You're a snob. You think you can wash away all the shit of the modern world if you do it in cold water at a stone sink. But you never think of us, do you? I can't even wash my hair. We get sacrificed just so you don't get proved wrong.'

Kitty ran from one parent to the other, clinging and complaining, attempting to extract guilt as well as the taken-for-granted grief.

'You don't love me or you wouldn't let me go.' 'If you really loved me you'd be thinking of my best interests instead of selfishly trying to hang on to me.'

Tim, at least, was enthusiastic. 'Just look at that operation, Mum!' He spied on the devastation of the earth with envy. 'This guy Stefan came up from nothing and he must be worth a million now. I bet if we stirred up some trouble we could get ourselves a cut of the action. Why don't you check on the planning laws or something instead of sitting around like a cream-faced loon?'

As well as attending to the emotional needs of her family there was a very great deal of housework to be done. Somehow she had never got round to discussing a rota of chores with the children. She couldn't expect her mother to help out – not with her heart; and Martin had never been domesticated.

With so many large people in the house shopping lists and meals were enormous. In between bouts of washing up there were cups of coffee to be made and wine poured and she tried to leave some sandwiches ready. It was natural for the men working the machines to drop into the cottage for some refreshment and Stefan and his family were friendly too. He tried to spread out his plans for the hotel on the kitchen table and point out to her the site for the ladies' hairdressing salon or the sauna. He never said no to a coffee or a brandy. Eleni, his wife, preferred a cup of tea and something savoury and the children silently raided the cupboards for soft drinks.

She did not really mind these services. Soon enough she would be all alone; plenty of time for thinking then, when they had left her.

Quite suddenly that time arrived and there was Kitty, a little girl in white shorts, her yellow nylon holdall slung over her shoulder. 'We're leaving now, Mum,' she said gruffly. 'You can see us off if you promise not to make a fuss.'

The twins joined the farewell party that accompanied the leave-takers to the harbour. Even Stefan was there, impressed by Martin's size and sternness. Harriet followed at a distance, lest her face betray a deficiency of fortitude. She kept an eye on Kitty. The child linked and butted Martin with an aggressive insistence that was beyond affection. All of Martin's attention was given over to Tim. The two of them were deep in conversation. They were probably talking about money. They each had the same loping, indifferent stride. Lulu, flanking Tim's side, had a rolling gait which seemed to offer a moll's support. Powerful Stefan was reduced to submissiveness and he merely carried their cases.

Kitty was getting tiresome. Soon she would bite or kick her father to extract her due tribute of attention. Martin would grow tired of her. The thought struck Harriet with grim satisfaction. Kitty needed a weaker soul upon whom to wreak her vanities. It's not goodbye after all, Harriet thought. It's good fortune. Kitty would always return to Harriet. Harriet would lose nothing. But Kitty, perhaps, would lose a measure of her hold.

All the same when the harbour came into view she began to panic. How could she give away her baby? Her feet refused to move and her jaw clamped in fright.

'Wait!' She managed to squeeze out a single word.

Her family paused and turned with a forbidding look.

'I ... think I'll say my goodbyes now,' she said briskly. 'Lulu! Tim! You'll see them off properly for me, won't you?' She made a little dash forward and gave Kitty a careless squeeze as if she was a dish towel. 'Goodbye, my darling.'

Kitty looked unsure of herself. She gave her father a worried glance. Her chin had begun to quake. 'Mum?'

The others grew bored with all this and continued their descent of the hill. Seeing them leaving her Kitty suffered a different anxiety. 'Well, 'bye, Mum,' she said awkwardly and she trotted after them.

For a long time Harriet remained where she was. From her high point on the track she watched the passenger boat sway into the harbour and its trivial disgorging of assorted life. She gazed until the little procession of her family had merged with the caravan of human and animal life that was waiting to be borne across the water. When she could no longer identify the goats and sheep from her own little ewe lamb she gave a great long dry sigh and headed back up the hill to the cottage.

The cottage looked dirty and in mourning. Unwashed breakfast cups littered the table and a letter lay abandoned on the mat in the hall. A letter! The postman had been! Joe, oh, Joe! Her heart clanged around in her chest like a kicked bucket as she noted the postmark and stooped to retrieve the envelope. But the lumpy loops of writing brought her quickly back to self-pity. It wasn't from Joe. She recognized the writing as her mother's. She stuffed the letter in the pocket of her dress and sat down at the untidy table, the better to feel sorry for herself. It was very quiet. The excavating machines were silenced for lunch. After a while she got up and cleared the table and put fresh coffee on to brew. She opened a window and let in a bolt of sun and the hot, honeyed air. She turned on the transistor and was astonished to hear, not the usual blast of bouzouki music, but Mozart's clarinet concerto. As she poured her coffee, she found herself whistling along with the music. It was very peaceful. Instead of being vanquished by Kitty's departure she felt herself blossoming in the harmonious quiet. Having assessed the poor yielding quality of Martin's personality against Kitty's emotional onslaughts, she could look on Kitty's going as an interlude of release. For a little while she could afford to think about herself.

Still humming, a cup of coffee in her hand, a freshly lit cigarette's fragrance stinging her nose, she wandered into her bedroom and began to tidy it. Halfway through this calming task, she caught sight of her canvas carrier in the open wardrobe and remembered her meeting yesterday with Anne on the beach and the other woman's offer to sell her paintings. In spite of what she had said, the prospect excited her. She took the carrier from the wardrobe and withdrew the stiff paper rolls. It was a solemn moment. These were her Keptos paintings, strokes of love – her legacy from Joe. She laid the paintings on the bed and surveyed them with awe.

'My God!' she said faintly.

The paintings were vile. A mush of pastels evoked spilt baby food. The pinks and purples effected actual nausea.

'Barbara Cartland art,' she said with a wry smirk and she stuffed the paintings back into their bag.

She found herself thinking not of the paintings but of Anne. She kept sneaking back to the place in her memory where this odd, likeable woman was lodged. Anne had taken the trouble to come and see her when her own family was getting ready to desert. Now that she had time on her hands, she looked forward to returning that visit. She was shocked by her own selfishness, to think in terms of enjoyment when she had just forfeited her daughter. She brought her mind back to the boat waiting in the harbour and concentrated on this, poking her heart in its damaged places to aggravate the pain, but instead of carrying off her child the boat only returned the memory of yesterday's visitor and her interesting pilgrim's tale.

Harriet had been intrigued to learn that Anne was one of the original villa-owners on Psiros and that she and her husband had stayed there summer after summer, while the island was still unspoiled – until their marriage broke up and the money ran out.

'After the villa was sold to developers, I thought I'd never see Psiros again,' Anne had told her. 'Then I heard there was going to be an hotel on the island and cheap package tours there. I saved every penny I had to go for a fortnight. I went without booze, soap, meat.'

In spite of her own troubles, Harriet had been impressed. 'How very sad!' she exclaimed with feeling. As always, she had felt her own burdens lifting in the gift of another's.

'Parts of it are sad,' Anne agreed. 'The villa itself was hell. All our friends came to stay and they brought their friends too. People who were ill or in trouble always landed on top of us. The kids brought other kids. All my time went on cooking and fighting. Everyone took me for granted except my husband who was disturbed by the superior sex lives of our guests and kept telling me I was letting myself go.'

'If you hated the place so much –' Harriet spoke cautiously; '– why did you want to go back?'

'No, I didn't say I hated it. I said it was hell. We went there first on our honeymoon. We travelled the last leg by rowing boat and we slept in a sleeping bag. I was astonished by such beauty. I thought that if one could keep contact with such a place, life would always be all right. I blamed everyone when things went wrong. If only all those people weren't hanging out of me, if I could be as free as I was that first time, I thought I would see it as I saw it then.'

'And . . . did you?' Harriet hardly dared asked the question. Anne seemed indifferent to her state. She looked away and drained her drink. 'Shit no,' she said softly. 'The Garden of Eden is for the innocent.'

'So you're giving up? You're going home?'

'I didn't say that. It's not Paradise, no matter what the sign says – but it's not so bad. I like it. As a matter of fact, I'm staying on a while.'

'What will you do for money?' Harriet was thinking of the meat and the alcohol she had sacrificed and the soap which she had clearly managed to do without.

'I'll get a job. Plenty of jobs on good old Psiros for English-speakers. I'll have my own room, free food – a little stack of drachs.'

'But those people!'

'They're people.'

'How do you know so much?' Harriet was suspicious. 'Where did you learn about life?'

'I never learned anything until I was on my own. At first I was terrified. I thought the feeling was loneliness. Then I realized I was

194

just frightened of all the stuff that was in my head. I was afraid it would come and get me in the night.'

'Don't you mind being on your own?'

'We're all on our own, kid,' Anne said. 'That was my big discovery. Each of us has a life to get through and no one can do it for us. You pile up the bed with men and kids and teddies – but it's every man for himself. When you're married it seems quite safe to say, "This is *my* husband. These are *my* children." But what do they say? "I am Anne's husband"? "We are Anne's children"? Not bloody likely! They say, "Anne is my wife", "Anne is our mother". So who's got whom?'

All on our own. The phrase brought Harriet harshly back to the present. What would Anne care if she told her her husband had turned up out of the blue and taken away her daughter? But Harriet found the words had lost their power to frighten. Try as she might to make herself guilty or unnerved, she was excited by her solitude. The knowledge that only the older children would be coming back absolved her of all domestic duty. No one could say the twins were still dependent. There was no longer any need to clean rooms or cook dinners. She could do as she liked. She might eat in the taverna tonight and do some sketches of its owners. She must make the most of her time for sooner or later Kitty would come back clamouring for notice and if she could judge correctly the brevity of Martin's tether it might well be sooner.

It was even sooner than she had imagined. As she lay back in a new, luxurious, guiltless repose, following the winged incline of Mozart's music the sweetly throbbing air was invaded by a lustier note.

'Mummee!'

She sat up abruptly. 'Kitty?'

'We came back!' Kitty burst in followed by her brother and sister. Martin's bulk in the open doorway consumed the daylight. Kitty bounced up and down. 'Mummy, I found I couldn't bear to leave you and Dad says he's worried about Lulu and Tim so we've all decided we're going to stay.'

'But for how long?' Harriet was beginning to tremble.

'For ever and ever and ever.' Kitty hugged her bruisingly.

Year after year after year.

'We'll be going home in a couple of weeks,' Harriet babbled, '– and then Tim and Lulu will be looking for a place of their own to live.'

'Oh, bugger that,' Tim said. 'If home's good enough for Dad, it's good enough for me.'

'Martin . . . ?'

'Poor old Ma – can't you take it in?' Tim laughed. 'We're coming home – all of us. It'll be a bit of a squash but I reckon if I move into your new studio there'll be plenty of room. Dad's got much better ideas than my hare-brained schemes. I'm going to work with him.'

'And Daddy says I can go to one of those crazy Cordon Bleu courses,' Lulu cut in. 'If we do well he's going to get us each a car.'

'What about money?' Harriet said angrily.

'Relax. Money's no problem,' Martin said.

She thought of all the years of working in a dull office by day and painting under a dull light by night. She had not wished to restrict his life.

'You have another family!' she remembered.

'My wife's got a bundle.' He chuckled and lit a cigar. 'I don't have to worry. Frankly, the way things turned out, she'd probably pay me to stay away.'

'And now you're paying us to come home.'

She could see the large adults who surrounded her stiffen with a sort of here-we-go-again disapproval. Once more, she was trying to spoil it for them.

'I don't want you to get the wrong idea, Hat,' Martin said. 'I'm coming back because of the children – no other reason. I don't have to remind you that the house is still in my name. Naturally you will be welcome to stay. I won't impose on you in any way although it goes without saying that a man in my position has to consider his wife's appearance. I hope I can encourage you to get a hairstyle more suited to your age and to stop wearing those beatnik clothes. And I won't have you embarrassing me with you meaning-of-life tripe in front of my friends.'

'Yes, Mummy, you're just going to have to learn how to behave,' Kitty said. 'It's too mortifying when you go around asking perfect strangers if they're in love. It's like picking other people's pimples.'

'Lulu, Tim? Have you got no improving plans for me?' Harriet whispered.

'Well you might at least try to look pleased,' Lulu coaxed. 'We're doing all this for you, you know, no matter what Dad says. Go on, give us a smile, old girl. Now what do you say?'

What could she say? Seeing them all together she could only observe with astonishment the striking resemblance between Martin and the children. Martin was no longer the stern, slim youth she had adored. He was a distorting-mirror caricature. Lulu and Tim were only children but already they showed the same truculent set of jaw, the same critical eye. All the children had inherited Martin's talent for confusing argument. They were part of a molecular structure gravitating by sympathetic force into a natural mass. In spite of the link of blood and the hospitality of her womb, they were scarcely any part of her. They were her charge. They were Martin's children.

'And it's time you cut down on smoking. It's a disgusting habit,' Tim added.

She reached, unthinking, for her cigarettes but it was her mother's letter that came into her hand. She sat down and stared at its bubbling script, tears of resentful cowardice beginning to blur her vision. 'Here, dear.' She handed the letter to Lulu. 'Read this. It's from Gran.'

After the ritual of tearing and crackling the envelope, Lulu began: 'Dear Harriet, I am sorry to hear that you are lonely on your holiday . . .'

'I never said I was lonely!' Harriet protested.

'Don't interrupt,' Lulu snapped. She bent again to her reading. 'Well, I am lonely too and as you have taken the trouble to mark the exact location of your cottage on the postcard you sent, I take it that you are hinting that I should visit. You will be pleased to learn that by the time this reaches you, I am on my way to your Greek island. Do not go to any trouble. I am glad to be of use. Loneliness is a woman's lot, due to men. Look at the way your father went. I shall be arriving . . .' – Lulu mouthed dates and did some mental arithmetic. 'Wow! She's on the mainland now. She'll be here tomorrow.'

'No!' Harriet cried but it was a voice in the wilderness. The news

197

had prompted a great outburst of excitement in the others. They were arguing over who would collect her, where she would sleep. By the time these matters had been settled Harriet was on her feet, struggling out of the depths of her confusion.

'I never said I was lonely!' she insisted afresh. 'All I said was, "It's lovely here"!'

'"Lovely", "lonely", what's the difference? The words look almost the same written down,' Lulu said crossly. Like most of her generation, she was impatient with cause, only interested in effect. Harriet could not argue. Motive was irrelevant, weighed against the enormity of outcome, especially as one rarely truly perceived one's own motives. She would never know why they had all come back to her. She only knew that she had lost (for good?) the capacity to adapt. She was no longer responsive to their whim.

'What did she mean about Dad?' she pondered faintly. 'What did Mother mean when she said, "Look at the way your father went"?'

'You mean you don't know?' Tim and Lulu had their clonish grin. 'Didn't Gran tell you?'

'She told me nothing. She never told me anything.'

'He ran off. He went peculiar,' Lulu said.

'He set fire to all your toys in the garden and he ran away,' added Tim.

'With a woman?' Harriet felt a strange tremor.

'Don't be ridiculous,' Lulu scoffed. 'With his fishing rod and the office pension fund.'

She could picture her father riding sombrely away, the fishing rod neatly bandaged to his bicycle, his small suitcase balanced in the basket. After a mile or two he might put out a diffident hand to secure the case and feel instead a buttoned cardigan, the starched awning of a cotton frock, the smooth and scabbed surface of a child's knee. He would start to smile. He would feign a dangerous wobble and sing: 'My Rose, my Rosemaree!'

The family had assumed its communal glare of doubt. 'Well then,' Harriet said pleasantly. 'I think I'll be off. You can all look after each other. And be nice to Gran, won't you?'

'I think she's gone off her head,' Lulu said flatly.

'Is she going the way her father went?' Tim wondered.

'That's right. That's exactly right,' Harriet softly endorsed.

'Where are you going? How long for?' Kitty demanded.

After a moment's hesitation she reached out for Kitty's hand. 'Come with me and you'll see.'

'Let me *go*!' Kitty cried so vehemently that she obeyed at once.

She packed economically, taking only the clothes she felt at ease in, her canvas carrier of paints with the awful paintings. After brief consideration she rooted about in Kitty's holdall and retrieved, for herself, the blue swimsuit.

She ran all the way to the harbour.

SEVENTEEN

Hot sand rose between her toes and there was music. 'Eleanor Rigby' was being served, some distance away, from a can. It made her want to dance.

There had been a moment of panic when she disembarked at Psiros. What if they came to look for her? What if they did not? What would she do for money? What would she do next?

She knew what she wanted. At least she knew that. She took off her shoes and squeezed the soft, pearly sand under her feet. She moved between the basted sunbathers. A man smiled at her. It irked her until she realized that her own face, upturned to the rippling sign of the Paradise, affected cheer.

When she reached the patio she set down her suitcase and signalled a waiter with a tray of cocktails. She put money on his tray and helped herself to a drowning garden. With her head bent to this alcoholic stew she began a leisurely inspection of the hotel's amenities. A small retinue gathered in her wake.

'Fancy seeing you!' Janice said. 'Your little girl's not run off again?'

'Not her,' Harriet said.

She peered down an alley between an arch of instant greenery. In this cool recess, hidden from the telescope's eye so that she had not seen it before, was a beauty salon.

She might get her hair done – not in the manner advised by Martin, but cut back to show her face and her eyes. As she stared a handsome figure came out of the salon, with a glossy bouffant. She waved in welcome. It was the lifeguard, gloriously coiffed. He joined the procession. 'So,' he said. 'You come back to lovely Psiros. Now we make love.'

'You never can tell,' Harriet said.

She passed lumbering tennis players on the lawn. A couple cavorted in their clothes beneath the mushroom-shaped fountain.

They reached the children's playground. Bars of brightly painted wood in a circus contained the infants. They had their own small swimming pool, swings, a sandpit, a dangerous frame of climbing bars. There were seats cut in shapes of animals. Harriet saw a dark girl of six or seven, gravely patting a mound of sand. She smiled, remembering a small, solemn Lulu. The children squinted briefly at the strangers and proceeded with their play.

She saw Anne coming towards her and they greeted one another happily. Anne seemed to have dressed specially for her arrival. Her black vest had been dramatized by one of the hotel's large pink blossoms. 'Welcome to the simple life!' Anne hugged her; 'though I think I should warn you off those cocktails or you won't live to enjoy it.'

More people arrived. She was very popular. At the swimming pool, a sinking Betsy was supported on land by Delbert and another gentleman. Betsy's little sandalled feet dribbled daintily on the concrete as the three hurried to greet her. 'Just in time,' Delbert said. 'We've a friend here with us. You'll make up the foursome.' He introduced the dapper, elderly man with oiled hair and a sad, lewd eye. 'I don't think you two know each other.'

'Oh, yes we do,' she said happily. 'It's Reggie Lantern!'

'Crispian de Witt!' The new arrival fended her off with his free arm, stiffly extended. But then he winked at her. 'Say, what kind of foursome do these folks have in mind?'

'Let's go somewhere *relatively* quiet and have a drink,' Anne said. 'A proper drink – not a Paradiso! I've discovered some nice white wine from Paros. Let me get rid of the Molotov cocktail.'

'I've got to get my bearings first.' Harriet kept hold of her drink and handed Anne, instead, the canvas carrier containing her paintings. 'And I've a favour to ask. I want you to see if you can sell some of these.'

'You've changed your mind?'

'My mind ...?' Harriet looked lost for a moment but then she nodded. 'Yes.'

Harriet bent to retrieve her suitcase.

'You're staying?' Anne said.

She nodded uncertainly. The weight of the case seemed to damage her resolve. She frowned and jiggled it slightly as if weighing its contents.

'How long?'

'I don't know.'

'It's all right,' Anne said.

'I haven't very much money. I'll have to look for work.'

'That's no problem. I've been through that. There's jobs all over the joint for English-speakers. What do you fancy, lady? Barmaid, bedmaker, child-minder, loo-cleaner? More spills than thrills, I'm afraid, but it's a living.'

'It sounds fine,' Harriet was smiling again. 'I have to go now. I have to go for an interview. I'll see you later.'

Clutching her drink and her suitcase she moved back in the direction from which she had come.

'Harriet!' Anne called after her. 'You're going the wrong way. You have to ask in the hotel if you want a job.'

Harriet paused briefly. She waved with her fruited glass. 'I know where I'm going.'

For a long time she stood outside, looking through the bars. A castle was being constructed. The builders laboured with devotional intensity. A bridge surpassed the muddy waters of a moat. They hoisted a flag on the tower but it leaned over like a music-hall drunk and the builders chuckled.

'Gallop, gallop, gallop,' came the first horse messenger, which was two plump fingers of a child of five or six.

Another messenger left the sandpit and came to look at Harriet.

'Hello.'

'Hello.'

'I'm Harriet.'

'I'm nearly four.'

'Can I come in?' Harriet said.

The little girl considered the request. She looked around the playground, reflecting. All its other occupants were children between two and seven, except for the bored teenager who supervised them over the top of her magazine and through the insulation of her Walkman. 'Why?' she said to Harriet.

'To play.'

'Okay.'

She opened the gate and let her in. Harriet put down her bags and took the hand the child offered her and allowed herself to be led around.

'Here is the sandpit. This is our swing. This is Joanne – she got sick this morning. This is Edward, my brother. What do you want to do?' 'I'll just look on for a while until I get the hang.'

She crouched by the sandpit and watched the small, squat bottoms and rubbery legs and fine, tufty, slept-upon hair. Now and again she indulged herself by reaching out and touching a head. Some of the smaller children needed their noses attended to or had swathes of plastic drooping between their legs. Her own, when small, had been nicely kept. 'Don't your Mummies come down at all during the day?' She addressed the largest child, a self-important girl of about seven.

'Of course not.' The girl looked up briefly. With her dark hair and earnest play she looked dreadfully like Lulu. 'Our Mummies are very busy,' she said proudly.

So this was another generation – serious and self-sufficient, brought up like Victorian children by indifferent strangers. Looking at the young women around the pool and in the restaurant it was impossible to tell which of them had children and which had not. They were not encumbered by motherhood. They had the love of children without the boredom, they had freedom and fun. Who was to say they were wrong? The children seemed quite contented. Certainly they were less disposed to complain and whine than hers had been at that early age.

'Don't you mind?'

'Only the babies mind,' said the ancient seven-year-old. '*He* minds.' She jerked a scornful head in the direction of a tiny boy who had just been hit with a spade. 'He's a crybaby.'

Harriet put down her drink and bent to pick him up. She still remembered how to hold a child. It was not merely built into her limbs, like the memories of swimming or riding a bicycle. Her arms still missed babies.

She put her mouth in his hair and patted his bottom. At first he gazed at her with monstrous indignation but then he became intrigued by her hair and put it in his mouth. 'No,' she murmured. 'I have something nicer than that for you.' She took the strawberry from her cocktail and handed it to him. 'What do you say to that?' she said.

'Yum.'

He ate the fruit and then he grew sleepy. She hoisted him up on her body and felt little patting palms comfort themselves on the back of her neck. She sat down in a wooden rocking chair which was painted to look like a kangaroo and watched the children living out the lives that were prescribed for them, falling helpless into the trap of generation-building, destroying, swinging, tumbling, laughing.

She squeezed the satisfying body in her arms and sipped her drink. 'Yum,' she said.

MORE ABOUT PENGUINS, PELICANS
AND PUFFINS

For further information about books available from Penguins please write to Dept EP, Penguin Books Ltd, Harmondsworth, Middlesex UB7 0DA.

In the U.S.A.: For a complete list of books available from Penguins in the United States write to Dept DG, Penguin Books, 299 Murray Hill Parkway, East Rutherford, New Jersey 07073.

In Canada: For a complete list of books available from Penguins in Canada write to Penguin Books Canada Ltd, 2801 John Street, Markham, Ontario L3R 1B4.

In Australia: For a complete list of books available from Penguins in Australia write to the Marketing Department, Penguin Books Australia Ltd, P.O. Box 257, Ringwood, Victoria 3134.

In New Zealand: For a complete list of books available from Penguins in New Zealand write to the Marketing Department, Penguin Books (N.Z.) Ltd, Private Bag, Takapuna, Auckland 9.

In India: For a complete list of books available from Penguins in India write to Penguin Overseas Ltd, 706 Eros Apartments, 56 Nehru Place, New Delhi 110019.

A CHOICE OF PENGUINS

☐ **Further Chronicles of Fairacre** 'Miss Read' £3.95

Full of humour, warmth and charm, these four novels – *Miss Clare Remembers, Over the Gate, The Fairacre Festival* and *Emily Davis* – make up an unforgettable picture of English village life.

☐ **Callanish** **William Horwood** £1.95

From the acclaimed author of *Duncton Wood*, this is the haunting story of Creggan, the captured golden eagle, and his struggle to be free.

☐ **Act of Darkness** **Francis King** £2.50

Anglo-India in the 1930s, where a peculiarly vicious murder triggers 'A terrific mystery story . . . a darkly luminous parable about innocence and evil' – *The New York Times*. 'Brilliantly successful' – *Daily Mail*. 'Unputdownable' – *Standard*

☐ **Death in Cyprus** **M. M. Kaye** £1.95

Holidaying on Aphrodite's beautiful island, Amanda finds herself caught up in a murder mystery in which no one, not even the attractive painter Steven Howard, is quite what they seem . . .

☐ **Lace** **Shirley Conran** £2.95

Lace is, quite simply, a publishing sensation: the story of Judy, Kate, Pagan and Maxine; the bestselling novel that teaches men about women, and women about themselves. 'Riches, bitches, sex and jetsetters' locations – they're all there' – *Sunday Express*

A CHOICE OF PENGUINS

☐ **West of Sunset** Dirk Bogarde £1.95

'His virtues as a writer are precisely those which make him the most compelling screen actor of his generation,' is what *The Times* said about Bogarde's savage, funny, romantic novel set in the gaudy wastes of Los Angeles.

☐ **The Riverside Villas Murder** Kingsley Amis £1.95

Marital duplicity, sexual discovery and murder with a thirties back-cloth: 'Amis in top form' – *The Times*. 'Delectable from page to page . . . effortlessly witty' – C. P. Snow in the *Financial Times*

☐ **A Dark and Distant Shore** Reay Tannahill £3.95

Vilia is the unforgettable heroine, Kinveil Castle is her destiny, in this full-blooded saga spanning a century of Victoriana, empire, hatreds and love affairs. 'A marvellous blend of *Gone with the Wind* and *The Thorn Birds*. You will enjoy every page' – *Daily Mirror*

☐ **Kingsley's Touch** John Collee £1.95

'Gripping . . . I recommend this chilling and elegantly written medical thriller' – *Daily Express*. 'An absolutely outstanding storyteller' – *Daily Telegraph*

☐ **The Far Pavilions** M. M. Kaye £4.95

Holding all the romance and high adventure of nineteenth-century India, M. M. Kaye's magnificent, now famous, novel has at its heart the passionate love of an Englishman for Juli, his Indian princess. 'Wildly exciting' – *Daily Telegraph*

HOLY PICTURES

In the Dublin of 1925 the holy scriptures are about to be superseded by moving pictures. To fourteen-year-old Nan the cinema appears as a miraculous rescue from the confines of her Catholic upbringing. But growing up into a world of immoral, unreliable adults is not easy, and the last year of Nan's childhood moves from the burlesque to the tragic ...

'Sharp as a serpent's tooth ... it is a very long time since a first novel of such promise, of such fun and wit and style, has come so confidently out of Ireland' – William Trevor

A NAIL ON THE HEAD

Fifteen stinging, erotic tales on the sexual tripwire, each tale sketched with humour and biting perception. At once comic and tragic, the men and women in these stories are forced up against the limitations of love and life.

'Short, painful tales of love's humiliations' – *The Times Literary Supplement*

'Drawn with a fiercely imaginative, original and accurate hand' – *New Statesman*